Praise for Diane Barnes

Praise for *Mixed Signals*

"A snappy tale with sweet undertones…Barnes has written another charming, funny romance that keeps its plot rolling while capturing workplace dynamics."

— *Kirkus Reviews*

"Clever, honest and endearing."

— *Chick Lit Central*

"Completely relatable and so well written."

— *Chick Lit Club*

Praise for *Waiting for Ethan*

"Fans of romantic beach-reads will find that this book's charismatic heroine makes it an engrossing page-turner."

— *Kirkus Reviews*

"The novel is written in a breezy fashion and is likely to keep you furiously turning the pages until the back cover is reached and you find yourself hungry for more."

— *Worcester Magazine*

"I didn't want to put it down."

— *Chick Lit Central*

"This is a great romantic read."

— *Chick Lit Club*

Praise for *More Than*

- **Ippy Awards 2020: Silver Medal: Best Adult Fiction Ebook**
- **Indies Today 2020: Best Book of the Year Finalist**
- **NYC Big Book Award – Distinguished Favorite**
- *Ms. Magazine* favorite holiday book to curl up with
- Booktrib selection celebrating women's midlife transitions

"Peggy is an inspirational character."
— *Chick Lit Central*

"A story that is truly inspired and truly inspiring!"
— *Indies Today*

"A book chockfull of heart!"
— Annie Hartnett, award winning author of *Rabbit Cake, Unlikely Animals*

"a pace that keeps the pages turning."
— Jennifer Klepper, *USA TODAY* bestselling author of *Unbroken Threads*

"fresh, crisp, and real."
— Kelly Stone Gamble, *USA TODAY* bestselling author of *They Call Me Crazy*

Praise for *All We Could Still Have*

"A deeply moving story...Barnes masterly weaves through darkness to discover light and takes the reader on a beautiful journey."
— Suzanne Redfearn, #1 Amazon bestselling author of *In an Instant*

"I read this book in one night, holding my breath until the very last line."
— Ann Garvin, *USA Today* bestselling author

"Diane Barnes is a masterful storyteller...Readers will fall in love with *All We Could Still Have* from the very first page."
— Barbara Conrey, *USA Today* bestselling author of *Nowhere Near Goodbye*

"Her story will leave you with the most redemptive emotion of them all: hope."
— Alli Frank & Asha Youmans, authors of *Never Meant to Meet You* and *Tiny Imperfections*

Also by Diane Barnes

All We Could Still Have
Waiting for Ethan
More Than

MIXED SIGNALS

DIANE BARNES

◇

BRIGHT DIAMOND
Division of Locomax Publishing

This is a work of fiction. Names, characters, organizations, places, events, and incidents are either products of the author's imagination or are used fictitiously. Any resemblance to actual persons, living or dead, or actual events is purely coincidental.

Text copyright © 2015 by Diane Barnes
Revised 2023
All rights reserved

No part of this book may be reproduced, or stored in a retrieval system, or transmitted in any form or by any means, electronic, mechanical, photocopying, recording, or otherwise, without express written permission from the author.

www.dianembarnes.com

ISBN-13: 9781736720097
ISBN-10: 1736720090

Cover design by Erica Lucke Dean
Printed in the United States of America

*For Shirley: We love and miss you.
You taught me about strength, courage, and playing
the hand you're dealt.
In my heart, you are kayaking, playing golf, and taking
long, pain-free walks along the rocky Maine coastline again.*

Chapter 1

"Have you set a date?" The phone line crackles with my mother's excitement. It's our regular Saturday morning call, and it's the first time we've spoken since Nico moved out. I twist the diamond around my finger, thinking about how to respond.

My landlord, Mr. O'Brien, is the only one who knows Nico's gone. He left last Sunday, exactly twenty-three days after giving me the ring. Packed all his belongings in the back of his pickup during halftime and drove off near the end of the fourth quarter, minutes after Tom Brady was sacked. Mr. O'Brien watched the whole thing from his living room window. After Nico drove away, he came out to the walkway where I was standing and trying not to cry. He pointed to an oil spot where Nico's truck had been. "If he comes back, you tell him no more parking in the driveway."

"Jillian, are you still there?" my mother asks.

I take a deep breath and relax my shoulders. "We haven't set a date yet."

"I guess it will depend on the reception hall." I hear pages turning and imagine her flipping through a calendar. "Dad and I are thinking of coming next month. I have a list of places we can visit."

"Next month's not good." I can feel my underarms getting sticky. "Work is really busy, for me and Nico both."

"You work too hard. Can't you take some time off?"

Outside the sound of a snowblower starting startles me. I walk to my bedroom window and lift the shade. There are about five inches on the driveway that Mr. O'Brien and his grandson Zachary are clearing, and it's still coming down. I didn't know it was supposed to snow. I guess I haven't been paying attention to the forecast, or anything else, since Nico left. "Come in the spring when the weather is better. Nico will get Dad Red Sox tickets. Up on the Green Monster." Nico produces *BS Morning Sports Talk*, a Boston-based radio show. Tickets are a perk of his job.

"I think he'd rather see the Bruins," she says.

"We'll take him to a game at the end of the season." Hockey goes for another three months. Nico will be back long before then. He is coming back. I'm sure of it because his favorite coat is still hanging on the back of the kitchen chair. That worn brown leather jacket is as much a part of him as his ever-present razor stubble. He never would have left it here if he didn't plan to return.

"How is Nico?" my mother asks. "Excited about getting married?" Outside, the snowblower stops.

"Nervous." That's not a lie. Why else would he do what he did?

She laughs. "Can I talk to him?"

In the nineteen months that Nico has lived with me, she has never once asked to speak with him. My shirt is now soaked under the arms. I'll have to take a shower when I hang up. "He's not here," I manage to say.

"Where is he?"

"At his sister's." Also true. He called Monday after he to tell me he's staying with her, his eight-year-old twin three-month old nephew, and Baxter, the minia- er. My doorbell rings. "Mom, I have to go."

Mixed Signals

I disconnect and rush to open the door. Mr. O'Brien stands there shivering in an unzipped Red Sox winter jacket and his grease-streaked blue baseball cap with the red B. I hold the door open for him to come in. He doesn't move. I swear he's looking at my ring. What he's thinking is so clear that there may as well be a thought bubble floating over his head: *Why are you still wearing that? He's gone and not coming back.*

Finally he lifts his head. His watery blue eyes meet mine. Every time we talk, I fight the urge to get my tweezers and pull out the wiry dark hairs that stick straight out of his bushy white eyebrows.

"I need you to move your car to the end of the driveway." He trudges back across the porch without waiting for me to answer.

The first six or so years that I lived on the left side of Mr. O'Brien's duplex, he liked me. Gave me tomatoes from his garden every summer and a break on my rent every Christmas. The day after Nico moved in, he stopped me on the staircase to the basement, where I was heading to do my laundry. "He's living with you now?" His expression and tone were the same as my mother's the day I told her I wanted to quit piano lessons. "More wear and tear on the property. Higher water bills. I'm going to have to raise your rent." He tugged on the bill of his dirty Red Sox cap. "Two hundred more a month."

"Two hundred!" It was a 25 percent increase.

"Okay, one fifty."

So now I pay more and don't get any tomatoes or December discounts.

I bundle up in my ski coat, hat, gloves, and boots and head outside to move my car and help Mr. O'Brien and Zachary with the shoveling. We didn't have to worry about snow removal last winter because Nico has a plow on his truck. He needs it because he leaves for work at four thirty in the morning and has to go in regardless of the road conditions. His show never gets canceled. Boston loves to talk sports.

"Where's your boyfriend with the plow?" Zachary asks. His voice is much deeper than I remember, and he must have had a growth spurt since the summer because he towers over me and his grandfather now.

Mr. O'Brien is bending over the snowblower, about to pull the cord that starts it. He straightens.

"He's away." I'm focusing so hard on clearing the snow from my windshield that you'd think the task requires a doctorate.

"I hope he's back before the next storm," Zachary says.

⚜ ⚜ ⚜

When I go back inside, I have a message from my best friend, Rachel, inviting me and Nico to her house for dinner. Rachel has called four times since he left. I've ignored all her messages instructing me to call her back. I don't want to tell her about Nico because she'll hold it against him long after he returns. Rachel didn't think it was a good idea for me to let Nico move in, not without a ring. When the one-year anniversary of Nico's move-in date passed with no mention of marriage, she told me I needed to give him a deadline. I didn't, but I did tell him what Rachel said.

"What kind of deadline?" he asked. He was watching a baseball game, and he didn't take his eyes off the television.

"If you don't propose within six months, she wants me to kick you out."

"Damn it, no!" he yelled.

"I'm just telling you what she said."

He climbed out of his recliner and headed toward the kitchen for another beer. As he passed me, he said, "He walked the bases loaded and then Sandoval swings on the first pitch and hits into a double play. Inning over. No runs."

I turned my attention back to my book, sure he had no idea what I had just told him, but five months later, after he proposed, he winked and said, "Now you don't have to throw me out."

Even though I wouldn't have asked Nico to leave, it was time for us to get engaged. I'm thirty-four. He's thirty-eight. We'd been dating for six years. Rachel says every year spent dating in your thirties is like three years of dating in your twenties because by your thirties, you know exactly what you want. I don't know why she thinks she's such an expert. She got married at twenty-seven and was a mother by twenty-nine. She has three children now and is talking about having a fourth.

The day before Nico moved out, he and I spent the afternoon babysitting Rachel's kids. On the ride home from her house, Nico was uncharacteristically quiet. When we pulled into our driveway, he killed the engine and turned to me. "I don't think I can do this."

The curtains in Mr. O'Brien's living room shifted, and the old man's face appeared in the window. "Do what?"

"The husband, father, family thing."

I pulled my eyes off Mr. O'Brien and turned toward Nico. Even though the truck was parked, he had a death grip on the steering wheel. "What are you talking about?"

"I just—" He stopped talking and pinched the bridge of his nose. "I'm sorry, Jill." Our eyes met. He had tears in the corners of his. "I don't want to be a father. I'd be lousy at it."

"But you're great with Rachel's kids."

Nico rested his head on the steering wheel. The motion lights clicked off, and the driveway turned dark. I touched his arm. "Hey, it's okay. You have a little case of cold feet. It's normal. I'm nervous too. We'll get through it."

"Yeah," he said. "A minor case of cold feet, that must be what it is." Early in our relationship I might not have recognized his sarcasm, but I was an expert at identifying it now. He opened the driver's door. The lights snapped back on as he stepped onto the driveway. "I wouldn't be a good husband, Jill." He slammed the driver's door with so much force that the entire truck shook. I unbuckled my seat belt but stayed put in the passenger seat, watching Nico as he made his way down the walkway, up the stairs, and across the front porch to our side of the house. If I hadn't seen him just leave the vehicle, I might have thought the retreating image was Mr. O'Brien, the way his shoulders slumped and his back hunched.

We didn't talk anymore about what Nico said that night. When I left for the tennis club just before noon the next day, he was settled on the couch watching the Patriots' pregame show. I got home about two and a half hours later to find his pickup filled with boxes of his belongings and his hideous orange recliner. I wanted to back out of the driveway, race back to the club, and smash fuzzy green balls all over the court.

Instead, I made myself get out of the car and on wobbly legs forced myself to go inside and hear whatever it was he was about to say. Nico was sitting on the couch watching the football game. On television, the sports announcer screamed, "And Brady's sacked. The ball is loose!"

Nico stood. "I'm sorry, Jill. I can't go through with it."

The talking head on TV was still yelling. "Was his arm going forward or was it a fumble?"

"Fumble," Nico said as he walked past me and out the door.

CHAPTER 2

Instead of sleeping, I lie in my suddenly too-big bed staring at the glow-in-the-dark star decals stuck to my ceiling, and replay everything Nico said to me since our engagement. I can't remember anything that even hinted he was unhappy or thinking about leaving. Rachel's kids were a little wild on the day Nico broke the news; her three-year-old, Laurence, cried almost the entire time she was gone. Is that what scared Nico off? On the drive home from Rachel's, we were stopped at a red light; Nico didn't notice it turn green because he was so lost in thought. I had to tell him the light had changed and he could go. Is that when he was deciding to leave, or had he made the decision long before then and was working up the courage to tell me?

Next door, the shower goes on. Without looking at the clock, I know it's ten thirty. Mr. O'Brien gets ready for bed every night at the same time. I don't understand people who bathe before they go to sleep rather than when they wake up. It's something I didn't understand about Nico either, apparently one of many things.

At one o'clock, I give up trying to fall asleep and instead open my book, *Growing Up Pedro*. Nico gave it to me for Christmas. It's about Pedro Martinez, his all-time favorite Red Sox player. If anything will help me fall asleep, it's this book. I prefer fiction. The next thing I know, my alarm is going off and my book is on the floor. My head pounds so much that I'm sure there are a bunch of little men inside my skull trying to jackhammer their way out. I stagger to the bathroom and open the medicine cabinet. All the shelves are empty except the top one, where a lone box of tampons sits. I slam the door shut, causing it to jump off its track. What kind of jerk takes all the aspirin and cold remedies with him?

Forty minutes later, I make my way across the front porch and down to my car. Mr. O'Brien has already sprinkled sand over the frozen walkway, and his Buick is gone. For a retired guy, he sure gets busy early. I pull my hood over my head before I begin scraping the ice off my Accord. I'm just finishing the back windshield when the tires of Mr. O'Brien's station wagon crunch over the hardened snow at the end of the driveway. Even with his car windows closed, I can hear he's listening to *BS Morning Sports Talk.* According to Nico, the old man phones into the program at least three times a week using the alias Frank from South Boston. I'm not really sure if the caller is Mr. O'Brien, because his first name is Walter and we live in West Newton, but Nico's convinced it's him by the caller's habit of clearing his throat. Something Mr. O'Brien does regularly when he speaks more than a few words.

"Good morning," I say.

Mr. O'Brien acknowledges me by lifting his Styrofoam Dunkin' Donuts cup in my direction as he plods his way past me. The smell of coffee makes me wish he had brought one for me, something he sometimes did before Nico moved in. When he reaches his front door, he calls out, "Did he leave his key?"

I throw the ice scraper into my backseat, feeling like I missed part of this conversation. "Who?"

"Who?" He repeats it in a way that makes me feel like the dumbest person in the world. He clears his throat. "The young man who's been living in my house with you."

"No."

Mr. O'Brien sighs loudly before slamming his door.

⚜ ⚜ ⚜

On the drive to work, I tune into Nico's show as I do every morning. The hosts, Sean Branigan and Barry Smyth, aren't discussing sports. Instead, they're insulting a female sideline reporter who covered one of the playoff football games over the weekend. "She's hideous," Smyth says.

"How many times do you think she hit the concession stands during the game?" Branigan asks.

My jaw locks. I don't like these guys. Then it occurs to me: I don't have to listen to them—not until Nico comes home anyway. I smile as I change the radio to another station. Take that, Nico! You just lost a listener. I keep changing channels until a song I like comes on. I sing along with Taylor Swift about haters hating.

I'm still singing when I lower my window to order coffee at the drive-thru window. "Shake it off and order," the voice from the speaker says.

⚜ ⚜ ⚜

As I walk across the pedestrian bridge that leads from the parking garage to my office building, an icy gust of wind stings my face. I lower my head and run the rest of the way. When I enter the lobby, I tell myself that I need to be on my game today. In addition to changes in my personal life, my professional life is unstable as well. The company

I work for, CyberCrimeBusters, was recently acquired by a venture capital firm, which immediately changed our name to Cyber Security Consultants. Clients hire us to assess the security of their websites and technology applications. Basically they pay us to hack into their systems and close up the holes that allowed us to do so. Our new owners have big plans for expanding our business, starting with refining our brand. As one of a four-person marketing team, I have a lot of work to do to change the company's image. My coworkers are Renee Boudrot, who, like me, is a writer, and Ben Colby, the graphic designer. The three of us report to Stacy Taylor, who is the vice president of marketing.

Now, as I board the elevator, Ryan and Tyler, two twenty-something salesmen, get on with me. "Tell Nico great show today," Tyler, the light-haired one, says. My body tenses at the mention of Nico's name. In the four years I've worked here, he has attended every holiday party with me and several of our frequent after-work outings. The sports fans among my colleagues are impressed by his job. All night long, they buy him drinks and talk about Boston's teams. Most of the men outside Sales and Marketing don't know me as Jillian Atwood but instead think of me as that girl who dates the guy who produces *BS Morning Sports Talk*.

The elevator stops. "Any chance you can hook me up with tickets to Friday's Celtics game?" Ryan, the tall one, asks as we all step out onto the fourth floor.

"Sorry, no." If Nico doesn't come back, my coworkers and I will mourn together.

At the entrance to my section of the building, I fumble through my purse for my access badge. When I find it, I hold it up to the card reader, and the door clicks open. As I walk by row after row of dull gray cubes, I hear the slogan for

Mixed Signals

BS Morning Sports Talk coming from several of them: "The number-one-rated sports talk show in New England—and that's not BS."

I push my diamond around my finger with my thumb. Nico saying he doesn't want to get married is BS. If he meant it, wouldn't he have asked for the ring back?

I reach the aisle by the windows, where my department sits. No one is there. My coworkers' jackets are hanging on the hooks outside their cubes, so I know they're somewhere in the building, probably getting coffee. I settle in behind my computer and log into email. An alert for this morning's meeting flashes in the bottom right corner of my screen, telling me I'm eleven minutes late. *So much for being on my game today.* I run to the end of the hall to Stacy's office and burst through the door. Ben's and Renee's heads both snap in my direction. Stacy looks pointedly at her watch.

"Sorry," I mutter.

"We're brainstorming images for the new website," Stacy says.

"So far we've come up with a lock," Ben says. As usual, his light brown hair is still damp, and he smells like Irish Spring soap.

"We'll think about the images later," Stacy says. "Let's spend some time coming up with buzzwords and catchphrases we can use in our messaging."

Renee and I throw out ideas. Ben remains quiet, doodling on his notepad. I look down and see he's drawing a picture of Renee with her short, spiky black hair on fire and smoke coming out of her nostrils and ears. Over the past few months, she has started having hot flashes, and Ben teases her mercilessly about them.

"Prevent penetration," he offers.

"Gross," Renee says.

I scrunch my nose. Although the words definitely relate to cyber security, coming from Ben, who never sleeps with the same woman more than once, they sound dirty. As far as I can tell, his relationships usually last the same amount of time as the company's pay period: two weeks.

Stacy's computer beeps. "I have another meeting. Email me a list of catchphrases and images ideas by Wednesday."

Ben, Renee, and I stand. "Jillian," Stacy says, "how come I haven't seen a draft of the article on security risks in the health care industry?"

Yikes! With all that's going on with Nico and the acquisition, I forgot I'm supposed to be ghostwriting an article for our CEO. "I'll send it to you at the end of the day."

"Send me what you have so far," she says.

"I haven't started it yet." Embarrassed by my oversight, I can't meet her eyes, and look at the ground as I speak.

Stacy pulls a red and yellow stress ball, with the old CyberCrimeBusters name circling it, from her top desk drawer. "It's due tomorrow." She's squeezing the ball so tightly that her knuckles are white. "Send it to me by three today," she says.

I nod. Renee, Ben, and I file out of her office.

"What's going on with you, Jillian?" Ben asks when we are out of Stacy's earshot.

"What do you mean?"

"You're coming in late, forgetting projects, and you look like you didn't sleep all weekend," he says.

"Concealer, sweetie," Renee says. She's a few steps behind us. "Cover those dark circles right up."

Dark circles are only part of the problem. My long brown hair refuses to hold a wave. My usually dark complexion is pasty. The dimple on my cheek seems shallower. Even the blue of my eyes seems muted. It's like Nico took my sparkle with him when he left. For a minute, I think about confessing that he moved out, but being dumped less than a month after getting engaged is too embarrassing to talk about. Besides, when Nico returns, Renee will make it her mission to convince me not to take him back. From the moment she first laid eyes on him, she didn't like him. *You'd think knowing he was meeting your coworkers, he would have bothered to shave,* she said. *He looks dirty.* She didn't believe me when I told her that he had in fact shaved an hour or two before we left the house. While Renee dislikes Nico's facial hair, to me, his fast-growing beard is the epitome of masculinity, part of his sexual prowess. I can't imagine him without it.

Ben and Nico aren't friendly either. They met at a holiday party a few weeks after I started. I was wearing a short black sleeveless dress that showed off my arms and legs. Ben told me I looked smoking hot. He said the exact same thing to Renee and Stacy, but Nico insisted he had a different tone and look in his eyes when he said it to me. I think Ben makes him insecure. Nico never would admit it, but he's jealous of Ben's good looks. A green-eyed devilish version of Bradley Cooper is what Renee calls Ben, and her description is spot-on.

⚜ ⚜ ⚜

When I get home that night, the driveway is empty and my side of the duplex is dark. The thick row of long, pointy icicles hanging off the roof makes the house look haunted. In a way it is, with memories of Nico.

Usually when I make my way across the front porch, I can smell dinner cooking—steak on the grill Nico used on the back deck all year long, or garlic and basil from the Italian dishes he liked to whip up. The lack of a scent tonight is another reminder that he's gone.

Inside, the apartment is quiet. *SportsCenter* isn't blaring from the television. Worse, Nico isn't there to greet me with a kiss or tease me by rubbing his razor-stubbled face over my cheek. The only sign that he was ever here is his jacket hanging over the back of the chair. I take mine off and slip into his. It's big and cozy and smells like his woodsy aftershave. I take a deep breath and imagine him hugging me. He always squeezes a bit too hard, as if he can't get a good enough grip on me. Turns out I was the one who should have been holding on tighter.

I push back the sleeves, reach into the pockets, and pull out a handful of cinnamon candies from one and a folded piece of paper from the other. I unfold the note. It's Sean Branigan's letterhead. Below his name, the number 4.6 is written in thick black ink. I pop one of the candies in my mouth while I try to figure out what the number means. I come up with a pretty good guess: Branigan and Smyth are fond of rating women. Like they did today, they often waste on-air time discussing women's appearances: the hottest sports wife, the ugliest female sports reporter, the actress they'd give up ten years of their lives to sleep with, the star that they would choose death over sleeping with. A female intern started on the show a few weeks ago. The 4.6 is probably Branigan's rating of her looks. The guy is such a pig, but Nico idolizes him. I imagine him laughing when Branigan slipped him the note. *That's a little harsh. She's not that bad,* he probably said in a halfhearted attempt to defend the poor girl. As I think about it, I'm chomping the sucker into tiny pieces with my back molars. It drives me nuts the way Nico never stands up to Branigan. I rip off the jacket and fling it back over the chair.

As if he can see what I'm doing, Nico chooses that moment to call. My phone vibrates on the kitchen table as I debate whether to answer it. What if he's calling to get his coat back, or the ring? I'd have to admit it's really over. Nope. I'm not answering. Maybe he'll think I went out with Ben after work for drinks. That would make him insane. I imagine him jumping in his truck and driving by the restaurants near my office. When he finds me, he muscles his way past Ben and confesses he's made a horrible mistake. By the fourth ring, I've convinced myself Nico wants to come home and that's why he's calling. I scramble to answer before he hangs up because Lord knows, he won't leave a message.

"Hello," I say in a voice that I hope conveys I'm put out by his calling.

"Hey," he says. "How you doing?" His tone is friendly, like he's calling from work to check in and didn't recently move everything he owns out of the apartment we've shared for the past year and a half—plus all the painkillers.

I decide to play the game with him. "I'm okay." It comes out much louder and more forceful than I usually speak. "Have a bit of a headache though and can't find any aspirin. Could have sworn there was a brand-new bottle in the medicine cabinet."

He hesitates before responding. "I didn't know if you'd want to hear from me." His voice is hoarse, which happens whenever he's tired. "But I've been worried about you."

I don't know whether to think it's sweet that he's worried or incredibly arrogant. "Why?"

"Well, I've been wondering what you're eating without me there to cook for you." He laughs like he's joking.

It makes sense that he'd be concerned about that though. I'm a disaster in the kitchen. "I'm eating fine." I glance toward the counter at the box of Rice Krispies I plan to have for dinner, if I get hungry.

Nico yawns.

"You sound exhausted," I say, being nicer because being angry with him is something that I haven't mastered yet.

"No kidding. Between the baby crying and that little yappy dog barking all night, it's hard to get any sleep."

Then come home.

Do not say that out loud.

"I don't know how much longer I can take it."

Do not ask him to come back.

"I'm gonna have to find my own place soon."

"Or you could just come home." Sometimes I hate myself.

The fifteen or so seconds that neither of us says anything seems longer than my entire workday. Finally Nico breaks the uncomfortable silence. "Okay, so bye for now, Jill."

I go to bed at eleven, wondering exactly what he meant by *for now.* Until he calls again? Until he moves back in? Until he unexpectedly runs into me on the street? At three o'clock, I'm still awake. Only now I'm berating myself for asking Nico to come home. The toilet flushes on Mr. O'Brien's side of the duplex. Somehow I'm sure the old man's telling me what he thinks of my telling Nico to come home too.

Chapter 3

"I'm calling to confirm your appointment for a tour tomorrow at ten." It's Janice from the Westham Country Club. It's Friday, just past nine. She called my office phone, catching me off guard because I don't remember giving her this number. Then again, I didn't remember that Nico and I were supposed to meet with her either.

We scheduled the appointment the day after we got engaged. It was Nico's idea. He's always wanted to play golf there, but it's a private club with the exception of the function room, which is open to the public for events with at least one hundred people.

"I heard if you have your wedding there, they give you a free round," he said. "We can get married in the late afternoon, and I'll play in the morning." He planned to have two groomsmen and a best man to complete the foursome.

"I have to cancel," I whisper, afraid to say it loudly because I don't want Ben and Renee to overhear and figure out that Nico and I are having problems. On some level, I realize this is ridiculous because even if they hear me, they would have no idea what I'm talking about.

"Excuse me," Janice says. "I couldn't hear you."

"Something's come up. We won't be able to make it." I speak louder, but my voice cracks.

"I see," Janice says. "Would you like to reschedule?"

I swallow the lump in my throat. "Yes, but I'll have to call you back." I hang up before she has a chance to respond.

Then, even though I know I shouldn't, I can't help myself; I text Nico: *Westham CC called to confirm our appt. Said we'd reschedule. When do u want to go?* As soon as I hit send, I wish I could reach into cyberspace and retrieve the message. Damn, why do I ignore my good instincts and listen to the bad?

I sit completely still, staring out the window waiting for him to respond. My office park is nestled in a wooded area behind the highway. In the spring, summer, and fall, the view of the trees is beautiful. This time of year though, there are no leaves. All I see are barren limbs, gray skies, and a waist-high covering of snow. As I knew it would, my phone remains silent on my desk. I shove it in my top desk drawer so that it will be out of sight, and I won't be tempted to send any more pathetic texts.

For the rest of the morning, I work on the website rewrite and don't leave my cube. Every now and then, Ben or Renee shouts something over the walls, and they both laugh. Usually I would join in on their banter, but Janice's call has further soured my mood. Sunday will mark two full weeks since Nico left. It's the longest we have been apart since we met. It might be time to face the fact that he isn't coming back.

"Yo, Jill." Ben is standing in his cube, looking down over the almost-six-foot wall separating it from mine. I hate that he's tall enough to see over it because I can't get any privacy. "Renee and I are going out to grab some grub. Do you want to come?"

"No, thanks."

"What are you going to have?" he asks, running a hand through his hair.

I shrug. "Cereal."

"Cereal's not lunch. Why don't you come with us?"

"Because I don't want to," I snap, immediately regretting my tone. It's Nico I'm mad at, not Ben.

Ben sways backward, as though my words hit him with force, momentarily knocking him off balance. We stare at each other without speaking.

"Sorry," I finally mutter, spinning my chair away from him.

"Did you and Nico have a fight?"

I whirl back toward him. "No! Why would you ask that?"

"Because he's in a terrible mood today too."

In the hallway, there's a stampede of footsteps and loud voices as people make their way toward the cafeteria.

"How do you know that?"

"Branigan and Smyth were talking about it this morning."

I stand and walk over to Ben's cube. "On air?"

"No, at the coffee shop where I had breakfast with them."

I look at him blankly.

"Of course, on air."

"What did they say?"

"That he's been miserable for a couple of weeks."

He's miserable because he misses me! "Did they mention why he's miserable?"

Ben shrugs. "Just that he took it out on the intern. He fired her."

"Nico fired the intern?" I can't imagine him doing that. On the other hand, maybe after dismissing me as his fiancée, he's on a power trip. Or maybe Branigan insisted on hiring someone he would rate higher than a 4.6 for the job.

"Yup. Branigan indicated he's not getting along with the women in his life." Ben cocks one eyebrow.

"Are you two fighting, honey?" Renee asks. I didn't realize she was standing in the aisle listening.

"No!" *Tell them*, a rational voice inside me urges.

"Are you sure?" Ben asks. "Because you haven't been yourself lately, and you've stopped listening to his show."

It's true that I haven't listened all week, but I'm surprised Ben pays enough attention to me to have noticed.

"And you look horrible," Renee says, entering his cube. "Could pack enough clothes for a week's vacation in the bags under your eyes." She taps Ben on the shoulder. "Doesn't she look awful?"

"Hey," I say.

Ben studies me. "You look sad."

"Cucumbers or tea bags will help with those." Renee swipes the area under her eye.

"What else did Branigan and Smyth say?" I ask. *Damn! Why haven't I been listening?*

"Chilled tea bags," Renee adds. "I have some in my cube that you can put in the freezer."

Ben sighs like he's had enough of this conversation. "That he made a big mistake that he intends to fix this weekend."

For the first time in weeks, I smile. "He's going to fix it this weekend." I'm giddy as I repeat the words.

I imagine Nico showing up at my door with a dozen roses, confessing that he can't live without me. Mr. O'Brien watches the apology from his side of the porch. *Take care of the oil leak before you park in the driveway again*, he growls.

Should I play hard to get? Make Nico grovel? No. I will accept his apology with class. We'll move on. Plan our wedding. Years from now, we'll laugh about this entire thing; I'm sure of it.

"So what happened?" Ben asks.

"Nothing. Just a minor misunderstanding." I glance down at my diamond, not sure if it or I am sparkling more.

"Expect to fight a lot while you're planning the wedding," Renee says. "Lenny and I had some knock-down-drag-out arguments. I would have dumped him if the makeup sex wasn't so good."

Sometimes when people say things, I automatically picture them. I feel myself blushing as I see Renee and her robust husband tumbling onto a bed. *Think of something else. A puppy.*

Renee continues, "All these years later, it's just as good."
An adorable little black Lab.
"Last night, he—"
The dog is wagging its tail.
"Let's go to lunch," Ben says.
"Good idea," I say, suddenly starving.

⚜ ⚜ ⚜

Later that afternoon, Ben, Renee, and I are in Ben's cube reviewing images he's considering for the home page. "I like this one," Renee says. "Do you like it, Jill?"

I didn't see which of the five she pointed to because I was looking at my phone, which just vibrated with a text from Rachel. Now that I know Nico plans to apologize, I keep waiting for him to call or text.

"Which one?" I ask.

"Give me that," Ben says, snatching the phone off my thigh.

I try to get it back, but he jumps up and holds it high in the air above his head. "You'll get it back when we're done here."

Standing on my tiptoes, I try to reach it. "Give it back."

"Nope."

"Fine." I pretend to return to my seat. When he drops his arm, I pounce, grabbing the phone.

"Hey," he yells, trying to wrestle it away from me.

"You two are worse than my kids," Renee says.

Ben pins me against the wall. I try to squirm free but can't. I place my hands behind my back so that he can't get to them. He reaches behind me with both his arms like he's hugging me.

Outside his cube, there's a throaty laugh. "What's going on here?" It's Ellie Gardner, the company's top salesperson and my best friend at work. Ellie and I started on the same day and went through orientation together. I'm not embarrassed to say that in those first days of working together, I developed a girl crush on her. With her trendy short blond hair and big blue eyes, she's adorable. Before Ben found out she was married, he used to always flirt with her. "Would HR approve?"

Ben releases me. "He stole my phone," I say.

"Because she's paying more attention to it than me," he says.

The phone vibrates in my hand. I look down at it.

"See. It must be from Nico," Ben says, placing all the emphasis on my fiancé's Greek name. "Look at how excited she is."

It's true that I have a big smile on my face and am bouncing up and down on the balls of my feet as I see Nico's name flash across my screen and read his message: *I need to talk to you. Will you be home tomorrow afternoon?*

My response is fast and brief: *Yes!* ☺

"You sound jealous, Benjamin," Ellie says.

"Jill's my work wife. I don't like him interfering with our time together." He wraps his arm around my waist and pulls me closer, making it clear that he's mimicking a possessive boyfriend. "When she's with me, her full attention should be on me. I don't want her thinking about Nico."

Chapter 4

For the first time in weeks, I'm able to sleep through the night on Friday and wake up well rested. It's going to be a long day waiting to talk to Nico. I've been trying to figure out why he wanted to meet in the afternoon instead of the morning. All I can come up with is that he's planning something special. He'll show up in a limousine and whisk me off to the airport, where we'll board a plane for Aruba. Maybe we'll even elope there. It's not that far-fetched. It's a slow time of year for him. Football season just ended, and it's still a few months before baseball starts. Branigan and Smyth don't like talking about basketball and hockey, so they sprinkle in discussions about politics, television shows, and movies. It's the time of year Nico dreads most because they usually get in trouble for saying something inappropriate on air.

At ten o'clock, my phone rings. For a split second, I think Nico's calling early, but then I realize it's time for my weekly call with my mother. "Any news on your wedding plans?" she starts right off.

"We're going to talk about it later today," I promise.

Thankfully, she drops the subject. She tells me she had dinner with my brother, Christian, and his family last night. He's the reason my parents moved to Atlanta—well, he and his daughter, my adorable niece, Molly. A few months before

Molly's second birthday, my sister-in-law, Susannah, decided she didn't want to raise her daughter so far from her parents, so she and my brother moved to Georgia, where Susannah grew up. My mother and father decided they couldn't live so far away from their granddaughter, so they left too. It's been four years, and I still can't believe they left me here by myself. I had always suspected Christian was their favorite child, and my parents' move south of the Mason-Dixon Line confirmed it. After they moved, Nico and I became our own unofficial family of two. He was there for me when no one else was.

My mother ends her discussion on my brother's family by bringing our conversation full circle. "Molly expects to be a flower girl in your wedding," she says. "She's excited about it."

"I have to go. I have a tennis match," I say, grateful for an excuse to get off the phone. I'll be much more comfortable talking about the wedding after I speak with Nico this afternoon.

Zachary's Civic is parked behind my car, blocking it in, so I have to knock on Mr. O'Brien's door. The old man answers with a donut in his hand. He takes a bite, chews but doesn't say a thing.

The cold wind feels like ice on my bare legs, making me wish I were wearing sweatpants over my tennis skirt. "Can you ask Zachary to move his car, please?"

Mr. O'Brien glances toward the driveway before shouting for his grandson. Dressed in red-and-black plaid pajama pants and a red sweatshirt, Zachary bounds to the doorway. Powdered sugar covers his mouth. "We were just talking about you," he says.

I imagine Mr. O'Brien and Zachary sitting at the old man's yellow Formica kitchen table, Zac's elbow inadvertently resting in a sticky old syrup spill as he listens to his grandfather. *The boyfriend left weeks ago and she's still wearing the ring.* Mr. O'Brien rotates his finger near his head to indicate I'm crazy.

"Why were you talking about me?" I'm not sure I should have asked that.

"Well, not really about you, about your boyfriend. I heard he fired the intern yesterday."

Mr. O'Brien takes another bite of his donut and chews deliberately while staring at me.

"Do you think—" Zachary pauses to brush the white powder off his chest. "I need an internship. I was thinking it would be really cool to work at a sports show." He looks at me expectantly.

I notice one black hair in his blond eyebrow and immediately look to the wiry dark stray hair in his grandfather's. Could it be genetics?

"Can you ask him? I haven't seen him around or I'd ask him myself."

Mr. O'Brien watches me through narrowed eyes.

"Oh, I don't know," I say. "I think you need to be eighteen and out of high school to work there." That's a complete fabrication. I have no idea if there's an age requirement. Lying has become a bad habit since Nico left.

"I am eighteen, almost nineteen," Zachary says. "I'm a freshman at Northeastern."

Whoa, how did that happen? He wasn't even a teenager when I moved into the left side of his grandfather's duplex.

"When will he be home?" Zachary asks. "I'll talk to him myself."

"Maybe later today."

Mr. O'Brien scowls. I swear I see the word *liar* flash through his mind. "You know, Zac," he says, "her boyfriend goes to work very early. In the middle of the night practically." He makes *boyfriend* sound like a dirty word.

Zachary shrugs. "I'm used to getting up early for hockey."

Mr. O'Brien walks away without another word. In my mind, I shout after him: *I'm not lying. He texted me yesterday. He might be coming home. This afternoon even.*

⚜ ⚜ ⚜

A crowd of members dressed in white surround the floor-to-ceiling window looking over court one. I wedge my way in to see what they're all watching. Down below, Sean Branigan and his wife, Tammy, are playing doubles against another couple whom I don't recognize. Tammy stands behind the baseline. The ball bounces near her. She uses a backhand to return it, but she swings wildly, and it lands out of bounds on the other side of the court. Sean bangs the net with his racquet and screams something at her.

"That guy hates to lose," the man on my right says.

"It's a wonder they stay married playing together," a woman on my left says.

It's a wonder she married him in the first place, I think.

Tammy tosses the ball up in the air for the next serve. She faults and tries again. This time the ball lands in the service box, and her male opponent returns it to her. She hits it back with a perfect backhand. The other side tries a drop shot on Tammy's half of the court, but Sean races crosscourt, cutting off his wife, and reaches the ball just before it bounces twice. The rally lasts for several strokes and ends when Sean smashes an overhead shot the other team can't return. He looks up at the crowd by the window and bows. He fancies himself king of the court out there.

A bell rings. Everyone in the lobby hustles down the stairs to the tunnels leading to the tennis courts. I wait for my opponent, Jenny Stanton, who just arrived and is checking in. By the time she finishes, a second bell has sounded. We race downstairs to court one, where the Branigans were just playing. Their opponents are making their way through the revolving door, but the Branigans remain by the court.

Sean is sitting on the bench eating a banana. Next to him, his sweatshirt and sweatpants are folded neatly. His unzipped tennis bag rests on the ground in front of him. His wife sweeps loose clay off the court's lines.

Jenny frowns and looks at the clock. Players are supposed to stop the game and clean the area at the first bell and be off the court by the second. She drops her racquet and walks around picking up balls scattered near the baseline, something that Sean should have already done.

He reaches for his sweatpants and slides them on over his shorts. I put my bag down on the bench next to him. He watches me open it. "How are you, Jillian?" he asks.

"Great," I answer.

"Really?"

I can tell by the surprise in Branigan's voice that unlike me, Nico is telling people about our breakup. I wish he weren't because I can see it now, Branigan whispering to the guests at our wedding: *He almost didn't marry her. Got a bad case of cold feet three weeks after popping the question.*

I busy myself taking the plastic cover off a new can of tennis balls. Sean watches me carefully. His wife waves as she hangs the broom on a hook on the wall behind us. She walks over to the bench where we're sitting. "Your ring is gorgeous," she says.

It really is. Two emeralds flank a two-karat diamond in a white gold setting. Nico picked it out without any input from me. It's exactly what I would have chosen on my own. After six years together, he knows me well.

Sean's mouth drops open and his gaze falls to my left hand. "Have you talked to Nico today?" he asks.

"Not yet." I yank on the metal tab on the lid of the tennis balls. The can hisses as it opens. I breathe in the new ball scent, something I've always liked.

Sean places a hand on my shoulder as he stands. "I didn't think so," he says.

⚜ ⚜ ⚜

Dressed in his usual black sweatpants and blue polo shirt, David, the owner and my best friend Rachel's brother, leans against the counter, talking to another member as I head toward the exit after my match. Despite its stupid name, WimbleDome is the most prestigious tennis club in the area. Members shell out more than four hundred dollars a month to play here. Luckily, I pay less than two hundred. David gives me a break in exchange for marketing work that I do for him and because I grew up with him. He motions with his finger for me to wait. While he finishes his conversation, I study the brochure for the upcoming annual WimbleDome Mixed Doubles Tournament. There's a picture on the cover of Sean and Tammy Branigan hoisting a trophy over their heads with the caption "Club Mixed Doubles Champions, 2007–2015." The club opened in 2007, so no one has ever beaten them, something Branigan takes great pride in and brags about on the air at the time of the tournament. "For the ninth consecutive year, Tammy and I are the WimbleDome mixed double champions," he boasted last year. I swear he purposely mispronounced the name of David's club so that his idiotic listeners would think he was talking about the famous grass courts across the pond. Branigan then went on to waste a full hour of his show recapping each of the matches leading to the championship.

When I asked Nico why he allowed it, he shook his head. "Didn't have a choice. Winning that silly tournament means everything to the guy."

Nico's answer made me think Branigan must have always been the last kid picked in gym during elementary school and is still haunted by the memories. Why else would winning a title at a local club mean so much? It almost made me feel sorry for the guy.

David taps my shoulder. "Rachel says you're not returning her calls. She asked me to find out what's going on."

"Work has been super busy," I say. "I'll call her today."

"Make sure you do. She's worried."

⚜ ⚜ ⚜

The only good thing about Nico being gone is that I can watch something other than sports on television. When I get home from tennis, I set up camp on the couch and queue up some of my favorite movies, starting with *Pitch Perfect*. Forty-five minutes into the movie, a car door slams outside. I rush to the window, expecting to see Nico. Nope. It's Mr. O'Brien, weighed down with four or five plastic sacks of groceries. One of them rips open. A bottle of cranberry juice rolls down the walkway and boxes of frozen dinners spill to the ground. I think about going outside to help him, but by the time I put my boots on, he'll have picked up everything. I make a mental note to get him reusable cloth bags. Before returning to my movie, I head to the kitchen for a scoop of ice cream.

The movie ends a few minutes after four. Nico still hasn't called. I think about Branigan this morning, asking whether

I had spoken to Nico yet today, and the condescending way he said *I didn't think so* after I told him I hadn't. The ice cream churns in my stomach. For the first time, I wonder if I'm wrong about the reason Nico wants to talk to me. I text him, but he doesn't respond. By six o'clock, all my nerves are frayed, and I'm tired of waiting. I decide to call him. His voice mail picks up. I hang up without leaving a message. Forty-five minutes later, he calls back.

"Sorry I didn't have a chance to talk earlier," he says. "It's been a crazy day."

"That's okay."

The line is silent. I imagine Nico working up his courage to apologize. Maybe he's afraid I won't take him back? Outside a car door slams. I look out the window. Mr. O'Brien's daughter and Zachary's mother, Colleen, is carrying a dish covered with tinfoil to her father's door. Whatever is on the plate has to be better than the TV dinners that fell out of his torn shopping bag.

"You know Zachary, Mr. O'Brien's grandson," I say, glad I have a way to end the silence.

"Sure," Nico answers.

I tell him about Zac wanting to intern at the station.

"That's great. We need someone. Give him my number."

My stomach churns again. If he were planning on coming home, I wouldn't need to give Zachary his number because Nico would see him in person.

"Jill, I need to talk to you about a couple of things."

Here we go. Finally getting to the good part.

I sink into the couch. "Yes?" I kick my feet up onto the ottoman, trying to relax as I wait for him to confess how much he misses me and wants to come home.

"I found a place," he says. "I was out all day looking."

A place for our wedding? Did he go to Westham Country Club without me?

"It's in Brookline. Not too far from the studio. I'll be able to sleep later."

My breathing becomes shallow as I realize what he's referring to. Is it too late to hang up? Pretend I never answered.

"Jill, are you still there?"

My back is perfectly straight. My feet are back on the floor. "You're moving out of Nina's into your own apartment." *Please tell me I misunderstand what you're saying.*

"Yup. I can't get in for a few weeks. They need to fix up the place, but it's really nice. Even has its own parking spot."

"You're really not coming home?" My voice breaks. I wish I could kick my own butt.

"Look, Jill, I know this all seems sudden to you, but it's not. I've been thinking about it for a while."

"How can that be, when only a month ago you proposed?"

In the background, dishes clank. Is Nico having this discussion in front of Nina and her entire family? Why aren't they trying to stop him? Surely they don't want him to break up with me. The girls love me.

"At the time, it seemed like the right thing to do," he says.

"And now it doesn't?"

"I knew it was what you were expecting. What you wanted, so I did it."

"Are you saying you never wanted to marry me?"

The line goes quiet. For a moment I think he hung up, but then he says, "It's killing me that I'm hurting you. That was never my intention."

I leap to my feet. "You've confused me, and you've pissed me off, but you didn't hurt me. I'm fine."

He sighs. "Whatever you say."

"I'm hanging up now."

"Wait." He swallows. "The show. Branigan has this idea. We're going to be do—"

"I don't care about Branigan or your stupid show!" I pound on the end key and hurl the phone against the wall. The back falls off as it crashes to the floor. I pick it up and snap it back together. It rings in my hand. I look down at caller ID expecting to see Nico's name. Instead it's Mr. O'Brien's. *Crap!*

"Everything okay over there?" Colleen asks.

It was stupid to throw the phone against the wall, especially one that I share with my landlord. "Fine."

"We heard a loud bang. Did something break?"

Only my heart. Into a billion little pieces. "No. I dropped my phone. Everything's fine." My response is met with silence, so I go on. "Tell Zachary to call Nico about the internship. I'll give you his number."

"Let me get a pen," she says. I hear drawers squeaking open and banging shut. "Okay."

I spit out Nico's number.

"Jillian, are you all right? My dad told me about—"

"Did you get the number?"

She repeats it back to me.

"I have to go," I say and hang up quickly.

Chapter 5

On Sunday morning, I wake to my doorbell ringing over and over again. I glance at the clock. It's quarter to nine. Early for anyone except maybe Mr. O'Brien, unless Nico's had a change of heart? I pull my hair into a ponytail, brush my teeth, and throw on sweats and the Brady Number 12 Patriots shirt he gave me our first Christmas together. The ringing has been replaced by pounding. I make my way downstairs and pull open the door.

"Why are you avoiding me?" Rachel yells.

"I'm not avoiding you."

Mr. O'Brien's door swings open. He steps outside, eyeing Rachel and her five-year-old daughter, Sophie, like he's trying to determine if they are friend or foe. I wave to him. "What's all the shouting and pounding?" he asks.

"It was knocking," Rachel says. She pushes her way past me with Sophie following behind her.

Mr. O'Brien backs into his house and slams the door.

"Hi, Aunt Jillian." Sophie reaches up to hug me. I scoop her up and plant kisses all over her tiny face.

Rachel studies me as she removes her gloves and coat. "Are you sick?"

I shake my head.

"Well, you look awful." She continues past the staircase into the living room. She freezes in front of the couch. "It looks different in here."

I lower Sophie to the ground and concentrate on removing her jacket so that I don't have to look at Rachel when I speak. "We decluttered."

Rachel's quiet. I sneak a look at her. She's staring at the empty spot where Nico's hideous orange recliner used to be. "Nico let you get rid of his chair?"

Rachel's known me since preschool and can always tell when I'm lying. She says my voice gets higher and I tilt my head to the right. I tell myself to keep my voice low and my head straight. "We're getting a new one."

She takes off her jacket and throws it on the couch. There's a blob of spit-up or something stuck to her gray sweatshirt, and her black yoga pants are dusted in baby powder. Seeing her like this makes it hard to believe that once upon a time, our Westham High classmates voted her best dressed. Since having Sophie, her wardrobe consists almost exclusively of clothes like she's wearing today. She calls them her mommy uniform. "Where's Nico?" she asks.

"Playing basketball." That's probably the truth. It's what he does most Sunday mornings after football season.

Sophie tugs on my arm. "Can I have a snack?"

The three of us head to the kitchen. Rachel stops by the chair with Nico's leather jacket and rests her hands on it like she's trying to figure out the last time it was worn, by touching it. *Why hasn't he come back for it? There must be a reason.*

I open the cabinet and take out a bag of Oreos, which are Nico's and Sophie's favorite. I'm surprised he left them behind.

"Just two," Rachel says. I hand Sophie three. She gives me one back. I don't blame her. I'm a little afraid of Rachel too. I pop the cookie in my mouth as I go to the refrigerator to get Sophie milk.

"So why haven't you been to the club?" Rachel asks. "David told me you haven't been playing."

"I was there yesterday. Work has been busy."

Sophie finishes her cookies and wanders out of the kitchen.

Rachel has that look she used to get when I watched her cross-examine witnesses in mock trials before she met Mark and quit law school. "What's going on?"

Maybe I should tell her. She is my best friend, and it would be good to have someone to talk to about this. Yes, when Nico returns, he will have to experience her wrath for a while, years really, but maybe at this point he deserves that. He got his own place!

A loud crash from the hallway interrupts my thoughts. A second later Sophie cries. Rachel and I rush to her. The door to the closet is open. All the games are scattered over the floor. Sophie sits in a pile of Monopoly money, Trivial Pursuit cards, and other game pieces. "I was trying to get Trouble," she sobs.

"You've got trouble now, missy," Rachel says, picking up her daughter by the arm. "Stop crying. You're not hurt."

"I just wanted to play."

"You should have asked," Rachel snaps.

"It's okay," I say. "We can play."

Rachel helps me pick up the games and return them to the shelf. I carry Sophie to the living room and set up Trouble. Sophie chooses the green pegs; I take the blue. We put them into their spots on the board. In the hallway, Rachel continues straightening the closet.

"I go first," Sophie says. She's kneeling on the floor in front of the leather ottoman where the game is set up and reaches for the dice bubble. She presses down on it so it pops. The dice flips and lands on three. Sophie frowns. She needed a six to be able to move one of her pieces.

I hear Rachel's footsteps moving away from us and climbing the stairs. I pop the dice. It lands on six. Sophie gives me the evil eye. I swear to God, it's just like playing with Rachel when we were that age. Sophie has Rachel's curly black hair, huge brown eyes, and exact dirty looks.

Upstairs, the bathroom door squeaks shut as Sophie takes another turn. The dice lands on five. She pouts. I get a four on my turn.

We play for a few minutes before Rachel calls my name. "Can you come up here?" she asks.

"Go ahead," Sophie says. "I'll go when you're gone." As I walk away and climb the stairs, the dice pops over and over again. Her mother used to cheat too.

I enter the bathroom. The medicine cabinet and linen closet are open. The shower curtain is pushed to the side. *What the hell?* "Why are you going through my stuff?"

"I was trying to fix the medicine cabinet's door." She puts a hand on her hip, her tell for lying. "Why is there nothing of Nico's here?"

I feel my eyes filling up and squeeze them shut to prevent tears from flooding out. I take a deep breath and open them slowly. "He moved out." My voice sounds like it's far away.

"He moved out. Oh, Jillian." Rachel pulls me into a tight embrace. "Why didn't you tell me?"

There is no stopping the tears now. "He said he doesn't want to be a husband or a father."

"But he loves kids," Rachel says. Her ponytail is now wet with my tears.

"Right!" I sniff loudly as I pull myself away from her to get a tissue from the box on the vanity. "He just has a case of cold feet. He'll be back. I'm sure of it."

Rachel's expression remains neutral, so I can't tell if she agrees. "How long has he been gone?"

I blow my nose. "He moved to Nina's the day after Mark's birthday."

"That was weeks ago! Is that why you've been avoiding me, because you didn't want to tell me?"

I nod.

"Have you spoken to him?"

"He called last night to say he got his own place." Saying it out loud causes me to panic more than I did last night. My pulse throbs in my throat. *He got his own place. He's not coming back. Ever.*

Rachel folds her arms across her chest. "Bastard."

"You said a bad word, Mommy. I'm telling Daddy," Sophie says. I have no idea how long she's been standing there. She looks at me. "I got a six. It's your tur— Why are you crying, Auntie?" She rushes by Rachel to hug me.

I pick her up and hold her close to me, resting my nose in her watermelon-shampoo-scented hair. For the first time since Rachel married Mark, I'm jealous of the family she has with him and afraid that I won't have one of my own. I'm almost thirty-five, and my boyfriend of six years, my fiancé, has dumped me.

Chapter 6

Maybe it's because I confessed to Rachel what happened, or maybe it's because of the awful phone call with Nico, but for whatever reason, I wake up Monday with a new attitude. For weeks I've been asking myself, what will I do without him? Today I replace the question with, who needs him anyway? Before I get out of bed, I slide my diamond off and throw it into the top drawer of my nightstand. A thin red circle scars my finger where the ring used to be.

As I apply moisturizer to the indentation, I think about the night Nico proposed. We were at Vincenzio's Cucina in the North End of Boston. After we ordered dessert, he dropped to one knee. Right there in the middle of the restaurant with all the other diners looking on. "Let's make this official, Jillian. Marry me." Remembering the proposal now, it doesn't seem all that romantic, but at the time, I was swept off my feet and joined him down on the carpet for a long kiss. People at nearby tables all applauded. Vincenzio brought us each a complimentary glass of champagne. How could I have known Nico would change his mind three weeks later? Should I have known?

Surely Renee will notice that I'm not wearing my ring, so I'll have to break the news to her and Ben as soon as I get into the office. In the shower, I rehearse what I'll say. I don't have to tell them the ugly truth. I work in marketing after all. I know how to spin a story. *Nico and I mutually decided not to get married. We're going to spend some time apart and see how it goes. It was an amicable split.* Of course, they're in the same profession and know BS when they hear it. No matter, they won't call me out on it.

Instead of jeans, I dress in a short black skirt, a fitted blue blazer, and tall boots. Looking good will make me seem less upset. I bundle up in my long coat, hat, and gloves and head out the door. As soon as I step outside, the bitterly cold air stings my exposed skin. I hurry across the porch and down the walkway to my Accord, thinking I should have started it early to give it time to warm up. I turn the key in the ignition. There's an irritating whining noise, but the car doesn't turn over. I try again with the same result. *Perfect!*

Mr. O'Brien, back from getting his morning coffee, pulls in next to me. I turn the key one more time and hold it. Mr. O'Brien, who is now standing in the driveway in front of my car, holds his hands over his ears. Instead of his usual Red Sox baseball cap, he's wearing a blue wool hat with red B that's pulled low over his forehead. I get out of my car and slam the door.

"Your battery is dead," he says. He places his cup on the roof of my Honda. "Do you have jumper cables?"

"No, but I have Triple A." I step toward the walkway, wanting to get inside. It's so cold that it hurts to breathe. I imagine my lungs icing over.

"On a day like today you'll be waiting for hours. Don't you have to get to work?" He returns to his car and lifts the hatchback to retrieve his cables. "Pop your hood," he instructs. He does the same to his station wagon.

I remain in my driver's seat, shivering while waiting for him to clamp the cables onto the battery terminals or whatever it is he has to do, but he beckons me to the front of the car. "Do you know how to use these?" he asks.

My eyes widen. I thought he knew. "I'll call Triple A."

His sour expression reminds me of something my mother always said to me when I was a kid: Be careful or your face will freeze like that! The things that pop up and make me miss my parents always take me by surprise.

"I know how to use them," he says. "You should too. Pay attention." He tells me the red clamps go on the positive terminals of my battery and his, and the black get clamped to the negative terminal of his battery and on a piece of metal somewhere under the hood. After explaining, he tells me to connect them. I'm hesitant to attach them, certain I'll electrocute myself or blow up both vehicles. I imagine a fiery explosion. "Go on," he urges.

His earlobes are bright red, and I can't feel my face. If I don't do this soon, we'll both end up with frostbite or worse. I take a deep breath, hook them up, and duck like I'm taking cover. Nothing explodes. "What the hell are you doing?" my landlord asks. "Get behind the wheel and try to start your car."

I retreat to the driver's seat and turn the ignition. Once we get my Accord running, he asks, "If this happens again, would you know what to do?"

"Yes," I say out loud. *Call Triple A*, I say to myself. "Thank you for the lesson."

"One thing I've learned through the years is you're better off learning how to do things yourself because most people will let you down." The look he gives me and the change in his inflection tell me he's not talking about my dead battery. He reaches up for his Dunkin' Donuts cup and takes a sip. "Good thing I like iced coffee," he says.

⚜ ⚜ ⚜

When I arrive at work, Renee is talking to Ben in his cube. The radio plays softly in the background. As I walk by them, their voices drop to a whisper, but they don't look at me. It's good that they're sitting together. It will make it easier to tell them my news. I go to my desk to drop off my belongings. When I join them, I fold my hands behind my back so that they won't notice the missing ring. Neither of them looks at me though. Renee stares down at the gray carpet. Ben turns away from me, reaches for the radio on the windowsill, and fumbles with its volume. A voice blasts from the speaker. Ben hits the power button to silence it. My brain takes a few seconds to process that the voice is Nico's.

"Why is Nico on the air?" I ask.

Renee taps the toe of her boot against the wall. Ben shifts uncomfortably in his chair.

"What's going on?"

They look at each other but not at me.

"Put the radio back on," I instruct.

"Not a good idea," Renee says.

"You're better off not hearing what they're saying," Ben adds.

Well, now I'm totally curious. What could Branigan, Smyth, and Nico be talking about that has my colleagues so worked up? I reach around Ben for the power switch.

"She didn't see it coming," Smyth says.

"Tom Brady got sacked and then you sack your fiancée," Branigan says.

My knees buckle. I grab hold of the edge of Ben's desk to steady myself.

A laugh I recognize as Nico's. "It wasn't exactly like that."

On the radio they're talking about how I got dumped. I won't be able to show my face in Boston, in the entire state of Massachusetts. Damn, the show's streamed all over the world on the Internet.

"But you did call off the wedding, and you're single now, correct?" Smyth asks.

"True," Nico responds.

Ben and Renee both stare at me. I look back at them, pretending I have nothing to be embarrassed about. Somewhere in the building, the HVAC system roars to life.

Branigan asks, "Are you sure she knows the wedding's off, because I saw her over the weekend, and she's still wearing the rock."

Renee and Ben both look at my bare finger.

"She knows," Nico says.

"So, Nico's feeling a little sad," Branigan says.

"A lot sad," Nico clarifies.

Branigan ignores him. "What he needs is to get back on the bike, so we're going to have a contest. Ladies, if you're single and want a date with our producer, send us an email with your picture. And I can't stress this enough, we won't consider applicants who don't send photos."

A metallic taste fills my mouth.

"Clothing is optional in these shots," Branigan says.

"The less clothing, the better," says Smyth.

I'm going to be sick, right here in Ben's cube. My eyes roam the small space, looking for his garbage can.

"And Nico has high standards," Smyth says. "His ex, Jillian, is a good-looking girl. What would you say she is, a seven? An eight?"

"An eight when she puts in some effort," Branigan answers.

Puts in some effort? What does that mean?

"I don't think you can do better, Nico. Why did you dump her?" Smyth asks.

Yeah, Nico, why did you dump me? And for the love of God, why are you talking about it on your show?

"Not good in the sack?" Branigan asks.

Ben raises an eyebrow. I give him the finger.

"No, no," Nico says. "Nothing like that." His whiny voice makes my ears hurt. I snap the radio off but can still hear the show coming from radios in the next aisles. Great. The entire office is listening.

"Are you okay?" Ben asks.

No, I'm not okay! I look at him without answering.

He stares back; the expression on his face is more appropriate for the receiving line at a wake than the office.

Don't cry. Don't cry. I chant it to myself. A blast of heat pours out of the vent embedded in the ceiling tiles.

Renee touches my arm. "Why didn't you tell us, sweetie?"

"I was going to tell you today." I should have told them sooner. To have them find out like this is beyond humiliating. How could Nico do this to me? I swallow the lump in my throat. *Do. Not. Cry.* I blink back a tear. I would rather die than cry at work.

The people sitting a few rows away erupt in laughter. I wonder if they're the same ones listening to the show.

Ben and Renee watch me without speaking. I can't stand the pity on their faces. They think I'm pathetic. I am pathetic. Outside, a plane leaves a trail of vapor in the blue sky. I don't care where the jet is going. I want to be on it.

I bolt out of Ben's cube. He calls after me, but I ignore him and head for the restroom, where I study myself in the mirror. My complexion is gray and the whites of my eyes are bright red. Worse, there are two nasty pimples on my chin and one on my forehead. Almost thirty-five and acne. I can't catch a break. *First-world problems,* I imagine Nico saying. Every muscle in my body tightens. I hate him. I really do.

I hear someone coming and duck into a stall because I don't want to make small talk with anyone.

"Jillian, are you in here?" Ellie calls out in her husky voice.

I swing the stall door open and step out.

"Why didn't you tell me?" she asks.

"Was everyone in sales listening?"

"Ryan's radio was loud." She studies me quietly. "What happened?" she finally asks.

"Nothing happened. He just said he didn't want to get married." Not having a good answer to her question makes the entire thing even harder than it should be. I'd be able to understand it if he met someone else, but he decided he'd rather be by himself than be with me. Am I that unbearable? I take a deep breath and step toward the sink, wanting to wash my hands because I touched the stall door. I place my hands under the automatic soap dispenser. It squirts out a third of its contents, leaving a foamy mess on the counter.

I try to turn on the water, but nothing happens when I wave my hands under the automated faucet. My waving becomes frantic, but the sink remains dry. "Why the hell can't they just have a normal sink in here?" I whine.

Ellie reaches into the bowl and wiggles her fingers. The faucet comes to life. Of course she has the magic touch.

I scrub my hands together so hard they burn. "What am I going to do, El?

"You're going to be strong, and you're going to move on," she says.

"I'm not sure I can do that."

"Of course you can." She pauses. "This is Nico's loss, and he will regret it."

She might be giving me a sales pitch, but I need to believe it.

"Whatever you need to get through this," she says, "I'm here for you. We're all here for you. Ben and Renee were really worried about you when I just stopped by your row."

⚜ ⚜ ⚜

Later, as Ben, Renee, and I walk down the hall for lunch, I can hear the din of conversation coming from the cafeteria. I slow my pace. There will be a mob in there, many of whom listened to *BS Morning Sports Talk* today. I'm not sure I'm up to facing them. As we get closer, a group of employees from IT holding takeout containers approaches us from the opposite direction. The smell of fried food drifts toward us. As they walk by, one of the men elbows another. "That's her," he says, tilting his head in my direction.

I freeze. Renee and Ben are several steps in front of me before they realize I've stopped. They look back at me. "I'm going to have cereal at my desk," I say.

"What happened?" Ben asks.

I point to the IT guys. "People are going to be talking about me."

Ben strides toward me. Renee follows. "Did they say something?" he asks.

I explain what happened. He shoves his hands in his pockets and glares down the hallway. "People will talk. You have to ignore them."

Renee wraps an arm around my shoulder. "People break up all the time, honey." We resume walking to the lunchroom. Renee keeps a protective hold on me. "Think of it as a blessing that things ended before and not after the wedding," she says.

Never married at age thirty-five or divorced by thirty-six. I think I would choose door number two. Divorcees are more accepted by society than spinsters. If you're a divorcee, people assume the problem was with the ex, but if you've never been married, they wonder what's wrong with you.

When we enter the cafeteria, I keep my head down. Ben and I take our place at the end of the long deli line while Renee elbows her way into the crowd hovering by the salad bar. As we wait, I cross my arms and then uncross them, rest my weight on my left leg, shift it to the right, and then balance it evenly on both. At the same time, my eyes dart around the room, searching for anyone who might be pointing at me.

"Relax, Jillian," Ben says, putting his hand on my wrist. "You're drawing attention to yourself."

"I can't help it."

"Deep breaths," he says, taking one himself, presumably to show me how.

Ryan and Tyler step into line behind us. "What happened with you and Nico?" Tyler asks. "I liked that guy."

I knew I should have stayed at my desk.

"On the radio, they said he sacked you," Ryan says. He has a loud voice. It echoes through the crowded cafeteria.

Conversations around us stop. The room becomes quiet. At least it seems that way.

"It makes no sense," Tyler says. "Didn't you just get engaged a few weeks ago?"

"It's like fumbling on the goal line," Ryan booms.

A few people standing near us laugh.

"Knock it off," Ben warns.

"I'm sorry, Jillian," Tyler says.

"Unless he met someone else," Ryan continues. "Then it's an interception." He looks around the room, smiling and nodding, like a comedian on stage looking for approval.

Ben steps closer to him. "I said knock it off."

I grab Ben's arm. "I'm going back to my desk."

"Come on. We're just having a little fun with you," Ryan calls as I make my way out of the crowded cafeteria.

⚜ ⚜ ⚜

Back at my desk, I navigate to *BS Morning Sports Talk*'s website. A headline runs across the top of the page that reads "Win a Date with Our Producer." Under it is a picture of Nico wearing a green T-shirt I've never seen before. He's clean shaven, and his hair is about a half inch longer than the last time I saw him. I fantasize about ripping it out strand by strand.

The text beside his picture reads, "Our producer recently dumped his fiancée and is looking for a new girlfriend. He's successful, smart, sexy, and sensitive."

Sensitive! What a pile of rubbish!

"Send a picture (clothing optional) with a description of your perfect date, and you could be the lucky woman who wins a night, and maybe more, with our handsome Nico."

I look at the picture again and fight the strong urge to punch my fist through the computer screen. I click on the link to enter the "contest" and begin a profanity-laced email. I feel someone looking over my shoulder and click away from the page. "You don't want to send that," Ben warns.

I whip my chair around to face him. "Don't tell me what I want to do."

He places a plastic container with a sandwich and chips in it on my desk. "Look, I know how you're feeling. I've—"

"Really, your fiancé went on the radio telling everyone how he dumped you while his idiot bosses rated your looks and then all your coworkers made fun of you."

"Ryan is a weasel. Everyone knows it."

"It's not just Ryan," I say. "It's the guys in IT." I bury my head in my hands. "Do you know how popular that stupid show is?"

"They're not going to talk about you anymore," Ben says. "They'll have their fun with the contest this week and then they'll get back to sports."

I keep my head down on my desk, fighting back tears. Ben rests his hand on my shoulder. "It's going to be okay," he whispers.

Die before you cry at work. I chant it to myself. When I feel I have myself under control, I sit upright again. "I know." I open the food he dropped off and take a bite. It's a chicken salad sandwich with roasted peppers mixed in, on toasted sourdough bread. Nico used to make my lunch so I hardly ever buy food in the cafeteria, but when I do, it's exactly what I order, right down to the salt and vinegar potato chips.

Ben picks up a picture on my desk of me and Nico. "You can do much better than this jamoke. The guy has a unibrow, for crying out loud," he says. "And what's up with his beady little eyes?"

I take the photograph from him. He's right about Nico's eyebrows. I tried to convince him to have them waxed, but he wanted no part of that. Ben's wrong about Nico's eyes though. They are definitely not beady. They're almond shaped. He always appears to be squinting. It's extremely sexy. I throw the picture in my desk drawer.

"You're better off without him," Ben says.

Without him, I'm alone. I'm most definitely not better off alone.

As if he knows what I'm thinking, Ben adds, "You'll meet someone else. No worries."

But I am worried. Where is a single woman in her midthirties supposed to meet a normal single man?

※ ※ ※

Rachel calls me on my drive home. "I heard what happened on Nico's show today," she says. "I'm so sorry."

I've been in bumper-to-bumper traffic since getting on the highway, but now my lane comes to a complete standstill.

"What a stupid idea for a contest. I bet no one enters," Rachel continues. "Like a date with Nico is any great shakes. Please."

She's trying to make me feel better, but she's criticizing the man I've spent the last six years of my life with, the person I wanted to be with forever.

"Come over after I put the kids to bed," she suggests. "We'll have drinks and talk about what a schmuck Nico is."

"Thanks, but I'm really beat." The cars in front of me are moving again. I turn around a bend in the road. A billboard for *BS Morning Sports Talk* comes into view. I tighten my grip on the steering wheel as I look at Branigan's and Smyth's faces. Branigan's short red hair is receding, and his forehead is large enough to house the billboard. Angry red pockmarks scar Smyth's chubby face. Of course no one criticizes their appearance while the two of them rip females in the sports broadcasting profession—or any woman, really.

I'm so busy staring at their pictures that I don't notice traffic has stopped again. I slam on my brakes and just avoid crashing into the Volvo in front of me. *That's all I need.*

By the time I pull into my driveway, a feeling of doom blankets me. Rachel doesn't listen to sports radio. How did she find out about the contest? Is everybody talking about it? Do my parents know? Does my brother? Sure, they're all the way in Atlanta, but sometimes they tune in to *BS Morning Sports Talk* over the Internet. Even if they weren't listening today, they're sure to find out at some point. I can't put it off anymore. I have to tell them that Nico and I broke up. I stride into the house determined to break the news to them.

A few minutes later, I'm settled on the couch with a big glass of wine and dialing my parents' number. It rings five times and then Molly picks up. "We're eating at Grandma's," she announces. Glad to know they're having a nice family dinner while I'm here in our home state, alone and miserable.

I was all hyped up to tell my parents the news, but I can't ruin their happy family dinner, can I? Maybe I should, because it will make them feel guilty for leaving.

"Auntie, do I get to be a flower girl at your wedding?" Molly asks.

The sofa is old and offers little support. I sink deep into its soft leather.

"I hope you're not going to pick Sophie instead of me because you see her more."

"Of course I'm not going to pick Sophie instead of you," I say, trying unsuccessfully to get comfortable.

"Maybe you could pick both of us," Molly suggests.

"Sure," I say because I'm certainly not going to break the news that Nico and I have split to my five-year-old niece. Then again, it might be easier for my mother if she hears about it from her beloved granddaughter rather than her spinster daughter.

"Mommy, Auntie said I could be a flower girl at her wedding." Her voice is farther away, but I can still hear the excitement in it.

I squirm on the worn cushions.

"Hey, Jillian," my sister-in-law, Susannah, says. She pronounces my name Jill Ann, like I'm a Southern belle she grew up with instead of a native New Englander. "Molly's really excited about your big day."

Tell her now before this gets even more out of control. "Listen Sus—"

"Hey, Sis." My brother must have grabbed the phone from his wife. "Still can't believe Nico manned up. When's the big day? Better get it done ASAP before he changes his mind."

Before he changes his mind? Once, when we were younger, Christian and I were racing across the yard. I tripped over a log and landed so hard on my stomach that the wind was knocked out of me. His comments today have the exact same effect. Was it that obvious to everyone else that Nico would change his mind?

"We're still trying to figure it out," I lie, because my brother is the last person I would break the news to. He'd make me feel worse than I already do.

"Not getting cold feet, is he?"

"Maybe I'm the one who's getting cold feet," I say, bringing myself to a standing position.

My brother laughs. "Right. You've been trying to wear him down for six years and now that you've succeeded, you're going to back out. Fat chance."

I'm pacing the hallway again, trying to make sense of my brother's comment. Wearing Nico down? Is that what I've been doing?

My sister-in-law says something in the background.

"Hey, we got to run. Dinner is on the table," Christian says. He hangs up without letting me talk to my mother.

The tears that I've been fighting back all day fall freely now, but they're not for Nico. I want to be sitting at the supper table with my parents, having a home-cooked meal. I bet my mom made pot roast with potatoes and carrots that have been simmering in a Crock-Pot all day. My dad probably contributed to the meal by making Pillsbury Poppin' Fresh rolls. Dessert is definitely some type of homemade pie. Before my family all bolted south, we used to have supper together at least once a week at my parents'. I miss those dinners. Damn Christian and his Georgia peach of a wife.

Chapter 7

"How long are you staying?" Ben's voice startles me, causing me to jump in my chair. "Didn't mean to scare you," he says, zipping his jacket.

At just after six thirty, we are the only two left on the floor. "I want to finish writing this." I've been working on the new brochure all week, but every word I write triggers a memory of Nico, sending me into a sinkhole.

Ben stares at the blinking cursor on the mostly empty screen in front of me. "Looks like it's going to be a long night then."

"Maybe." I've worked until nine every day this week, mainly because I don't want to go home to my empty apartment, where there's nothing to do but think about Nico and listen to Mr. O'Brien coughing on the other side of the wall. It's unusual for Ben to be here after five though. "Why are you still here?"

"I had to finish the mock-up of the home page. Stacy wants to see it tomorrow." He stands behind me, fiddling with his key fob. "Why don't you wrap things up so we can walk out together."

His suggestion is tempting because crossing the pedestrian bridge from the office building to the parking garage is creepy this time of night. The lights that are supposed to illuminate the path are all buried in snow. Each time the maintenance crew digs them out, we get another storm, and they have to shovel them out all over again, so they finally gave up.

"I'll be fine."

"You sure?"

I nod, and Ben reluctantly says good night.

Instead of going back to writing the brochure, I visit the radio station's website to check on the number of entrees in the win-a-date-with-Nico contest. There's a running tally by the button where contestants submit their photographs and description of their ideal date. Right now the total is up to 67,504. Last time I looked, which was about five minutes before Ben came to say goodbye, the total was 67,501. Even though my level of angst increases along with the number of respondents, I can't make myself stop checking. I wish I could. In all, I must have checked more than a hundred times since Branigan announced the stupid contest. For a split second it even crossed my mind to enter, submit a fake picture and write an entry so good that they have to choose me. On the night of the date, when Nico finds out that I'm the contest winner, he'll smile and say *I was hoping it was you*. I guess I've seen *You've Got Mail* too many times.

The door at the end of the hall clicks open. At first, I think it's the cleaning crew, but there is only one set of footsteps. They are moving much too quickly for anybody to be doing any cleaning. Whoever it is turns into my aisle. I roll my chair backward to the opening of my cube and peek out. Ben walks toward me with a determined expression. "You're not working late again tonight," he says. "You're leaving now. We're going to dinner."

❧ ❧ ❧

We each drive our own cars to a steak place on the other side of town. The setting is much more romantic than the sports bars where Nico and I usually ate. The restaurant is dark, and each of the tables, including ours, is covered in a white linen tablecloth and has a lit candle in a hurricane-glass holder placed in the center.

"I feel like we're on a date," I say.

Ben looks up from the wine menu he's been studying and smiles. "Is it a first date, or have we been together for a while?"

"We're an old married couple going to get something to eat because neither of us feels like cooking," I say.

"Where are the kids?"

I grin, stupidly happy that he's playing along with me. "Amanda's away at school and Trevor is at friend's."

"I must really love you if I let you name our son Trevor," he says. "That's a dog's name."

"You wanted to name him Ben junior, and call him BJ, but I wanted no part of that."

Ben laughs. "It's a good thing you talked me out of it because he's at the age now when he might get teased for having a nickname like that." He gives me a suggestive smile that causes me to blush.

Our waiter arrives and introduces himself as Ian. We each order a glass of cabernet that Ben suggests. Nico never drank wine because he didn't think it was a manly drink.

A few tables away, there's a man in his fifties sitting with a woman half his age. Their clasped hands lie on the table, and they lean toward each other with big grins. "Wife number two," I say. It's a game I've been playing with Rachel since we were kids. We guess the stories of random people we see in public places. I tried it with Nico a few times, but he refused to go along with it.

"Nope," Ben says. "Wife number one thinks he's working late. She's the nanny." He points out a table where a young man of about twenty, wearing a baseball cap, is sitting with an older gentleman.

"Father visiting his son at school. The kid goes to Brandeis," I say because the college is not too far from where we are.

Ben shakes his head. "The kid's dating his daughter. He wants the old man's permission to marry her."

I smile, enjoying Ben's romanticism.

"The father's going to say no," he adds.

I frown. "What? Why?"

Nico never asked my dad. *You're thirty-four. We don't need your daddy's permission,* he argued.

"He thinks they're too young," Ben answers. "And he knows his daughter is much too good for that slob. Punk kid doesn't have enough respect to take off his hat at the table."

"I hope you'll go easier on the young man who eventually asks for Amanda's hand," I say.

"Amanda's smart enough not to date a guy who's always hiding under a baseball cap."

I think about Nico's collection of hats that used to hang on the outside of our closet door. He must have close to one hundred. I stare at Ben, wondering if he's passing some sort of judgment on me.

The waiter returns with our drinks and to take our order. "We haven't even looked at the menu yet," Ben says.

The waiter leaves. I open my menu, expecting Ben to do the same. Instead he points to two middle-aged women. "Sisters reunited fifty years after being given up for adoption by their birth mother," he says.

The waiter has to return two more times before we're finally shamed into stopping our game and choosing our dinners. Ben gets the bone-in rib eye, while I order the filet.

"Wasn't that much better than the cereal you were going to eat?" Ben asks when I finish.

"How do you know that's what I was going to have?"

He gives me a challenging look. "Are you going to tell me it's not?"

"Rice Krispies," I admit.

"Well, I'm sure Snap, Crackle, and Pop missed you tonight, but I enjoyed your company."

In the parking lot, he hugs me good-night. Although he's hugged me plenty of times through the years, tonight feels different.

I drive home singing to the radio. When I pull into the driveway, the motion lights snap on. Mr. O'Brien must have knocked the icicles down today because they no longer hang from the roof and the house looks less ominous. As I walk across the porch, I see him sitting in his recliner watching the hockey game. He checks his watch as I pass, making me feel like I missed curfew. It's just past ten o'clock. Ben and I were at the restaurant for more than three hours. I had no idea so much time went by.

Not until I get inside and see Nico's jacket hanging over the back of the kitchen chair do I realize that tonight is the first time I've had fun since he left. I place my hand on the coat's soft worn leather, wondering what Nico did this evening. "You'd be mad if you knew who I went out with," I say.

On the other side of the wall, Mr. O'Brien claps and cheers. The Bruins must have scored.

Chapter 8

Rachel still lives in the town where we grew up. To get to her house, I have to pass my childhood home, a brown split-level ranch. When my parents first moved away, my eyes would well up each time I drove by, and I wondered if I was the only person who felt homesick in the town where they were raised.

As I ride by on this mid-February evening, I see the new owners still have their Christmas lights up—red, green, and blue bulbs, a colorful contrast compared to the white lights my mother insisted upon. She would go crazy if she saw the house now because she firmly believes the Christmas tree should be down and the decorations packed away by New Year's.

On the day the moving truck drove off with all my parents' belongings, my father and I stood on the front landing watching it roll down the street. He draped his arm around my shoulders and pulled me close. "I wouldn't be able to leave you behind if I didn't know you had Nico to lean on," he said.

Tonight, I briefly imagine that after our weekly call tomorrow, when I tell my parents that Nico and I split, my father will sit my mother down in the living room of their English Tudor. *It's not right that she's there by herself,* he'll say. *She needs us. We have to move back.*

Smoke billows from Rachel's chimney, and the smell of the fire permeates into her yard. She rarely uses her fireplace because she worries the kids will get hurt, but she's pulling out all the stops tonight in an effort to cheer me up, making my favorite roast beef dinner with crème brûlée for dessert. I take my time walking up her driveway, breathing in the smoky smell, my favorite scent of winter. When I reach the front door, I rap on it once before entering the house. "Hello," I call out.

I sit on the bench in the foyer and pull off my boots because I don't want to drip water on her hardwood floors.

Sophie is the first to greet me. She climbs up next to me and hugs me. I'm surprised to see that she's already dressed in her pink footie pajamas. Usually Rachel has to battle with her to change. "Auntie Jillian, Mommy said I'm not allowed to ask about Uncle Nico," she says.

The mention of Nico's name pierces my heart. It's strange to be at Rachel's for dinner without him, but I guess I will have to get used to doing everything without him now.

"Sophie!" Mark yells. He's coming down the stairs. Jacob, the baby, is cradled in his arms. Laurence trails behind, sucking his thumb and carrying a toy minion. There is also a picture of the little creature on his pajama top.

"What did she do?" Rachel hollers from the kitchen.

"Nothing," I say.

Mark trades me my coat for Jacob, who immediately starts crying when handed off. I place him over my shoulder and rub his back, wishing someone would do the same to me.

"Auntie, do you want to play Connect Four?" Sophie asks.

"Auntie came to talk to me tonight," Rachel says. She's standing in the hallway, wiping her hands on a dish towel.

"Mark, bring all the kids into the living room and keep them there until supper."

He takes Jacob from me.

"Don't let them too close to the fire," Rachel calls out as I follow her into the kitchen. She checks on the roast before pouring me a glass of wine.

In the other room, Mark and the kids break out into belly laughs. I peek in and see him crawling on all fours with both Laurence and Sophie on his back. Rachel and I both grew up in the same sort of family, with loving parents and brothers who teased us in good fun. We wanted the same things out of life, a husband and a household filled with kids. She got that. Today, her home is filled with love and laughter, a stark comparison to my quiet, lonely apartment. I wonder if I had never met Nico, would I have met someone else and have what she does?

She interrupts my thoughts. "I can't believe Nico blindsided you by announcing your breakup on air."

"I think he tried to tell me about the contest, but I hung up on him." I get up from my stool to finish setting the table while Rachel makes gravy.

"Don't defend him. It was unacceptable for them to talk about you like that."

"It really was," I agree.

"You should do something to get back at him," Rachel says. *Vengeful* should be her middle name. In high school she dumped ten cans of Chef Boyardee spaghetti and meatballs over the hood of a Ford Mustang belonging to a boy who had the nerve to break up with her. His car was parked in the school lot at the time, and she got detention for a week.

"Believe me, I'd love to. Any ideas?"

"What did you do with the ring?"

Instinctively I touch the finger I used to wear it on. "It's in my bureau drawer."

"He paid a lot of money for it," she says in a way that makes me think she knows exactly how much it cost him.

"How do you know?"

She sighs. "Who do you think picked it out?"

"Nico told me he picked it out by himself." I point a knife at her. "You never told me you helped."

There I was, thinking how well he knew me because he selected my dream ring. I am such a fool.

She sighs. "He made me promise not to tell. The point is, you should sell it."

I can't do that. I'm going to wear it again someday. The thought pops into my head with no warning. I imagine striking it with a mallet to send it back to the crevice of my brain it crawled out of. "Why do you think he hasn't asked for it back?"

Rachel's spoon clanks off the side of the pan as she stirs the gravy. "Don't even go there," she says as if she's reading my thoughts. "I can see you waiting around for another six years because you think if he really didn't want to marry you, he would ask for it back."

No one knows me better than Rachel. Maybe she's my soul mate.

"After he humiliated you like that, you can never take him back," she says.

"I know that." Even to me though, my words don't sound convincing. She gives me a look that says she doesn't believe me.

⚜ ⚜ ⚜

After dinner, Rachel and I are sitting by the fire in the living room. Mark is upstairs, putting the kids to bed. "I'm going to show you something, but you have to promise not to be mad," she says. She empties the remaining pinot noir into my glass. "Do you promise?"

I swear her expression is the same as when we were seventeen and she was trying to convince me to steal a bottle of vodka from my parents' liquor cabinet. "They'll never know," she promised. Meanwhile, the very next day they noticed the alcohol was missing; I got grounded for a month.

I get up to throw more wood on the fire, wondering what she's up to. "No, I don't promise."

"Well, remember that I'm trying to help you." She reaches for the iPad that's sitting on the coffee table in front of the couch and swipes at the screen. As I watch her fiddle with it, I figure out she had the same thought that I did to create a fake entry for the *BS Morning Sports Talk* win-a-date-with-Nico contest. Great minds think alike.

She hands me the tablet. My own face stares back at me. The words *30-Something-Love* appear above my picture. "What is this?" It can't be what I think it is.

"I created an online dating profile for you." It's exactly what I think it is. Rachel sounds pleased with herself, like she's giving me her kidney instead of soliciting dates for me on the Internet.

"Why would you do that?" I scroll though the page searching for a way to delete my profile.

"How else are you going to meet someone?"

"I don't want to meet anyone."

A bang comes from the fireplace as a log falls against the glass door. I get up to reposition it.

"Do I have to remind you that you're going to be thirty-five in April? Ticktock. Ticktock."

"Screw you!" I jab at the log repeatedly with the poker. Embers shoot out of the fire onto the hearth. "I'm not doing Internet dating."

"It's how single people our age meet people these days."

I give her a look that means *How the hell would you know? You've been happily married for eight years.*

She reads my expression accurately. "Mark's sister met her boyfriend on this site and Sophie's preschool teacher met her husband." She's listing other people who work with Mark who do online dating, but I'm not paying attention because I'm reading the description she wrote of me. She called me "hopelessly optimistic"; no doubt that's a reference to my waiting six years for a proposal that lasted three weeks.

"There are other sites too," she says. "I think you should be on them all to increase the odds of meeting someone you like. It's a numbers game after all."

"I'm not doing any!"

"Shh, you'll wake the kids," Rachel whispers.

I search all over the dating site for a delete button. Finally, I found it in the Account Settings tab. I click on it. A message instantly appears: *Are you sure you want to delete your profile?*

Damn straight I am. I click on yes.

Another message: *We hope you're leaving because you found someone. We hope it works out, but because love's unpredictable, your profile will remain in an archive and can be reactivated at any time.*

I won't be reactivating it. That's for sure. Then, just to be sure Rachel doesn't either, I ask her for the password she used to create the account and change it.

Mixed Signals

❧ ❧ ❧

The hardwood feels cold on my bare feet as I pace up and down the hallway listening to my mother. I was up all night, worrying about how I'm going to break the news to her that Nico and I broke up. I meant to do it as soon as I answered, but she began the conversation by telling me she stopped into a bridal shop to look at dresses. She found one she thinks will be perfect on me.

"It's an empire silhouette with a sweetheart neck," she says, making me feel like a disappointment as a daughter because I have no idea what either of those things means—not to mention that I have no use for the dress anymore but can't bring myself to say it.

"Mom," I interrupt.

She keeps talking. "The one I saw has short sleeves—"

"Mom, I have to—"

"But they can alter them to cap—"

"Mom!"

To my surprise, she stops speaking. The line goes quiet. Here's my chance. I'm going to tell her now before she starts up again. I take a deep breath. "Nico and I broke up. There's not going to be a wedding." I exhale loudly, feeling better now that it's out there. I wait for her response. She says nothing. I give her a few seconds to digest the news. One. Two. Three. Nothing but silence from the other end. Four. Five. Six. "Mom?" Seven. Eight. Nine. "Are you still there?"

The other line clicks in. I glance at caller ID. It's my mother. *Unfreakinbelievable!*

"I must have lost you," she says.

"Did you hear anything I said?"

"No. I was telling you about the dress."

I take a deep breath and prepare to say it again. *Keep your voice calm.*

"They're getting more in next week. I'm—"

"Nico and I broke up," I blurt out in a shaky voice.

"Going back—What did you say?"

"I don't need a dress. Nico and I broke up." I repeat it without a trace of emotion this time, like I'm telling her about our horrible winter weather.

"Are you arguing about wedding plans? Because all couples do. You'll work it out."

"We won't. It's over."

"Did you fight today?" she asks.

"He moved out almost a month ago." Not sleeping last night catches up to me all at once. All I want to do is go back to bed and pull the covers up over my head. Instead, I fall onto the couch.

"That can't be," my mother says. "We've spoken every week. You never said a word about it."

"I thought we would work things out, so I didn't want to worry you with it."

"Oh, honey," she says.

I can't fight back my tears, because really all I want right now is my mother to hug me, but she's a thousand miles away because she'd rather live near my brother than me.

"Did he meet someone else?" she asks.

"What? No! It was nothing like that."

"Men don't leave unless they have someone to move on to."

Except Nico did. "Well, he did."

"Don't be so sure," my mother says like she knows something I don't, and I briefly wonder about her life before she met my father. "Are you able to afford your rent on your own?" she asks. "Didn't your landlord raise it when Nico moved in?"

"I'm fine, Mom."

"Are you sure? I can send a check."

"I'm good."

"You should have never let him move in with you," she says. Her words remind me why I sometimes don't mind that she followed Christian, Susannah, and Molly all the way to Atlanta.

Chapter 9

The next morning, Mr. O'Brien rings my doorbell. He has bags from the hardware store in one hand and an electric drill in the other. "Need to change your lock." He pulls open the storm door and steps inside.

Feeling awkward in my flannel pajamas, I fold my arms across my chest. "Why? Did something happen?"

He walks down the hallway to put the bag on the entryway table, leaving a trail of wet sand from his boots. "Did something happen?" he repeats. "He left without leaving the key. He can get in anytime he likes." He shrugs out of his wool Red Sox jacket and hands it to me. The stench coming off it makes me wonder when he last washed it. Maybe I should offer to do it for him?

"I don't think he wants to get in." After the conversation I had with my mother yesterday, I don't think I can handle Mr. O'Brien right now.

"Better safe than sorry," Mr. O'Brien says. He presses the drill's on switch and watches the bit spin before turning it off.

I go to the closet for a broom and begin sweeping up the trail of dirt he is leaving behind him. "I really don't think this is necessary," I say.

Mr. O'Brien lifts his baseball cap and immediately returns it to his head. "Why did he leave?"

Mind your business! Someday I'm going to be the kind of woman who says exactly what she's thinking, but for now I remain the girl who doesn't want to be rude. "He wasn't sure he wanted to get married."

Mr. O'Brien clears his throat. "That's something a fellow should know. If he doesn't know, he knows."

My bottom lips quivers. I tell myself to hold it together. God only knows what Mr. O'Brien would do if I break down crying in front of him.

For a half second I think the old man might realize that I'm on the verge of tears, because his expression softens so that his face doesn't look as wrinkled, and I can almost imagine the young man he once was. "I knew from the moment I first saw Carol. Asked her to marry me on our second date."

I whisk the sand into the dustpan. "Your second date?"

"Only because I thought it would have been ridiculous to ask her on the first."

Now my eyes are filling up. Nico's had six years' worth of dates, and he's still not sure. I look down at my bare ring finger, knowing that's not exactly true. He is sure, sure he doesn't want to marry me. Why not? Is there something wrong with me?

There's tapping on the storm door. Zachary stands on the porch with two cups of coffee and a box of Munchkins. He and his grandfather alone keep our neighborhood Dunkin' Donuts in business. Mr. O'Brien opens the door for his grandson. "Morning," Zachary says.

I wave at him and flee to my bedroom before my tears fall. Why aren't I good enough to marry? Why did Nico lead me on for so long? I rip off my pajamas and put on my tennis whites. Smashing a ball around the court is exactly what I need right now.

Back at the front door, Mr. O'Brien teaches Zachary how to replace the lock. The boy looks up at me. "They think it will keep people tuned in," he says. "Especially females."

Just like when I'm having a conversation with his grandfather, I have no idea what Zachary's talking about and stare at him blankly.

"I started at the morning show this week," he clarifies. "Branigan came up with the contest as a way to keep listeners tuned in until the Sox start. Now that the Pats are done."

"And Nico went along with it?"

"He didn't want to, but ratings are really low. Four point something."

I think of Branigan's letterhead in Nico's jacket pocket. "Four point six."

Zachary nods. "And they want us to grow the number of female listeners to increase advertising opportunities."

Mr. O'Brien interrupts. "Did you come to gab or to help?"

⚜ ⚜ ⚜

Every time I swing my racquet, I pretend the ball is Nico's head and smash it back over the net. The ball soars over the baseline. My opponent, a woman named Jane Chen, sighs each time the ball lands out of bounds. I don't blame her. It's boring playing with someone who can't sustain a rally. I don't even win a point in the first game. "Sorry," I yell across to her.

We start a new game. She serves. As the ball heads back to me, I hear Nico: *I can't do this, the husband, father, family thing.* Whack! The ball bounces off the wall of the bubble on the opposite side of the court. I'm losing fifteen–love.

Jane serves again. *Brady got sacked and then you sacked your fiancée.* Slam! The ball flies into the net. Thirty–love.

Jane's next serve lands deep in the service box. *Win a date with our producer.* Smack! The ball flies over my head backward. Forty–love.

Jane tosses the ball into the air and taps it to me. *Send pictures. Clothing optional.* Smash! The ball soars high in the air and lands in the court next to ours. "Damn it," one of the players yells. He picks up our ball and without looking at me whips it over the net separating our courts. "Sorry," I mumble.

I hear knocking on glass and look up. David stands in front of the window in the reception area that overlooks our court. He extends both arms in front of his chest and moves his hands in a downward motion.

I take a deep breath and pace back and forth on the baseline, trying to clear my head. Usually when I'm playing, the only thing I think about is tennis. In fact, I play because the courts are the one place I don't bring any of my worries. I'm mad at myself for allowing Nico to ruin this sanctuary. When my pulse slows, I return to the baseline and serve. Jane hits the ball back with a backhand. I use a forehand to return it. The ball hits the top of the net, teeters, and then falls onto her side. I pump my fist, excited to win my first point of the set. I look up at the window. David gives me a thumbs-up.

⚜ ⚜ ⚜

"You were playing with a lot of anger," David says to me in the lobby after my match. I'm distracted by Branigan entering the club, his wife trailing a few steps behind him. He's dressed in his white shorts, a white short-sleeved shirt, and a Patriots wool cap with a pompom over his big fat head.

He walks toward David and slaps him on the back. "We're looking forward to renewing our title as the club's mixed-doubles champions," he says.

David laughs.

Branigan looks at me. "Did you hear we're trying to find a date for Nico?" he asks.

"Sean," his wife warns.

Branigan flashes a huge smile, showing all his capped teeth. "We could have the same type of contest for you," he offers. "I bet your picture would get a lot more attention than Nico's. Although you'd be surprised by the number of women who want a date with him."

David nudges me toward the lounge. "Let's go," he says.

Once we're seated, he says, "I'm sorry. For what you're going through with Nico."

"Thanks."

"Consider yourself lucky that you figured out things wouldn't work before rather than after the wedding."

Things were working just fine, I think. "I guess."

"You guess? Let me tell you, divorce sucks." David got married right out of college and was divorced a year later. He seems to have figured it out the second time around though. He's been married to wife number two for eight years.

A waitress arrives at our table. David tells her to bring a glass of water and a strawberry smoothie, which is my favorite.

"Rachel asked if there is someone I can set you up with here at the club," he says.

I look down at the court where two men are playing singles. "Yeah, she's on me to start dating right away. Even signed me up for online dating, but I'm not up to any of it right now."

Across the room, the bartender fires up the blender.

"I figured that," David says.

We both stop to watch a rally on the court below us. It ends with a shot that lands in the back right corner. "Out," I say as David calls it in.

He refocuses on me. "I do think it's important that you keep busy to distract yourself from what's going on."

"Distract myself, how?"

"The doubles tournament is coming up."

"I'm horrible by the net. That's why I play singles," I remind him.

The waitress returns with our drinks. She puts the smoothie in front of him and gives me the water. He motions for her to switch the glasses. "I know. I need linesmen."

"No way!" Every year it's a struggle to get people to ump the matches because there are always heated disagreements about whether a ball was in or out.

"Do I have to remind you of the break I give you on your membership fee?" David asks.

"So unfair," I answer.

⚜ ⚜ ⚜

I expect Mr. O'Brien and Zachary to still be fiddling with the lock when I arrive home, but both their cars are gone. With my tennis bag flung over my shoulder, I make my way to my side of the house. I twist the doorknob, but the door doesn't open because it's locked. *Unbelievable!*

I dig my cell phone out of my bag and call the old man. His phone doesn't even ring. Instead, an automated message tells me the number I've reached and instructs me to leave a message. "It's Jillian. You locked me out! Call me when you get this." I repeat the same message on his home phone and retreat to my car. I cruise around the neighborhood. The huge snowbanks and coating of hard snow and ice on the roads make driving on the side streets treacherous, so I head for the highway.

Unlike during the week, there are few cars on the road with me. Before too long, I pass a sign for Lexington, the town where Nico's sister lives. My car drifts to the right lane. My blinker goes on just before the exit. *Don't do this*, the rational voice inside me warns. As usual, I ignore it and turn onto the off-ramp. *Don't do this!*

A few miles later, off in the distance, I see the street sign for Nina's road: Harrington Circle. Adrenalin surges through my body. *What do you think you're going to accomplish?* the rational voice asks. I just want to see if he's there. *What if he is there? Then what?* I drown out my competing thoughts by turning up the radio and singing along with Adele.

I flip on my directional and turn onto the cul-de-sac. In the distance, I see Nico's Tundra parked on the side of the road. My hands get sweaty on the steering wheel. The closer to Nina's I get, the slower I go. Finally, I'm directly in front of her house. I turn down the radio. Someone is standing in the driveway. It's Nina with the dog on a leash. *Crap!* She stares at my passing car. I step on the gas and race by. The street dead-ends. There's nowhere to go. *Son of a beeyatch!* As I turn around in the circle, Nina, still staring at my car, marches down her driveway into the middle of the road. She's carrying Baxter now.

Two houses away from her, I jam on my brakes. She continues walking toward me. We stare at each other through the windshield. *Absolutely brilliant, Jillian.* I think about shifting into reverse and hightailing it through the snowy woods.

She makes it to my car and comes to the driver's window, knocking on it. She has the same dark, squinty eyes as Nico. Looking into them causes my own to fill with tears. I should drive away.

"Jillian, are you okay?" she asks. "What are you doing here?"

What the hell am *I doing here?*

"Jillian, what's going on? Are you all right?"

I remain motionless in the driver's seat. Tears roll down my cheeks.

"Put the window down," Nina says. "Please."

I lower it.

The dog barks at me while Nina stares. Finally she says, "Oh, Jillian, you shouldn't be here."

"I miss him." I didn't plan to say this and hate that I did.

Nina lowers Baxter to the ground but doesn't say anything.

"Did he tell you why he left?" I ask.

She shakes her head.

"I need to know," I demand.

The dog is barking incessantly now.

"I need to talk to him."

She shakes her head. "He's not even here. He's out with George and the kids." She picks up Baxter and looks back at her house. A car turns down the street and comes toward us. "Are you okay to drive?" Nina asks.

I nod.

"Text me when you get home."

She crosses the street in front of my car and carefully plods her way over the slippery snow-coated road to her house. I stomp on the gas. My tires squeal and my back-end fishtails as I accelerate down her street and out of her neighborhood. I'm crying so hard that I gulp for breath.

As I pull over to the side of the road to compose myself, my phone rings. Mr. O'Brien's name flashes across the screen. I let him go to voice mail and then listen to his message. "I told you before you left that I was taking the key to make duplicates and would leave them under the mat." He sounds like he's talking to the dumbest person in the world. In this case, he really might be.

Chapter 10

I hate Valentine's Day, and I swear, I'm not saying that just because I'm single. I didn't like it back when Nico showered me with a dozen roses and chocolates either. It's a schmaltzy fake holiday that's depressing for people without a partner and puts too much pressure on those with them. Even going out to dinner is a chore; reservations at good restaurants are impossible to get, unless you live for the day and make them months in advance, and there are waits of over ninety minutes at crappy chains like the Olive Garden. Nope, Valentine's Day has never been for me. I don't need Hallmark dictating when I'm supposed to shower my boyfriend with love. And okay, maybe because I don't have a boyfriend this year, I'm more repulsed than usual by the slow-moving caravan of florist vans driving up the hill leading to my office.

Inside the building, Barbara, the receptionist, has pasted hearts on the door of the reception area. I experience a strong urge to rip them all off as I walk by, and have to admit that my dislike for the holiday is more intense this year. On the fourth floor, Renee crashes into me, rushing to board the elevator as I step off. No doubt she's on her way to reception to pick up the dozen roses her husband, Lenny, had delivered here.

"Happy Valentine's Day, sweetie," she says. She's wearing a red dress, and there's a gold chain with a heart pendant circling her neck.

Instead of ripping it off her like I'm tempted to do, I force a smile. "Same to you." Despite my best effort, it comes out as a snarl.

Ben's talking on his cell phone when I pass his cube. "I'll be there at six," he says. I imagine he's talking to the girl he met at the gym over the weekend, who I think is a bodybuilder. I overheard him telling his friend Lucas about her earlier in the week. Apparently she asked him to spot her on bench presses. How many women do those?

I blink twice as I enter my cube. There's a vase of pink carnations sitting on my desk, next to it a small box of Godiva chocolates. For just a second, I picture Nico sneaking into the building early this morning to drop them off, never mind that he doesn't have the access card needed to unlock the door to my area. I reach for the small card sticking out of the flowers. When I see my name written across the envelope in black fountain pen, I know the gifts are not from Nico. They're from Ben. I think about our dinner last week. Maybe it really was a date? He did pay. I tear open the envelope. Written in the same black ink, the message in the card says *Happy Valentine's Day. Renee and Ben.*

Of course Ben didn't get me the flowers. Renee did. She feels bad because I'm single on this freaking fake holiday. Still, her thoughtfulness causes a lump in my throat. *Do not cry at work!*

"Morning, Jill," Ben says, staring down at me over the wall.

I can't look at him because there are tears streaming down my cheeks. *It's just flowers and chocolate! Get yourself together.* "Thanks for these." I motion to the vase and candy.

"Renee's idea," he says, quickly sinking back into his chair. A second later, he flees the area like a fire truck pulling out of the station in response to a 911 call. I can't blame him. No man wants to be near an emotional single woman on Valentine's Day.

I dive into my chocolates, looking for one filled with caramel. Instead, I get a nasty fruit-filled one, the one people usually take a bite of and return to the box. I toss it into the garbage and choose another. This time I get what I want.

The smell of flowers suddenly overpowers the area. I glance down the aisle and see Renee turning into her cube carrying a huge number of roses. I go to her desk, where she has arranged them in the corner. I can't believe how many roses are in that beautiful glass vase. I count them. Thirty-six! "They're beautiful!" I say, trying to make up for my unfriendly greeting earlier.

"They are!" she agrees.

"The carnations you gave me are too, and the chocolates are delicious."

"What carnations and chocolates?" she asks.

"The ones you and Ben gave me."

She bites down on her lower lip. She does that a lot when she's thinking. I'm always afraid she's going to puncture a hole in it and the collagen will leak out, dripping down her chin like wax from a melting candle. "You're welcome," she says.

"Whoa!" Ben turns the corner into Renee's cube and spots her flowers. "What did Lenny do wrong that he's trying to make up for this time?"

Renee playfully hits Ben in the arm. "Lenny sent them because he loves me, which reminds me." She reaches into her suitcase-sized pocketbook and extracts two envelopes, handing one to me and the other to Ben. "We're having a party to renew our vows on our twenty-fifth anniversary."

The muscles in my back stiffen as I read how the envelope is addressed: *Jillian Atwood and Guest.*

"Sounds like fun," Ben says.

I force myself to smile, but in fact can't imagine anything more dreadful. I can see it now, me sitting alone at a table watching a roomful of happy drunk couples dancing. No way am I going. What reason can I give? "It does, but I have to miss it." They are looking at me like I need to say more. "I'm going to Atlanta that weekend." Damn, Rachel is right about my voice getting high when I lie. I sound like I swallowed helium.

Renee and Ben stare at me like they too have picked up on my tell. The silence is unbearable so I keep talking. "I haven't seen my parents since the summer. Or my brother. And I miss Molly. She's getting really big. I saw pictures on Facebook." Apparently Rachel is also correct about me tilting my head when I fib, because it's practically resting on my shoulder.

Renee and Ben exchange a look. Damn. I wish I were a better liar, but until Nico left, I didn't do it that often.

"You haven't opened the envelope," Ben says. "You don't even know when it is."

"You don't have to make up excuses, honey," Renee says. "I understand. You don't want to go by yourself."

God, it sounds pathetic hearing it out loud.

"I'll be your date," Ben says. "One night with me, and you'll forget all about Nico." I expect him to wink or smile, but the look he's giving me isn't playful at all. It's downright seductive, sending a most unexpected jolt between my legs. Damn, where did that come from? Must be because it's Valentine's Day.

Although, I have to admit that I have thought about Ben that way before. Just once, but it was recent and couldn't have been at a worse time, the day after I got engaged. It was the night of the company's holiday party at a fancy downtown hotel. As soon as we arrived, Nico planted himself on a stool in the bar in front of the television. He claimed he had to watch the football games for work because they had playoff implications. I spent the night in the ballroom with Ben, who inexplicably didn't have a date. We were at a table drinking and talking with our coworkers. Ben made sure my glass was always full. At the start of the evening, he was bringing me wine, but at some point my beverage switched to Captain Morgan and Coke, something I only drink when I want to get drunk. Eventually, our group moved to the dance floor, trying to outdo each other with ridiculous moves that didn't at all go with the country music the DJ was playing. Each time the music slowed, Ben and I took the opportunity to refuel with alcohol. Right before the party ended, the Garth Brooks version of "Make You Feel My Love" came on. I headed back toward our table. Ben grabbed my arm. "I get the last dance," he said, placing one hand on my shoulder, the other at my waist. I looped my arms around his neck. At first, we were careful to leave room between our bodies, but as the music went on, Ben pulled me closer so we melded together. His lower hand slowly circled around my waist while the one high on my shoulder drifted downward. Soon his fingers were splayed across my backside. He thrust ever so slightly forward and whispered my name. I thought I heard desire in his voice, and when he pressed against me, I was sure. He quickly took a small step backward and repositioned himself as though he remembered he was dancing with a coworker, not with one of his usual floozies, but the damage was done. The brief moment of feeling him against me had sparked a drunken, unquenchable desire. I leaned into him, grinding my pelvis into his and again felt how hard he was. A few feet away Ellie was dancing with her husband. I felt her watching us but didn't care. Ben closed his eyes, thrusting against me the same way I was bumping against him. I felt like I was back in the cafeteria at a school dance with my high school boyfriend, doing all we could to arouse one another while fully clothed. "This is dangerous, Jill," Ben whispered, his words slightly slurred, but he held me tight against him until the song ended.

Nico appeared in the ballroom doorway, motioning for me because it was time to leave. Ben and I walked toward him. Nico and I were spending the night at the hotel so that neither of us had to drive after drinking, which was a good thing because I was having a hard enough time navigating the walk across the ballroom. Just before Ben left my side, he leaned close enough so I could smell the scotch on his breath. I'm not sure I heard him correctly, but what I thought he said was, "I wish I were the one going upstairs with you."

In the elevator up to our room, I backed Nico into a corner, kissing him and stroking him over his pant leg, desperate to fulfill the desire that had ignited on the dance floor. We were staying on the twenty-seventh floor, and the elevator's climb up was painfully slow, our passion heightening as we slowly made our ascent. "I need you so bad right now," I whined, guiding his hand deep inside the waistband of my black velvet skirt.

"I thought you were going to be angry with me," he said.

"I am," I gasped.

"Then I need to piss you off more often. I like angry Jill."

We staggered out of the elevator toward our room, stripping out of our clothes as soon as the door shut. Eagerly

Nico led me to the bed. After six years together, I knew where and how he would touch me, knew the exact path his hands and mouth would travel over my body, and still I couldn't wait. As he climbed on top of me, I closed my eyes and Ben's handsome face popped in my mind. And then I couldn't stop myself from fantasizing it was Ben in bed with me, my body shuddering more violently than it ever had before. When Nico moaned my name, it was Ben's voice I heard back on the dance floor.

Even though I didn't technically do anything wrong, I felt guilty for days after. Now, after Nico leaving me, I'm happy for that betrayal and thinking that a night with Ben might be exactly what I need to get over him. Ben gives me a cocky grin that makes me wonder if he can see inside my head to the X-rated images of him and me together that are playing over and over again, making me all hot and bothered. I fan myself with the invitation.

"I'm glad it's not just me," Renee says. Her neck and face have turned the same color as the roses on her desk. There's a thin line of perspiration above her lip.

"What do you say, Jill? Is it a date?" Ben asks.

Would Ben and I behave the same way we did at the holiday party? What would happen without Nico there waiting for me this time? Would I become just another of Ben's one-night stands? If so, would we be comfortable working together after, or would the entire dynamic of our four-person department change? "I'll think about it," I say.

Ben and I never talked about what happened between us on the dance floor that night. At breakfast the day after the party, I heard from Ellie that Ben spent that night with the pretty-but-dumb blond human resources temp. I was sure Ellie got it wrong because Ben made a point of never hooking up with anyone at work, but the temp's frequent visits to Ben's cube the following week seemed to confirm Ellie's information was accurate. Later I overheard Ben's friend Lucas asking Ben why he broke his rule about sleeping with a coworker. Ben said the girl wasn't a coworker she worked for the temp agency and he'd never have to see her again after her assignment at our company was over.

    I chalked up our behavior at the holiday party to the heavy drinking we had both done. That and maybe I was rebelling against Nico for ignoring me all night long. I honestly never thought about Ben that way before that night and haven't since. Not until right now anyway.

Chapter 11

It used to make me happy when I heard *BS Morning Sports Talk* coming from my coworkers' radios. Today, hearing the show blasting from their cubes feels like a betrayal, like they've chosen Nico over me. Only Renee seems to be Team Jillian, and that's because she doesn't have a radio on her desk.

I drown out the sound of Branigan's voice with music, and busy myself responding to emails. Before I can get through them all, Ryan, Tyler, and Ben break into explosive laughter. It doesn't surprise me that Ryan and Tyler are listening, but hearing Ben howl like that stings. He should boycott the program to show his allegiance to me.

Because the three of them are practically busting their guts, curiosity gets the best of me. "What's so funny?" I call out.

Ryan yells a response, but his giggles jumble his words.

Ben takes a few seconds to compose himself. "The idiots calling in about the contest," he answers. "Branigan is having them describe their best features."

"Who knew so many chicks have such bodacious ta-tas?" Ryan asks.

A wave of anger rushes over me as I realize that women are actually trying to win a date with Nico. "What kind of person would enter a contest like this?" I ask.

The guys are too busy laughing to respond, but Renee answers. "Single females in their thirties to forties. They're desperate because there are so few good men available."

Her words land like a sucker punch to my abdomen. I am one of those desperate women now. I met Nico when I was twenty-eight. He wasted six years of my life, six of my child-bearing years, a time when I was at my best physically, lean and muscular with no wrinkles or cellulite. At thirty-four, I can already feel body parts shifting downward, see the beginning of a roll in my once flat abdomen. This morning, I plucked two gray hairs from the front of my head and a long dark one from my chin. My chin!

As if he knows what I'm thinking, Ben calls out, "If it makes you feel any better, some of the male callers want a chance to win a date with you. Branigan says you should call in if you're interested."

In fact, what Ben just told me makes me feel worse because there's an urgent voice whispering to me that I shouldn't pass up the opportunity. *How else are you going to meet a normal single guy?* the voice whispers.

In the hallway, a soda can snaps open. A few seconds later, the top of the bright blue skullcap that Ben's friend Lucas always wears bobs over the wall in Ben's cube. "What's going on, Brother?" Lucas asks. There's the sound of palms slapping together, and I imagine the two shaking hands

In my mind, there is no friendship more unlikely than Lucas and Ben's. Ben is preppy and seems more likely to fit with the J. Crew or Ralph Lauren crowd. With his skullcap, jeans, and flannel shirts, Lucas looks like he should be living in Seattle back in the grunge era. He's definitely not what comes to mind when I think of an engineer, but no company other than our new one, trying to sound sophisticated, would give hackers the title of cyber security engineers.

Mixed Signals

"You have to hear this," Ben says. He turns up the volume of his radio.

Branigan's baritone voice booms through the area. "If we pick you, how will you make it worth Nico's while?" he asks.

Jesus H. Christ! I do not want to hear the answer to that. I stomp over to Ben's desk and rip the radio's plug from the outlet. "I don't want to listen to that!"

"Whoa, chill," Lucas says, taking a large sip of Mountain Dew. He's six feet tall and thin as a pencil, surprising considering he drinks his first sugary soda before nine in the morning and goes through about ten a day.

"Sorry," Ben says, "but it's really funny."

"Not to me." The quiver in my voice gives away how upset I am over this. *Get it together*, I tell myself.

Lucas turns away and busies himself rearranging the collection of toy cars Ben has displayed on his shelf.

"Sorry," Ben says. "I didn't mean to upset you. I'll get headphones."

A few rows over, Ryan bursts into laughter again.

I mutter under my breath and return to my cube. Behind me I hear Lucas saying to Ben, "She's all riled up about this."

"Can't really blame her," Ben answers. He whispers something to Lucas that I can't hear.

Lucas's enthusiastic response is loud, though. "I'll take care of it. It will be fun."

⚜ ⚜ ⚜

The sound of a plow wakes me the following morning. Outside, there are at least five inches of fresh snow on the railing. On days like this, I often wonder why I didn't move to Georgia with my brother and parents, not that they asked. Nope. One Sunday afternoon at the end of lunch, my mother dropped the bombshell that she and my dad had made an offer on a house in Christian's Atlanta neighborhood. "We feel like we're missing out on Molly's childhood," she said.

"What about me?" I asked. "You're leaving me here alone?"

"You're hardly alone," she said. "You have Nico and all your friends."

It's true that I would never leave New England. Miserable winters and all, I love it here. Still, it would have been nice to have been asked.

Staring out the window, I see Mr. O'Brien on the driveway, surveying the damage from this latest storm. He glances up at the window and shakes his head, like he's had enough. *Me too, Mr. O'Brien.* If I'm right about the five inches of new snow, our total for the season will pass one hundred, and we still have another week in February and the entire month of March to get through.

As I head for the shower, I hear the snowblower starting. By the time I'm dressed for work and out the door, the driveway is clear except for the end, where the plow has deposited a large icy bank of snow. Mr. O'Brien uses a pick to hack away at it. After starting my car and blasting the heat, I grab a shovel to help him.

"Couldn't wait for Zachary to get here to help. He's going to be at work later than usual," Mr. O'Brien says. He almost sounds like he's blaming me because I helped Zac get his job.

"Something happened to the station's website," he mutters. "Damn technology."

I watch a plow turn onto our street, praying he doesn't block us in again. "What happened?" I ask.

The plow passes the house next door. I watch it make its way toward us, hoping the driver will take pity on me and the old man and clear the end of the driveway. The truck slows as it gets closer. The driver's dour expression brightens. He flashes us an ice-melting smile as he pushes another gigantic pile of snowy mush off the street toward us. My landlord and I both mutter under our breath.

"Zac called me this morning. Said he has to stay late to work on the website because someone did something to the contest page and what's-his-face's picture."

As far as I know, Mr. O'Brien has never used Nico's name. I'm not even sure if he knows it. "What do you mean, they did something to his picture?"

Mr. O'Brien clears his throat. "It was replaced with a, um, vulgar one."

I think about Ben whispering to Lucas yesterday and Lucas's enthusiastic response. Did Ben tell him to hack the radio station's website? Even if they had nothing to do with it, Nico will suspect me. He knows what my company does and how good Lucas is at his job. Through the years, I told him several stories about the sites Lucas was able to access. Of course, usually the companies know what he's trying to do. He doesn't do it illegally.

My shoveling shifts into high gear so that I can get out of my driveway and to the office. After Mr. O'Brien and I clear away enough of the snowbank to get my car out, he looks at his watch. "You're going to be late for work. You should go." I feel bad leaving him with the rest of the shoveling, but he insists.

As I begin to back out toward the street, I flip the station on my radio to *BS Morning Sports Talk*. I'm paying more attention to what Branigan is saying than driving.

"Turn your wheels to the right," Mr. O'Brien hollers.

"Who did you piss off in our IT department, Nico?" Branigan asks.

"The other way!" Mr. O'Brien shouts.

"No one," Nico answers.

My car hits an icy mound of snow. Mr. O'Brien frowns. I imagine the thought bubble over his head says *Where did she get her license?* I pull the car forward and try again. This time, I make it to the street. I beep and wave at Mr. O'Brien as I drive off.

"Well, someone's mad at you," Branigan says.

"No one but Jill," Nico answers.

⚜ ⚜ ⚜

By the time I pull into the parking garage at work, I have learned that someone replaced the picture of Nico with a photoshopped image of his head on a big body with, as Branigan put it, "a tiny male anatomy." There's no doubt in my mind that Lucas is responsible. With his ability to hack into sites, he's our company's biggest asset. We usually start a sale with an assessment of a prospect's technology. After we present them with a list of their applications and data we were able to breach, the sale is easy to close.

Once I get in the building, I travel down the maze of hallways on the first floor that leads to Lucas's windowless office. He stands when I enter the room and adjusts his blue cap. Stacks of empty Mountain Dew cans, each about twenty high, line the side of his desk. "What brings you down to the slums?" he asks.

"Did you hack the *BS Morning Sports Talk* website?"

He reaches into the small refrigerator under his desk and pulls out a soda. "I heard about that. They messed with Nico's picture." His grin gives him away.

I stuff my gloves into my coat pocket, wondering if I should hit him or hug him.

"Lucas, you can't mess with their site. Nico will know I had something to do with it."

"If I were the one who hacked it, I promise you that I'm good enough not to get caught, but I didn't do it," he says.

"I don't believe you." I head back for the door.

"Jillian, I'm an engineer. I don't know how to change a picture."

When I arrive in our area, Ben has a dopey smile on his face "Did you hear?" he asks. "They had to take the radio station's website down because it was hacked."

"Yeah, by you and Lucas." I try to make my voice sound like I'm annoyed, but truthfully, I'm touched that they're trying to do something nice for me. "I appreciate you trying to help me, but you can get in big trouble. Don't do it again."

Ben's expression and words are almost identical to Lucas's. "I'm a graphic artist. I don't know how to hack a website."

"The picture was fantastic," Renee says. She's sitting in Ben's cube eating her oatmeal. I can tell by the aroma that brown sugar is her flavor of choice today. "I saw it just before they took the site down."

I bet she saw it. She's probably involved too. I imagine her drafting talking points for Ben's and Lucas's denials in case they get caught. All three of them are going to get arrested. I'll have to bail them out.

I return to my cube and log into the show's website. All that is there is a Page Cannot Be Found error, so there's no way for women to submit their pictures or state the reasons they want to go out with Nico. Just like that, Ben and Lucas have stopped the contest. Instead of the website, I wish they could find a way to hack into Nico's heart, pull a few strings, and make him love me again, or maybe they could find a way to access my memories and delete all the ones relating to Nico.

Later that morning my phone buzzes with a text. It's just after ten, a few minutes after Nico's show ends. I know without looking that the message is from him because for six years he texted me precisely at this time to see how my morning was going. His message today is not as friendly:

I was hoping for an amicable split. Disappointed you involved your coworkers to publicly humiliate me. GAME ON!

Chapter 12

Because participants can't submit pictures to the contest until the website is fixed and its security is enhanced, the radio station extends it. For two weeks, Branigan and Smyth sandwich calls from women who want to go out with Nico between listeners who want to talk sports. According to the show's website, the contest has close to 140,000 entries. Crazy considering most of the audience is male.

By the time the show is ready to announce the winner, "WinADateW/Nico" is trending on Twitter in Boston. On the morning of the announcement, Ben, Renee, and I are sitting in his cube listening to the show. A few rows over, Ryan and Tyler are snacking on foul-smelling sausages and eggs from the cafeteria, waiting to see pictures of the winner.

Branigan has been milking the interest in the contest since I started listening at six this morning. Now, he concludes his interview with a hockey player. "Okay, we know you've all been waiting to find out who the lucky lady is who has won a date with Nico," he says. "We'll tell you right after this commercial break. Stay tuned."

This is really happening. For six years, Nico has dated no one but me. Now he's going on a date with a listener. I reach for the slinky on Ben's desk and extend it between my hands, compress it and then repeat. The sound of the metal rings collapsing on each other comforts me but annoys Renee. She grabs the toy from me. "Don't worry, honey," she says. "It's just a PR stunt. Nothing will come of it."

I'm not so sure of that. The winner will be a woman who willingly listens to Nico's show, unlike me, who tuned in under duress. If she listens to sports talk, she'll probably love watching games with him. I usually sat on the couch next to him, reading. Only when he jumped to his feet, cheering for a play, would I glance at the television. I imagine that whoever the winner is, she'll be jumping right beside him. Damn, she's more likely to be his soul mate than I ever was.

The commercial ends. "First, I want to thank all the young ladies who participated in our contest," Branigan says. "The response was overwhelming."

Smyth pipes in. "Who would have thought so many women would be interested in a date with Nico. The guy's a schmuck."

Ben elbows me.

"Exactly right," Renee mumbles.

"So it took us several days to go through all the pictures, but Smyth and I have studied them all carefully," Branigan says.

"Some more carefully than others," Smyth adds. He and Branigan both laugh.

"Nico hasn't seen any of the pictures," Branigan says. "We didn't want our decision influenced by his preferences, because frankly we know better than he does."

I'm sure Branigan means that as a jab at me, and give the radio the finger.

"Maybe you shouldn't be listening, Jillian," Ben suggests.

Listening to the show is like looking at an accident I pass on the highway. I know that it's going to upset me, but I can't help myself. "I'm okay."

"Our sponsor, Vincenzio's Cucina, has generously donated dinner for Nico and the winner."

It's like Nico is slamming my heart with a sledgehammer. Why there, of all places? Won't the memory of the night we got engaged bother him?

"And the winner is—drum roll, please," Smyth says. "Bonnie Carmichael."

"Ms. Carmichael is a yoga instructor and sent photos of herself in some very interesting positions," Branigan says. "Our intern, Zachary, is in the process of posting them to our website."

"Not the good ones," Smyth says. "We would get in trouble for that. Big trouble."

"How is it even possible to spread your legs like that?" Branigan asks.

"She's obviously very flexible," Smyth answers.

"So Nico is looking at her pictures now," Branigan says. "What do you think, you lucky dog?"

Nico's hoarse voice comes over the airway. "I'm blessed," he says.

The pictures go up a few minutes later. I know because the sales guys whistle like construction workers. "I want a piece of that!" Ryan shouts.

"She is hot, don't-get-too-close-or-you'll-get-scorched hot," another says.

Do not look, my rational voice warns. She's probably beautiful.

Branigan has horrible taste. She might be hideous, says the voice that always gets me in trouble.

I take a deep breath, navigate to the radio station's website, and click on the link for the morning show. Across the page, in big bold letters, the type reads Nico's Date. Under it is a full body shot of a lean woman dressed in nothing but a leotard. She has a heart-shaped face with a flawless complexion. Her thick, long blond hair flows over her left shoulder. Just above her right breast, there's a tattoo of a shamrock. She's sitting with her muscular tanned legs fully extended out to each side of her body. There is a one sentence caption under the picture: "Tune in Monday to find out if Nico scores."

Damn, I should have listened to my rational voice. My eyes well up. Ben enters my cube. He looks at the screen. I can tell by how quickly he turns away from it, feigning no interest, that he's already seen the photograph. "That picture's been photoshopped, and her rack, definitely not real," he says.

I click off the page.

"Hey," he says, noticing my watery eyes. "It's going to be okay." He places his hand on my back and moves it in small circles. His kindness makes it harder to fight back my tears. "You're going to end up with someone so much better than Nico."

"Sure," I say.

⚜ ⚜ ⚜

The last thing I feel like doing after work is partying with my coworkers, but our new owners are hosting an event for us at the Time Machine, a restaurant down the street. Stacy warned us that not attending would be like committing career suicide, so I have to suck it up for an hour or so.

Renee and I wait until everyone else has left the office before we make our way over. "Try to forget about Nico and have a good time," Renee says as she pulls open the door to the restaurant.

"Okay," I say, but it will be hard to forget about him here, because it's one of the places he loved to go with me.

Stepping inside is an instant sensory overload. Machines ding and beep, colored lights flash. Waiters and waitresses race around the crowded room carrying trays with onion rings, french fries, and buffalo wings, all emitting strong aromas. The idea behind the restaurant is that while you're there, you go back to when you were a kid, so there are all sorts of video games you can play while you eat and drink.

A new woman in Human Resources, the one who replaced the HR temp Ben slept with the night of the holiday party, greets us and gives us free drink tickets. "Have fun," she says.

Renee takes our jackets to the coat check while I scan the crowd, looking for our coworkers. Cheering breaks out in the back of the room, and then an electronic voice comes over the speaker: "Team three wins." I turn my head toward the commotion and immediately see Lucas's blue cap in the crowd. Next to him, Tyler and Ryan high-five each other.

Just beyond them, Ellie has Ben pinned in the back corner of the bar. He sees us and waves his arms high above his head. His frantic movements remind me of someone shipwrecked trying to get the attention of the search crew in a helicopter flying overhead. I imagine Ellie bending Ben's ear about ideas she has for the new website. She rarely stops thinking about work. I'm sure that she even forwarded her work phone to her BlackBerry before she left the office this evening.

"Looks like Ben needs to be rescued," Renee says.

We navigate our way through the dense crowd, brushing shoulders with many other people here to start their weekend. "I was getting worried that you weren't coming,"

Ben says. "Let me get you a drink." He pushes his way past Ellie and heads toward the bartender.

"Ben was just telling me the two of you are going to Renee's twenty-fifth anniversary party together," Ellie says.

Renee's face turns bright red. At first I think she's embarrassed because she didn't invite Ellie, but then she rips off her long black cardigan, grabs a menu, and fans herself. "It's like a hundred degrees in here," she says.

Ellie and I look at each other because it's cold, like the air conditioner is on instead of the heat. Hot flashes. They can hit you anytime, anyplace. That's what I've learned from watching Renee over the past few months.

"I don't know if I'm going," I say.

"Going where?" Ben hands me a glass of red wine and Renee, white.

"To my party," Renee answers.

"You're going," he says. "You're my dance partner."

"We'll see," I say.

"You should go," Ellie says. "You two had a great time dancing together at the holiday party."

Ben casts a sideways glance at me. My cheeks redden thinking about how I behaved that night. Damn Ellie for bringing that up. She called me the day after the party. Her voice was a mixture of disgust and judgment. *What the hell were you thinking, grinding with him like that? What if Nico saw?*

Now, I wish he had, not just because it would have hurt him, but because it would have given him a reason to leave, one that I would understand.

The group of coworkers who were playing games stream toward us. Lucas and Ryan edge their way into our circle. Ryan bumps Ellie's arm, causing her to spill beer on her shirt. She goes to the bar to get a napkin. He stares at me with a smirk. His dark brown eyes, which are set too close together, are already bloodshot. I'd bet anything he's already burned through the three free-drink tickets Human Resources gave us on the way in.

"So, Jill, did you see the woman who won a date with Nico?" he asks. "She is one hot little dish."

I tighten my grip on the glass in my hand, causing the wine to slosh back and forth along its sides. For a split second, I imagine tossing it at Ryan, watching the red liquid drip down his face onto his gray sweatshirt.

"I don't know," Ben says. "She looks like Miss Piggy to me."

"A strong resemblance," Lucas says. The two clank glasses.

I get a sinking feeling in my stomach. "What did you guys do?"

"We didn't do anything," Ben says. Lucas laughs and the two clank their beer mugs again.

I take my cell phone from my purse and navigate to the radio station's website. Instead of Bonnie's picture, there's now a photograph of Miss Piggy lying on a pink exercise mat with her open legs high in the air above her head. The picture is funny, but I don't want to encourage Lucas and Ben, so I try to stifle my laugh. It comes out as a snort, which causes them both to burst out laughing.

"Nico already blamed this on me. If he figures out a way to prove it, we could all be in big trouble."

Ben wraps his arm around my waist and pulls me toward him. "You didn't do it, so relax."

Ellie returns, looking pointedly at Ben's arm around me. "Jill, let's go to the ladies' room." She takes my glass and places it on the table.

When we get to the restroom, she asks, "What's going on with you and Ben?"

"Nothing."

Whenever she's excited, two curved lines that look like parentheses appear between her eyebrows. They're there now. "He's definitely into you," she says. "Told me to convince you to go to the party with him."

A toilet flushes.

"That's because he doesn't want me sitting home feeling sorry for myself." I tell her how he asked me to go to dinner with him because he thought I was spending too much time at work.

A stall door swings open, and Renee steps out. "Ben's had a thing for you since you started," she says. "Haven't you ever noticed the way he looks at you?"

How does he look at me? "No!"

"Oh, I've noticed," Ellie says.

Maybe at the Christmas party he looked at me a certain way, but other than that, he hardly notices me.

"And I had nothing to do with those flowers and chocolates on Valentine's Day," Renee says. "All his idea."

"We're friends. He's trying to cheer me up." That has to be the reason he gave me a gift.

As Renee washes her hands, she checks out her flushed reflection in the mirror. "Be careful around him," she says. "You're vulnerable right now, and he doesn't always use the best judgment."

Other than when she's having hot flashes, Renee looks and acts young, so I often forget that she is twenty years older than me and has two teenage kids. Right now, though, the way she's looking at me and the concern on her face definitely remind me that she's a mother. She rips a paper towel out of the dispenser. "I don't want you to do anything you'll regret." She touches my hand on her way past me. I can feel that hers is still wet.

"You should definitely hook up with him. Let him cheer you up," Ellie says, and laughs.

Even though the thought crossed my mind, I shake my head.

"You know what they say: The best way to get over someone is to get under someone else," Ellie persists.

"What happens the next day when we have to work together?"

"You can always find a new job," she answers.

⚜ ⚜ ⚜

When I return from the restroom, Ben is standing by himself watching two men shoot basketballs. The game they're playing continuously spits balls at them. They have two minutes to get as many as they can through the net. Ben motions with his head for me to join him. Ellie nudges me in his direction. "Be crazy. Go for it," she says.

Nico's voice on the radio this morning replays in my head: *I'm blessed.*

Maybe it is time for me to do something crazy.

I inch toward the game, watching Ben's expression to see if there's anything to Renee's words about the way he looks at me. I don't notice a thing.

"Why are you staring at me like that?" he asks when I reach him. "Do I have something on my face?" He wipes his mouth.

"I wasn't staring," I say, feeling ridiculous.

We both turn our attention toward the game. Usually the silence between us is comfortable, but tonight it's awkward. Thank you, Renee and Ellie. So that we're not just standing there staring at each other, I begin to narrate each shot with my best sports-announcer voice. "That's an air ball. He's going to have to focus more if he's going to pull out a W."

Ben laughs, so I continue. "Nothing but net on that last shot."

The player misses a shot and looks over his shoulder at me. My narration may be distracting him, but I don't stop.

"He's on fire now," I say.

"Shooting the lights out," Ben says in a gravelly voice, which I think is an imitation of the legendary Boston Celtics' announcer Johnny Most.

"He's making a living behind the three-point arc," I say.

"It's raining threes," Ben says.

"He can nail the trifecta."

"He's the hot hand," Ben says.

"He can really shoot the three-ball."

Ben has run out of banal expressions, but I have more. I guess I didn't completely tune out the games during all the hours I spent next to Nico on the sofa, reading while he watched. "He's money, a pure shooter. He can fill it up," I say.

The guys who were playing basketball give us a strange look and move on to another game. Ryan sneaks up behind us. He smiles at me appreciatively. "Nico sure trained you right for the next guy," he says.

Just like that, all the air is sucked out of the room. If anything, Nico has soured me on sports. I glare at Ryan, fantasizing about twisting his head off and shooting it through the net. His and Nico's.

Ben steps up to the abandoned machine and digs two quarters out of his pocket. "Let's see you put your money where your mouth is, Jillian."

Ryan wanders back to the table at the bar. Good riddance!

"Loser buys lunch next week," Ben says.

I nod in agreement, certain I will win. I used to beat Nico all the time. Boy, did my winning annoy him. He'd make us play for hours because he refused to quit until he won. By the end of the night, my arms would hurt from shooting so many baskets.

Ben presses the game's start button. The score lights and timer flash on. Music and an annoying whining voice, which I guess is supposed to be cheering, blast from the speakers. Ben spins a ball on his index finger before shooting his first basket. As he lifts his arms over his head, preparing to take his first shot, his shirt rises, revealing the elastic band of his Jockey briefs and a patch of smooth skin on his strong lower back.

He looks back at me over his shoulder. I worry that the cocky grin he gives me is because he knows I'm admiring his body. "Haven't missed one yet," he says. I glance at his score, thirty-eight, which means he's hit nineteen in a row. I turn my attention from his back to his shooting. He's like a machine, throwing basketball after basketball through the net. As he does, I notice the way his muscular biceps flex each time he shoots the ball. I think about Ellie's words in the restroom. Maybe I should take her advice. *So hey, Ben, what do you say we upgrade this friendship. Add some benefits.*

"Beat that!" Ben says. I didn't realize his turn ended. He has 118 points.

"Oh, I got this," I say, running my hand up his arm because I suddenly need to feel it. It's as rock solid as it looks. Why haven't I ever noticed that before?

"Well, let's see." He playfully smacks my butt as I approach the machine.

Would he touch another coworker there? I try to imagine him grabbing Renee's butt. Nope.

"Where will you take me for lunch?" he asks.

I shake my head and press the start button. Spinning a ball on my finger, I cock my head sideways and smile. "Watch and learn." The first ball I shoot swishes through the net.

"So you got lucky," he says.

I score twenty-eight consecutive shots. With thirty-one seconds still left on the clock, I have already tied Ben's score.

"Damn," he whines. "You are freakishly good at this."

Again, I imagine taking Ellie's advice and coming on to Ben. *I'm freakishly good at a lot of things*, I would say, playing with my hair and trying to look seductive. The thought causes me to laugh because I could never pull it off.

When my score is ten points higher than Ben's, he tries to distract me by tossing popcorn at me. Instead of throwing the basketballs toward the net, I turn and hurl them at him. He catches the first, but the second ricochets off the ball he's holding and bounces through the room. An employee dressed as a referee returns it to us with a scolding.

"Two out of three," Ben says.

This time when he shoots the balls, the tip of his tongue hangs out of the right corner of his mouth. I've seen the same thing at work when he's concentrating hard on an illustration he's drawing. His seriousness makes me laugh. I inch closer to him. He glances at me sideways. I bump my hip against his. He bumps back, undistracted. I lean into him with all my weight. He laughs, leans back, and keeps scoring. Finally I yank on his arm and pull it backward.

He drops the ball he's holding and grabs me, pushing and twisting me so that my back is pressed up against the machine and he's facing me. He pins my hands high above my head. "Afraid you're going to lose?" he asks.

"No chance." I try to squirm away. He tightens his grip on me. We both laugh as I try to shove him off me. The more I try, the harder he presses against me. His thighs are as rock solid as his biceps.

Our faces are less than an inch apart. Our eyes lock. There are specs of gold in his green irises that I've never noticed before. His soapy clean smell from the morning is gone, replaced with a sweaty, provocative scent that is stirring up desires that have been dormant in me since Nico left.

"If I let you go, are you going to behave?" he asks. "Let me start over, with no cheating?"

He's so close that I feel his warm breath on my face as he speaks. If I move just a spec forward, our lips would touch. *Do it.* The thought pops into my head. *Damn Ellie!*

"Jillian?"

My mouth goes dry at the sound of Ben's voice saying my name. I struggle to swallow. "Okay."

He releases me. While he feeds the basketball machine with coins for our next game, I try to compose myself. *What's wrong with me?* I watch him shooting baskets, everything below my waist tingling, thinking about how good his hard body felt pressing against mine.

I glance away from him toward the bar. Ellie and Renee are both staring at me. Ellie has a huge grin, but Renee looks concerned. This is their fault! They planted these crazy thoughts in my head.

Ben's turn ends. He scored 132 points. I step up to the machine, but can't focus. Shot after shot, the ball bounces off the rim. My final score is eighteen points.

"What happened?" Ben asks.

"I have no idea," I say without meeting his eyes.

Chapter 13

The WimbleDome Mixed Doubles Tournament begins on Saturday morning with a continental breakfast. When I arrive, all the players are gathered around the bulletin board in the back of the Club Café checking out the brackets to see whom they are playing.

David is meeting with the umpires by the bar, giving them their assignments and passing out shirts with the navy-blue WimbleDome logo, a D that looks like a dome with an uppercase W going through it. Ben designed the logo as a favor to me years ago.

Ben. Last night after our basketball game, he sat at the bar, chatting up the bartender, who kept finding reasons to bend toward him, giving him an up-close view of her ridiculous cleavage. At one point, I saw her scribbling on a napkin and handing it to him. He cocked his head and a sly smile crossed his face as he tucked it into his pocket. Before he left for the night, he touched her hand. "See you tomorrow," he said.

"Can't wait." She giggled.

There's no doubt what he'll be doing tonight or who he'll be doing it with. Meanwhile, Nico will be at the restaurant where he proposed to me, with Bonnie, the Namaste Nitwit. I should have taken Ellie's advice last night and figured out a way to go home with Ben. That way, I wouldn't be obsessing about Nico's date.

"Jillian," David says. "You're on court one." He tosses a shirt at me. "So you better do a good job." The windows in the café overlook court one. It's also where the finals are held, so there's no doubt I'll be here all day.

I leave to change into my shirt. When I return, there's a commotion by the bulletin board. Branigan has penciled his name into the winner's spot on the bracket. The other players all laugh. "You overly confident bastard," someone says, slapping him on the back. Tania and Jeff Long, who have been runners-up to the Branigans the last two years, walk away whispering to each other.

Branigan and his wife work their way through the crowd to where David and I are standing. Tammy's blond hair is perfectly coiffed, flowing freely over her shoulders. Her face looks tanned, and she's wearing eye shadow, mascara, and lipstick. In comparison, most of the other women are wearing white baseball caps over their heads. Those with hair long enough have ponytails sticking out the hole in the back. Their complexions are the typical New England late-February transparent, and none of them have bright colors painted over their eyelids.

"Sean. Tammy," David says, shaking their hands.

Tammy hugs me hello. The overpowering scent of her lavender perfume causes me to sneeze.

"Jillian," Branigan says, nodding his head. "What do you think about the response to our little contest? None of us at the station were expecting anything like that."

"I hope prostituting Nico is worth the jump in your ratings," I say.

Branigan laughs. "If you were listening this week," he says, "you heard there's a lot of interest in a date with you too."

"Thanks, I'm all set," I say while imagining ripping his tongue out of his mouth so he could never speak again.

"Really, does that mean you're dating someone?" He smirks as if what I'm telling him is impossible.

"It does." I purposely keep my voice low, hoping I sound convincing. I know I shouldn't lie, but he makes me crazy.

"Who is he? How did you meet?"

Good going, Jillian. "I'd rather not say."

Branigan studies me for a moment. "Is that because it's someone Nico knows?"

I keep my expression neutral. "Maybe." Now that I've started, I may as well continue with the lie. Branigan is bound to tell Nico. Maybe Nico will even be jealous.

"I'll make sure to let Nico know." The bastard actually winks like he knows my lie is all a ploy to try to get Nico back.

Well, isn't it? asks the voice in my head that never lets me get away with anything.

David whistles. The loud conversations end abruptly. Everyone turns toward him. "Welcome to the tenth annual WimbleDome Mixed Doubles Tournament." He explains the rules and talks about the prizes: a gift certificate to a five-star restaurant down the street from the tennis club, tickets to watch the Red Sox home opener in WSPR's suite, and a month's free membership for the winning couple. "Good luck to all the opponents. Win or lose, I hope everyone has fun today," he says.

The bell rings. The crowd hustles out of the café, only to get caught up in a line on the stairs. David and I wait behind the mob. "You're dating already," he says. "Good for you."

"Yeah." I know I should tell him the truth. He's good friends with Branigan, though, and I don't want Branigan to know I was lying. He can suspect it all he wants, but I'm not going to confirm it for him.

"How did you meet?" David asks.

Ben's face pops into my head. "Work."

"Be careful with that," David warns. "Things can get tricky if you break up."

⚜ ⚜ ⚜

The morning matches are uneventful. I sit in a chair by the net, looking down on the court, calling balls in or out. Most of the shots land clearly inbounds or out, so there are no disputes. At the end of long rallies, the crowd watching from the café upstairs pounds on the glass, showing their appreciation of the well-fought points. Opponents shake hands at the conclusion of the matches and wish each other well in the rest of the tournament.

When we break for lunch, there are only eight couples left. The Branigans are one of them. Sean edges in behind me in the buffet line. "Have you heard how the Longs are doing?" he asks.

I use the tongs to drop a sourdough roll on my plate. "They haven't lost a set yet."

Sean picks up an onion roll with his fingers. "Tammy and I haven't lost a game." He winks and pushes his way past me to the deli meat.

⚜ ⚜ ⚜

No one is surprised that the Branigans are taking on the Longs in the final match. As he does every year, David assigns a second umpire to call the match with me. I'm a bit surprised to see that he's appointed Jordan Kaufman though, because Jordan owns a jewelry shop that regularly advertises on *BS Morning Sports Talk* during the holidays. In fact, Nico purchased my ring at his store. I know because he presented it to me in the telltale blue velvet box with the letter K printed on top of it in a cursive gold font.

When Jordan walks onto the court, Branigan shakes his hand and turns to me. "When you return the ring to Nico, I'm sure Jordan will give him back most of what he paid for it."

"Or," Jordan says, "I can turn the diamond into earrings or a necklace for you."

"That wouldn't be right," Branigan says, shaking his head before returning to the side of the court to get ready for the last match.

Jordan and I decide that he'll be responsible for calls on the side of the court closest to the outside wall and I'll handle those on the side of the café window. The Branigans and Longs wish each other good luck, and the match is set to begin. The large group of members gathered in front of the window in the café cheer wildly when the teams walk onto the court. Branigan pumps his fist at them, and they pound the glass harder. I guess I'm the only one rooting against the guy.

The match is well played, both teams fighting hard for every point. The rallies are long, with the Longs and Branigans both running all over the court to make seemingly impossible returns. Most of the games go to deuce several times. After more than two hours, the players all look spent. Tammy's eye shadow and mascara streak down her face, and her blond hair is wet with perspiration. Sweat drips down Branigan's face, legs, and arms onto the clay surface. Jeff is moving with a limp, and Tania keeps rubbing her right shoulder and elbow.

The match is winding down though. The Longs are only one point away from unseating the Branigans as the club champions. The crowd in the café is silent. Most of them are watching with their hands covering their mouths or their arms folded across their chests. Tania prepares to serve to Branigan, who glides up and down on his tiptoes waiting for the ball. She bounces the ball four times, tosses it high in the air, extends her racquet, and taps the ball toward Sean. The serve has no speed or spin. The ball floats in the air like a hot air balloon. Branigan's eyes light up as he gets ready to slam it. He brings his racquet back and then accelerates it forward through the ball. He swings hard. The ball soars over the net, whizzing between Tania and Jeff. It bounces near the outer edge of the baseline and skids out of bounds. The crowd in the café all swipe their hands horizontally, indicating the ball was in. Jeff and Tania both yell, "Out!"

Branigan pumps his fist like he knows the shot is good. He looks at me, waiting for me to confirm his call. I too know that the ball was in, but every hideous thing he has said about my breakup over the last six weeks runs through my mind in an endless loop. *Tom Brady was sacked and then you sacked your fiancée. Win a date with our producer. Send pictures, clothing optional. When you return the ring to Nico...*

"Out," I say. It's barely a whisper.

Branigan squeezes his eyes closed.

"Did you call it?" Tania asks, moving across the court toward me.

"It was out," I say again, louder.

Tania jumps up and down. Jeff pulls her into an embrace.

"It was in!" Branigan roars. "Jordan, do something!"

The crowd at the window bangs on the glass, screaming the shot was good.

"I couldn't see it," Jordan says. "Jeff was blocking my view."

"Damn it, Jillian. You know it was good," Branigan yells.

"Sorry, it just missed. By like a millimeter." My voice is as high as Minnie Mouse's.

He smashes his racquet against one of the net's poles. The sound of metal on metal echoes around the dome. He drops his mangled racquet to the ground and stalks over to me. His face burns red. The veins in his neck bulge; his pulse throbs in his forehead.

I step backward. He moves along with me, backing me into the curtain separating court one from court two. He jabs his fingers in my face. "Do the right thing here, or I swear to God, I'll make you pay for it." He's baring his teeth.

Jeff, Tania, and Jordan watch with wide eyes, too stunned by his outburst to react. Tammy runs toward us, grabbing his arm. "Don't be a poor sport, Sean," she says.

He shakes her hand off. "I'm warning you, Jillian!"

David races into the dome and wedges himself between the two of us.

He grabs Sean, trying to calm him. "She knows it was in!" Branigan screams, trying to wiggle his way free of David.

"Go, Jillian," David says.

Yikes! What have I done? Sunken to his level, that's what. Maybe I should admit I made a mistake? I look over at the Longs. Jeff is massaging Tania's shoulder. Nope, that wouldn't be fair to them.

As I head toward the exit, Branigan stops screaming. The bubble becomes eerily quiet. I look back toward the court and make eye contact with him. "You're going to pay for this," he says.

CHAPTER 14

Sometimes when I'm sad, I watch movies that are tear-jerkers so that I can have a good sob without feeling like I'm crying because I feel sorry for myself. On this Saturday night, after what I did at the tennis club and while Nico is out on a date, that is my strategy. I'm settled on the couch about three-quarters of the way through *Terms of Endearment* with a giant glass of wine and a big box of tissues, bundled up in Nico's coat because I'm cold.

Outside, I hear a car pull into the driveway. For a minute, I imagine it's Nico. He had a horrible time on his date and wants to get back together. Before I can convince myself of that, two doors slam. Definitely not Nico, unless the Namaste Nitwit is with him. Maybe it's Sean and Tammy Branigan, coming to get their revenge? I tiptoe toward the window and lift the shade. Rachel and Mark make their way past Mr. O'Brien's to my side of the duplex. The old man must be looking out the window because Rachel waves. I picture him looking pointedly at his watch. It's almost ten, too late for visitors in his mind.

I open the door before they ring the bell. "We had dinner in Boston and thought we'd stop by," Rachel says. Her eyes widen as she notices that I'm wearing Nico's leather coat. "Why do you have that on?"

"Because it's cold in here."

She eyes the thermostat. "Then turn up the heat." She stares at me for a few seconds. "Have you been crying?"

"Sad movies."

Mark hands me a box from Mike's Pastry. "This will make you feel better."

I grab it from him. Mike's cannolis are my favorite. I haven't had one since the night Nico proposed. We went there after going to Vincenzio's Cucina. The hairs on the back of my neck stand straight up. I study Rachel and Mark carefully. "You went to the North End tonight?"

Mark looks at his feet. Rachel heads to the living room without answering. I chase after her. "Where did you have dinner?"

"Vincenzio's Cucina. I had the pappardelle. Mark had—"

"Why would you go there tonight of all nights?"

Rachel shrugs. "Mark's mom was available to babysit."

"You knew Nico was going to be there." I say it through gritted teeth. "He'll think I sent you there to spy."

"Who cares what he thinks?" Rachel says. She throws her long wool coat over the arm of the sofa and sits.

Mark slinks into the room and joins his wife on the couch. His dark gray jacket remains zipped up to his chest.

"How could you go along with this?" I ask, looking at him. I drag the ottoman into the center of the room and position myself on it so that I'm facing them. I drop the pastry box to the floor. It lands with a thump.

"I told her it was a bad idea. She insisted," Mark says.

"You said you're glad we went," Rachel says to Mark. "Your veal was delicious."

I imagine Rachel confronting Nico while he's eating his spaghetti. She picks the plate up and dumps it over his head.

It's the Chef Boyardee incident all over again. I'm almost afraid to ask, but I have to. "What happened?"

"He wasn't there," Mark says.

Okay, I wasn't expecting that. Why wouldn't he go? Did he decide he's not ready to date again yet? Maybe he realized he made a big mistake by letting me go. Maybe the entire contest was a publicity stunt and he never had any intention of going, or maybe Nico is sentimental after all and decided to go to a restaurant other than the one where he proposed to me. "Are you sure?"

Mark nods. "You know how small that place is, and we were sitting by the door."

My heart rate returns to normal. "That could have been disastrous. What were you going to do if you saw him?"

Rachel picks up one of the blue throw pillows and hugs it to her chest. "I hadn't thought that far ahead. I just don't want him to get away with what he did to you. You don't date someone for six years and then dump them less than a month after proposing. We need to get back at him."

Dump! I hate that word! "There's nothing I can do," I say as I take the pastries to the kitchen and put them on a plate.

"Those are for you," Mark says when I return. "We already had ours." I take a chocolate-filled one. Rachel has the traditional ricotta filled. The room is silent as we bite into them. Debra Winger's face is frozen on the television screen at the point where I paused the movie.

"Since you're not interested in online dating, I asked David to fix you up with someone at the tennis club," Rachel says when she finishes chewing. "He told me about a dermatologist who sounds promising."

The piece of cannoli tastes sweet in my mouth, but my mind fills with bitter thoughts: *I don't want to start dating again.*

I can't believe Nico is putting me through this. I hate Branigan and am glad I called the ball out.

"That's the last thing I want right now."

Rachel reaches for the dish of pastry and helps herself to another half. "Jillian, if you want to have kids, you have no time to lose." Mark shifts uncomfortably beside her on the couch. "You're going to be thirty-five soon."

"I have plenty of time."

"At the very least get your eggs tested." Rachel wipes her mouth with a napkin. "Or freeze some."

Mark jumps up and excuses himself to go to the bathroom.

"Maybe I should just pick out a sperm donor," I say. Rachel and I stare at each other. The only sound in the apartment is the sound of Mark's footsteps climbing the stairs.

"Jillian, you wasted six years of your life with Nico. You should have cut bait a long time ago. You can't diddle around now."

Wasted six years. Is that what I did? What about the good times Nico and I had together? Don't those count for something? I gather up the plates and head to the kitchen.

When I return to the living room, Rachel and Mark are standing. Rachel buttons her coat. "Sorry if we upset you," Mark says.

"You didn't," I say, because he didn't. Rachel did.

"Call me," Rachel says before going through the front door. "We'll go to a movie or out for drinks."

I watch them walk down to their car. When Rachel reaches the driveway, she yells up at me. "Love you, Jillian."

I know that she does, and I know that's why she tried to find Nico tonight and said the things she did. So no matter how misguided her effort is, I really can't be *all* that mad at her.

"Love you too," I call out.

Chapter 15

On Monday morning, my alarm goes off to *BS Morning Sports Talk*. Branigan's voice fills my room, sending chills down my back. He's talking about the Celtics, but I have an overwhelming feeling that something is terribly wrong. Whether my nerves are frayed because I fear Branigan is going to extract revenge on me, because I'm afraid Nico will announce on air that it was love at first sight with Bonnie the Namaste Nitwit, or because I'm worried about seeing Ben again after my crazy thoughts on Friday night, I'm not sure. All I know is, I'm so nervous that my left eye won't stop twitching.

I remain in bed under the covers, listening to the radio, and fall asleep again. When I wake up, Smyth is still talking about basketball. Branigan interrupts. "The intern screwed up my coffee again. Zachary, two sugars, two creams. How hard is that?"

Feedback from a microphone and then Nico's voice. "Maybe it would be easier if you got your own coffee. Zac's busy with me in the control room."

Through the wall, I hear Mr. O'Brien break into a coughing fit. He's probably choking on his breakfast, hearing Nico talk back to Branigan.

Branigan chuckles. "If Zac's too busy, you can get it."

I look across the room at the alarm clock but can't make out the numbers without my contacts.

Branigan and Smyth resume talking about the Celtics. A few minutes later, Branigan says, "Thanks, Nico."

Why doesn't it surprise me that he actually fetched his boss's coffee? He'd do anything Branigan told him to. I head to the bathroom for my shower but make sure the radio's volume is loud enough to hear over the water. I need to know what happened on Nico's date, if he even went on it. By the time I leave for work, they still haven't mentioned it, convincing me that he didn't go.

They actually talk about sports on my drive to the office, but as I pull into the parking lot at eight thirty, Branigan teases that they will have the can't-miss details about Nico's date in the next hour.

"Good morning," Ben calls out as I pass his cube. He's sitting with his legs up on his desk next to his computer, sipping a coffee and reading Boston.com. His radio plays softly behind him.

After I deposit my bags and coat in my cube, I go to his. He's wearing a crisp green oxford shirt and tan khakis with a perfect crease ironed into them. I always wanted Nico to dress like Ben. Instead, Nico has a bureau filled with T-shirts branding Boston teams' championship seasons and a closet filled with jeans. While most men match a tie to their shirt, Nico coordinates his baseball cap.

"Sit," Ben says. "I got you breakfast." He hands me a coffee and a pastry from a bakery he passes on his way to the office. At least once a week, Renee and I plead with him to stop there, but usually he saves his visits for someone's birthday or when one of us returns from a week-long vacation. I wonder what the special occasion is today as the jingle for *BS Morning Sports Talk* plays in the background. It occurs to me then that he stopped at the bakery for me, as a way to make me feel better when Nico recounts his date on air.

"Thanks," I say, biting into my pastry.

He nods. "So Friday night was fun."

"Yeah, I saw you chatting up the bartender."

He grins. "We went out Saturday night."

I'm surprised by the sinking feeling in my heart. "Good for you."

"Oh, it was good for her too." He laughs.

Renee's been in the kitchen making her oatmeal. Now she joins us, sitting on Ben's desk and stirring the lumpy white mush in her bowl. "I need to give the caterer a head count for the party. Jill, are you coming? Ben, are you bringing a date?" She looks at us expectedly.

I shake my head. "Sorry, no."

Ben nudges my foot with his. "Come on."

"Why don't you take the bartender?" The suggestion leaves a bitter taste in my mouth.

"Maybe I will."

"Who's the bartender?" Renee asks.

"The one from Friday night," I say.

⚜ ⚜ ⚜

One of the sales assistants is using the copier at the end of our aisle. The constant groaning of the machine drowns out my radio playing softly in the background. I turn up the volume so that I can hear Branigan and Smyth. It's just before nine. They're interviewing a football reporter about possible moves the Patriots will make in the off-season and still haven't talked about Nico and his date.

Minutes later, Branigan thanks the guest for appearing on the show. "After the commercial break, Nico's going to tell us about his date," he says. "Believe me, you don't want to miss this."

Tyler, Ryan, and Ellie have congregated at the copier to talk to their assistant. They laugh at something she says. I turn up my radio even louder.

The commercial ends. Branigan speaks again: "We've been getting texts all morning from listeners wanting to know how you made out with Bonnie. So, let's not keep them waiting any longer. Nico, tell us what happened."

Feedback from a microphone and then Nico speaks. "So I got lost on the way there." His voice is much softer than usual, and I wonder if he's nervous. I lean toward the radio. "My GPS took me to the total wrong place."

When did he get a GPS? He has a stack of old dirty maps in the pocket of the driver's door because he doesn't trust technology.

Ben's head appears over the top of the wall. "Are you sure you want to listen to this?"

Renee enters my cube and makes herself comfortable in the guest chair. In the hallway at the end of our aisle, the sales team breaks into laughter again.

"So I finally find the place," Nico continues. "She lives in one of those fancy brownstones. An amazing place. Brick wa—"

Branigan cuts him off. "We don't want to hear about her house. Tell us about her. How did she look?" He pauses. "I assume she looked like the original picture we posted and not the one of Miss Piggy that somehow appeared over the weekend."

"Nothing like Miss Piggy." Nico whistles. "She's wearing this itsy-bitsy black dress. Killer body. I mean supermodel material."

"Well, she does work in a gym," Smyth says. "Yoga instructor and all."

"She hugs me hello." Nico's voice is louder with a trace of amusement now.

Branigan interrupts. "Was it a loose hug or a tight one, where she's pressing every bit of her body against yours to let you know how much she wants it?"

Renee shakes her head and mutters, "What a pig."

"She was rubbing up against me," Nico says. "She kissed me hello."

"Tongue?" Branigan asks.

"Affirmative. This girl was ready for a good time."

Ben sinks back into his seat. Renee scratches her cheek.

"You lucky dog," Smyth says.

Nico continues. "She takes me for a tour of her place. We go in every room but the bedroom." He laughs. "She says, I'll show you that after dinner. And now I'm really revved up, wondering if I should suggest ordering in."

Who is this imposter pretending to be Nico? This is how Branigan talks, not my Nico.

"But I don't. We leave for the restaurant. We end up going to another place in the North End, not Vincenzio's. And this girl, she orders a tray of olives, telling me they're an aphrodisiac."

"Whoa, whoa," Branigan says. "Why didn't you go to Vincenzio's?"

Oh no.

"We just didn't." Nico's voice breaks as he says it.

"They're one of our biggest sponsors. They deserve to know why you didn't go to their place."

It's suddenly a hundred degrees in my cube. Sweat pools above my lips, and my cheeks feel like they're on fire. I look at Renee, expecting to see her shedding layers of clothing and fanning herself, but she's sitting there with her arms wrapped around herself like she's chilly. Maybe I'm having my first hot flash?

"Well, we get to Vincenzio's. We're just about to go inside, and I see—" He stops.

My stomach turns. I may get sick in my cube. I pull the trash can closer. Renee gives me a sympathetic look.

"Don't keep us hanging," Smyth says. "What did you see?"

"My ex's best friend and her husband."

"No!" Branigan and Smyth both scream.

I'm going to kill Rachel.

"Jillian must have sent them there to spy," Branigan suggests.

Please God, let me spontaneously combust right now.

Renee nudges my leg with her boot. "You didn't?"

"Jesus, Jillian," Ben mutters.

"I don't know," Nico says. "Maybe it was just coincidence, but I figured we sh—"

"There's no such thing as coincidences," Branigan says. "A woman scorned. Who knows what she's capable of."

Ben looks down into my cube again.

"I knew nothing about it," I say.

I can tell by the skeptical expressions on Ben's and Renee's faces that they don't believe me.

"I don't think so," Nico says.

"Oh, I saw Jillian at the tennis club Saturday night. Let me tell you, she's definitely not taking this well. She looks like she's gone crazy and is hitting the Ben and Jerry's hard," Branigan says. "A woman in her midthirties. She knows you were her last hope. She's desperate."

At some point the sales team must have moved away from the copier because the only sound in the room now is my blaring radio, letting the whole company know what's going on in my personal life. I scramble to turn it down, knocking over a glass of water on my desk.

"Let's keep Jill out of it. She—"

Branigan cuts off Nico. "She even made up a story that she's dating someone else."

Renee wipes up the spilled liquid with tissues.

"Maybe she is," Nico says.

"I'm pretty good at detecting BS. She was lying," Branigan says, his voice notably louder than it was before. "She's a lying bi—" The name he calls me is bleeped out.

"Sweetie, did you tell him you were dating someone?" Renee asks while Ben stares down over the cube wall at me.

"Um, I might have."

Renee and Ben exchange a look that I guess means *she's so pathetic*. Imagine if Ben knew he's the one I was pretending to date.

"She's so mad at me about us helping you move on that she stole the tennis match from me," Branigan says. "Called a ball out that was clearly in. The entire club saw it. Believe me, Jillian will get hers."

A chill runs up my back as I imagine Branigan bludgeoning me with his tennis racquet.

"Did you purposely make a bad call against him?" Ben asks.

"I couldn't tell if the ball landed on the line." I close my eyes and see the green felt on the white chalk.

Branigan is still blathering.

"Calm down, Sean," Smyth says.

The show breaks for commercial. Renee jabs at the radio's power switch. Ben sinks back to his chair. They both disappear into their cubes, leaving me with my anger. I want to kill Rachel. Murder Nico. End Branigan's life. Triple homicide. Details at eleven.

After the humiliation I suffered on *BS Morning Sports Talk*, Ben and Renee insist on taking me out to lunch, so the three of us pile into Renee's SUV and head to an Italian restaurant not too far from the office.

While we wait for our meals, Renee entertains us with stories about her son, Joel, whom she's teaching how to drive. "I need to take a Valium before getting in the car with him," she says.

I break off a piece of my roll and dip it in the oil, wondering if I should ask to borrow some of her pills to get over the jittery feeling I've had since Branigan promised revenge. The waitress arrives and hurriedly passes out our meals. Ben ordered sausage on his pizza, but the one she throws down in front of him has pepperoni. "Excuse me," he says, but she's already gone, on her way back to the kitchen on the other side of the restaurant. He watches her, shaking his head. The table goes quiet as Renee and I wonder if we should start eating. "Go ahead," Ben says, but we don't. After several minutes, he decides to eat the food in front of him.

Every now and then, I catch him watching me. When I meet his eye, he looks down. "What's up?" I ask after this happens three times.

"Why would your friend go to the restaurant where Nico was taking his date?" he asks.

I just picked up my chicken panini, but I return it to my plate to answer his question. "I didn't ask her to do it, if that's what you're getting at."

He holds my stare and raises one eyebrow.

"I didn't!" I pick up my sandwich again. Before I take a bite, I add, "She wants to help me get him back."

Renee reaches for the salad dressing and pours more on her plate. The lettuce is already drowning. "Why would you want him back?"

Ben and Renee both stare at me, waiting for an answer. I swallow before clarifying. "Get back at him for what he did. Revenge."

"Ah, good!" Renee stabs a carrot onto her fork. She makes a loud crunching sound as she chews it.

"Just let it go," Ben advises.

"No," Renee says. "I like the idea of getting back at him. He deserves it."

The waitress reappears at the table next to ours, delivering their food. Ben's on his third slice and doesn't try to catch her eye, which is probably a good thing because she uses the same dump-it-and-run delivery style she used with us. "I wanted pepperoni," I hear the man at the table saying as she walks away. He whistles to get her attention. She continues walking in the opposite direction.

Ben leans toward him. "Did she give you sausage?"

"Yeah," the guy says.

"Want to trade three slices of yours for mine?" Ben points to his pizza. "It's pepperoni."

"No, I don't." The guy scoots his chair away from Ben and closer to his table. Renee and I laugh. Ben shrugs.

While we finish our meal, Renee directs the conversation back to me. "The best way to get back at Nico is to start dating someone else immediately," she suggests. "Which is probably why you told Branigan you were dating someone."

"I'm not sure why I said that."

"Well, you should start dating again," she says.

The thought of having to date again leaves a nasty aftertaste in my mouth. I gulp down my remaining water. Flirting. Hoping he'll ask me out. And then when I get a date, trying to figure out what to wear, right down to my underwear and bra. Thinking up clever conversation. The whole wondering if he'll call, waiting for the first kiss, shaving my legs before every date, and worrying about the first awkward time we sleep together. No, thanks. I'm not up for any of it. "I'm pretty sure I'm done with dating," I say.

"Nonsense," Renee says. "You need to get right back to it. You don't have any time to waste."

It's like she's conspiring against me with Rachel.

"Think how pissed Nico would be if you started dating me." Ben winks.

"That's brilliant," Renee says, rubbing her hands together.

"You have something on your face," Ben says to me, touching his cheek.

I wipe mine.

"The other side," he says. He reaches toward me and wipes away whatever was there. The spot where he touched me tingles.

"You don't really have to date," Renee says. She bounces up and down in her chair she's so excited. "You just have to make Nico think you are."

"How are we going to do that?" I ask.

"You're still Facebook friends, right?"

I nod, thinking I need to unfriend him.

"Fake posts!" She looks pleased with herself.

Ben does that thing where he raises one eyebrow. "OMG! Slept with Ben for the first time tonight! I didn't know sex could be so good!" He says it in a voice much deeper than normal. "It was better than the millions of times I fantasized about him."

"Finally gave in and made Ben's dreams come true." I wink at him. "Pretty sure I've ruined him for all other women."

Renee covers her ears with her hands. "Enough," she says. "You're grossing me out, but you get the idea."

Ben leans closer to me and whispers, "Can't get enough of Ben. Want to do him morning, noon, and night."

I put my hand on his thigh. "Blew Ben's mind with that thing I do with my—"

The waitress finally returns to see if we need anything. "The check," Renee says. "And hurry."

Ben waits for her to leave. "Tell me about that thing you do," he says.

Renee points at me. "Not another word."

"Do you do it with your tongue?"

I lean closer, stare into his eyes, and slowly trace my tongue over my upper lip. Ellie would be proud.

He arches backward in his chair.

"Enough!" Renee warns.

Ben lets it go, but as we drive back to the office, I see him watching me through the rearview mirror, and I know I've stirred his curiosity.

Chapter 16

When I get home from work that night, Rachel's blue Odyssey is parked behind Mr. O'Brien's Buick. She's leaning into her backseat, removing Laurence from his car seat. Sophie stands next to her, holding a bouquet of tulips, and rushes across the driveway toward me. "Auntie Jillian, don't be mad at Mommy. She was just trying to help."

"I'm not mad at Mommy, honey," I say as I bend to hug her.

"Good, because she says it's all Uncle Nico's fault. Mommy says he was mean to you."

"Sophie, take this bag," Rachel says, handing her daughter a small grocery sack. She lifts Laurence out of the car. "I really didn't know he saw us," she says. "And I had no idea they'd talk about it on air. I mean, why would they?"

Because Branigan is going to take every chance he can to humiliate me, after Saturday.

On the other side of Rachel's car, Jacob cries. I go to get him, with Sophie trailing behind me.

"I'm sorry," Rachel says as she collects a cooler from the back of the minivan.

"We made you dinner to 'pologize," Sophie adds. "And brought you flowers." She tries to hand them to me, but I'm carrying Jacob in his car seat and ask her to hold on to them until we get inside.

Mr. O'Brien's door opens as the five of us traipse by. "How long are you going to be here?" he asks Rachel.

"An hour. Maybe a little more." She points to the cooler. "I made vegetable lasagna. Would you like a piece?"

"It's yummy," Sophie says. "You should have some." Laurence stands next to his sister, staring up at Mr. O'Brien, who looks down at them.

"Did you two help make it?"

"Mommy made it for Aunt Jillian because the men on the radio weren't nice," Sophie answers.

Mr. O'Brien touches the bill of his baseball cap and clears his throat. I'm sure he knows exactly what Branigan and Smyth said. He looks at me but quickly turns away when I meet his eye. "I'm leaving for Keno at seven thirty," he says to Rachel. "Move your car before then."

Inside my apartment, I help the kids out of their coats, mittens, and boots while Rachel brings the food to the kitchen. By the time I join her, she has emptied the cooler on the table. In addition to the lasagna, she's made a Caesar salad and garlic bread. She instructs me to play with Sophie and Laurence while she heats up the food. She keeps Jacob in the kitchen with her.

Sophie sets up Concentration on the living room floor with my deck of cards. We played this game for more than an hour the last time Nico and I babysat. It was Sophie and me against Laurence and Nico. Jacob was asleep in his crib. He woke up crying around the same time Laurence went into meltdown mode. That's when the fun ended. Nico tried to soothe Laurence, picking him up, carrying him on his back. It didn't work. I suggested he take Laurence outside to build a snowman. When I peeked out the window, Nico seemed to be enjoying himself, laughing as he lifted Laurence into the spot for the head of the snowman and snapping a picture with his phone. I wonder what he did with that photo? Does he ever look at it now and miss the time we spent together, or did he take the shot to mark the moment he no longer wanted to be part of my life?

"It's your turn, Auntie," Sophie says, bringing me back to the present.

"What do you think, Laurence?" I ask the boy. He takes his thumb out of his mouth and places it on the back of a card in the row closest to Sophie. I flip it over. It's the queen of hearts. "Pick another one." He chooses the one directly to the right of the queen. It's the joker. Sophie always insists on keeping them in the deck. I flip the two cards back over.

Sophie takes her turn. She selects a card in the left-hand corner on my side. It's the queen of diamonds. She studies the board, trying to remember where the queen of hearts is. With his thumb back in his mouth, Laurence makes sucking noises. Sophie looks at him and then down at the board again. It takes her a moment to notice the big wet spot on the back of a card right in front of her. She turns it over, revealing the queen of hearts and smiles at me.

"Dinner's ready," Rachel calls from the kitchen. She has made up an extra plate and is covering it with tinfoil. "Take this to your landlord," she says, handing it to me.

"He said he didn't want it," I remind her.

"He'll eat it," she says as she helps Laurence into his seat.

I really don't feel like facing Mr. O'Brien again after what happened on *BS Morning Sports Talk* this morning. *You sent your friend to spy*, I imagine him saying. *What do you even see in him? I could tell he was no good from the moment I laid eyes on him.* He'll shake his head, grab the plate out of my hands, and slam the door in my face.

Rachel tries to give me the covered plate, but I won't take it. "Why don't you bring it to him?" I ask.

"I don't think he likes me. Laurence, knock it off!" He has his fingers in the lasagna.

"He doesn't like anybody," I say.

"Sophie, wait until we're all at the table."

"But I'm hungry," Sophie whines. She's biting into a piece of garlic bread.

"I said wait." Rachel thrusts the plate at me. "Just take it to him," she snaps. "Sophie! Laurence! Knock it off."

Jacob starts to cry. I figure it might be safer over at Mr. O'Brien's, so I head outside with the food without putting on my jacket.

I run across the porch and knock on his door. My teeth are chattering by the time he answers. "Where's your coat?" he asks. He's not wearing his baseball cap, and one piece of black hair among his thick white moss stands straight up behind his ear. It's like a distant relative of the wild hair in his bushy eyebrows.

I hold up the plate. "You might want this later." He pushes the door open, and I extend the dish of food to him. "Enjoy."

I start to make my way back across the porch. "Jillian," he calls, startling me because he rarely uses my name. In fact, sometimes I wonder if he remembers it. "Now that's it's just you over there"—he points his thumb in the direction of my apartment—"I'm reducing your rent. Twenty-five dollars less."

"Thanks." He doesn't hear me because he has already closed the door.

We've finished eating, and Rachel and I are cleaning the kitchen. Sophie and Laurence are in the living room watching television, and Jacob is sleeping in his car seat.

"What is that still doing here?" Rachel asks, pointing to Nico's jacket.

I can't believe I've left it hanging over the back of the kitchen chair for almost two months. When Nico lived here, I always got mad at him for throwing it there. *Put it in the closet*, I'd pester. He'd ignore me, so I'd end up hanging it up myself, muttering under my breath just loud enough for him to hear about how lazy he was. He'd counter with *Jillian, you need to relax*. We would definitely end up fighting about it.

"I'm waiting for him to realize he forgot it and come get it," I say.

"You should get the scissors and cut it into a hundred tiny pieces."

I imagine handing Nico a bag of leather scraps, enjoying his crestfallen face. Jacob lets out a small cry. Rachel rocks his seat, and he falls right back to sleep. I wish it were that easy for me, but once I wake up, I'm usually up for hours.

"Or donate it to Goodwill," she says.

"It's his favorite coat."

The look she gives me is similar to the one she gave Sophie earlier for eating the garlic bread before we were all at the table. "You know, Jill, that's the problem with you. You wait for things to happen."

I'm on my way to the sink to rinse out a soda can; instead I crush it between my hands. "What are you talking about?"

"You waited six years for Nico to ask you to marry him, and now you're waiting for him to come back."

"I'm not waiting for him to come back." I yank on the faucet and run the dirty dishes under the water.

"Well, you're not moving on with your life."

"What do you want me to do?"

"I want you to start dating again," she says. Her voice softens. "Seeing that jacket every day can't be good for you. It's a constant reminder of Nico."

"I don't think getting rid of his jacket is going to help me forget about him."

"Well, you need to figure out something that will."

Ellie's words pop into my head. *The best way to get over someone is to get under someone else.*

"Ben wants me to go to Renee's party with him," I blurt out.

"Ben, the guy you work with?"

I nod.

"Didn't you tell me he's a player?"

"I think I said he burns through women."

"Same difference," Rachel says. "You need to make a smart choice this time."

This time. Like she knew Nico wasn't a smart choice when I was dating him.

Chapter 17

I know as soon as I wake up the next day that Branigan is up to something. *Don't listen.* I chant it to myself over and over again, and the mantra works. I immediately switch off my alarm and get ready for work, with the television on instead of the radio. The morning news show is chronicling all the problems the MBTA, Boston's public transportation system, has had this winter, making it impossible for people to get where they need to be. "The weather, the late trains. They're making everyone cranky," the female anchor, who is rumored to have had an affair with Branigan, says.

It must have snowed last night because there is a fresh coating on the driveway. Mr. O'Brien's Buick is gone, and there is a set of tire tracks from where he backed out this morning. As I hurriedly clear the inch or so off my windows and windshield, he returns from his daily trip to Dunkin' Donuts. Unlike every other morning, there are no voices blasting from the speakers of his car. When he gets out of the station wagon, he's carrying two cups of coffee. He makes his way to my car and hands me one without saying anything.

Not listening to BS Morning Sports Talk? *Buying me coffee? Whatever it is Branigan and Smyth are saying must be bad, very bad.*

Mr. O'Brien sighs as he makes his way to his door. Before he disappears inside, he offers me advice. "Listen to music today," he says.

Of course I'm not going to do that now. I jump into my car and tune the radio to 108.4 WSPR. Shouldn't I know what they're saying about me? As I back out of the driveway, they're not talking because an advertisement is playing. It's for an attorney who specializes in divorce, representing men only. I don't understand how that's even legal.

"I'll help you keep what's yours," the lawyer says. The commercial causes my back to tense as I picture the show's angry male listeners plotting with this vengeful man to ruin their soon-to-be ex-wives' lives. I imagine most of them have children, and my heart breaks for these kids with the bickering parents.

Three miles up the road, as I turn onto the highway, the advertisements end. Branigan's deep voice fills my car. "Today, we're talking to noted psychiatrist William Decker, an expert in stalking. Dr. Decker, welcome to the show."

A stalking expert? Surely this can't have anything to do with me. I pick up my coffee from the center console to take a sip.

"Stalking is repeated, unwanted attention. It can take the form of harassing the victim with repeated phone calls, emails, texts, or gifts," the doctor explains.

Branigan interrupts. "Jillian has been harassing Nico with phone calls and texts."

I flinch, causing coffee to trickle down my chin and drip on my jacket. I return the drink to the cup holder, thinking about that one day I left Nico a bunch of voice mails and text messages. Certainly one time does not make me a stalker. I accelerate while moving from the right lane through the center to the left lane.

"That behavior is certainly consistent with stalking," Dr. Decker says. "The thing to remember is if the initial actions are ineffective, the stalker may escalate to more intrusive behavior."

"Like driving by his sister's house or having a friend spy when he's on a date?" Branigan suggests.

"Sending a friend to spy is bit unusual," Dr. Decker says. "More often the person does the stalking themselves."

"I didn't send her!" I step on the gas as I scream at the radio.

"The interesting thing," Dr. Decker says, "is that we don't know what causes a person to stalk. Sometimes it's because they want a close relationship with the victim, and sometimes it's because a close relationship, often romantic, has just ended and the stalker doesn't know how to respond to that in a healthy manner."

"In Jillian's case it's because she bullied Nico into proposing by giving him an ultimatum, but soon after he gave her the ring, he dumped her."

Bullied him? Is that what Nico told him, or is Branigan purposely twisting Nico's words?

Focused on the radio show, I don't notice the police car sitting in the median until I fly by it. I spike the brakes and glance in my rearview mirror. The cruiser is pulling out with its blue lights on. *Please don't be coming after me.* On the radio Branigan asks, "So how can Nico stop Jillian from stalking him?"

"I'm not stalking him!" I scream as I move from the left lane to the center lane, hoping the cruiser will pass. Instead, it follows me. *For Christ's sake. I can't catch a break!*

I turn down the radio's volume and make my way to the breakdown lane and stop. Traffic whizzes by as the police car pulls in behind mine. In high school, when we studied the constitution, my history teacher told the class if we're ever pulled over to always keep our hands in plain sight and not to make any sudden moves. I keep mine on the steering wheel, but after several minutes of waiting for the trooper to get out of his car, I get bored. I reach for the glove box and pull out my registration and then fish around in my wallet for my license. Meanwhile the police officer hasn't left his vehicle. I turn the radio back up. Dr. Decker is explaining the first thing a stalking victim should do is make it clear to the stalker that the attention is unwanted.

The officer finally steps out of his car. He's wearing aviator sunglasses even though the sky is covered in metallic-gray clouds with no chance of the sun breaking through anytime soon. I turn down the radio again and lower my window, letting in a blast of cold air. The trooper's boots click on the pavement as he makes his way toward me. When he reaches my car, he bends into the window. "Do you know why I pulled you over?"

I shake my head, figuring I might have a better chance of getting away with my lie if I don't speak.

"Clocked you at eighty-three in a fifty-five zone." He straightens himself and adjusts his glasses.

"Sorry, I had no idea."

"Where you going in such a hurry?"

"Work."

He points to my license and registration so I give them to him. He returns to the cruiser with my information. I turn the radio back up while he's doing whatever it is he's doing.

There's a commercial on for hair restoration. Branigan is the spokesperson, which, if you ask me, is not a good choice considering his forehead is spacious enough to use as a backboard to practice forehands and backhands. I turn to look at the trooper. He's staring down at something in his lap. My car shakes as traffic whizzes by.

The advertisement ends. Branigan speaks. "Before we let you go, Doctor, what advice would you give to Jillian?"

"When relationships end, we have a lot of mixed emotions—anger, fear, sadness. It can be a very tough time. Instead of thinking about the relationship that didn't work, focus on ones that are. Stay connected to family and friends. Tell them what you're feeling. Take care of yourself. Eat right, exercise, and sleep. Laugh whenever you can."

"Thank you, Doctor," Branigan interrupts. "Jill, if you're listening, we hope you'll take his advice."

I give my radio the finger. There's a knock on the car window. "Was that intended for me?" the trooper asks when I lower it.

"No! Of course not!"

He has both hands on his belt but isn't saying anything.

"The radio show. They were talking about me. Not even telling the truth."

He takes off his glasses and slips them into the pocket of his black patrol coat. "They're talking about you on the radio?" The way he asks the question leaves no doubt he thinks I'm crazy or under the influence. He stares at my coffee cup in the center console. I expect him to ask me to pass it to him so he can sniff it. Instead, he studies my eyes, looking at my pupils to see if they're dilated, no doubt. He's probably going to ask me to step out of the car and walk a straight line or search my car for drugs. "What are they saying?" he finally asks.

"My ex and I broke up a few months ago, and they're accusing me of stalking him."

As he folds his arms across his chest, the piece of paper he's holding flops in the wind. "The people on the radio know you and your ex broke up?"

"Yes, and they think I'm stalking him."

"Do the, um, people on the radio, talk about you often?"

"Lately, they do."

"Turn up the volume," he says.

"What?"

"I want to hear."

I spin the knob. Branigan's voice booms out of the speakers. "So, Nico, you're going to have to make it clear to Jillian that the attention is unwanted so that she stops stalking."

I turn the volume back down. "See."

The police officer looks down at my license like he forgot my name on the walk from his patrol car back to my Honda. "Jillian Atwood," he reads. "Well, I'll be." He stares at me for a moment. "Are you stalking him?"

"No, my friend showed up at the restaurant he was having dinner at, so they think I'm a stalker."

"She just happened to show up there? You didn't know he was going there?"

"Well, yeah, I knew he was going there, but I didn't tell her to go there and spy."

"So it was all one big coincidence."

"I had no idea she was going to the restaurant." I rest my head in my hands.

"I'm going to let you off with a warning," the trooper says. "Two of them actually. Slow down and don't stalk your ex. It could lead to big trouble."

⚜ ⚜ ⚜

Branigan and Smyth are taking calls when I pull into the parking lot at work. Even though I'm almost twenty minutes late, I remain glued to the driver's seat, listening to their show.

"Robbie from the FJ Cruiser, you're on," Branigan says.

"First time, longtime," the caller says. Nico had to explain to me that it means first-time caller, longtime listener. "Tell him he needs to change the passwords for his e-mail and voice mail accounts. My ex was a stalker too. She broke into mine. Sent some nasty messages to the new girl I was seeing."

"Good advice," Branigan says. "Nico, have you changed your passwords?"

"Affirmative," Nico answers.

Like I wouldn't be able to figure out his new password. Redsox 2013 or Patriots2015 instead of Bruins2011.

Frank from South Boston is next. I lean closer to the speaker, anxious to see if the caller is Mr. O'Brien using an alias, as Nico claims. "I thought this was a sports show, not a soap opera," he says and then pauses to clear his throat. "When are you going to talk about the Bruins?"

Well that sure does sound like something my landlord would say.

"Frank, we promise we'll get back to sports after one more call," Smyth says. "'Cause we're pretty sure our listeners want to hear from our next caller."

Branigan's smug voice comes back on. "On line two, we have a caller claiming to be Rachel, the friend of Jillian's who was at the restaurant on Saturday night."

No, no, no! Why would Rachel call?

"How long have you known Jill?" Branigan asks.

"Since before I was old enough to talk." Her speech is clipped.

I fumble through my purse for my phone and send a frantic text to her: *HANG UP. NOW!*

"I want to be crystal clear," Rachel says. "Going. To. The. Restaurant. Was. My. Idea. Jillian knew nothing about it."

Branigan laughs. "You expect us to believe that?"

"It's the truth."

A silver BMW pulls into the parking garage next to me. It's Kurt Bryan, the head of human resources.

"Did Jillian tell you to call?" Branigan asks.

"No!" Someone in the background says something to Rachel.

"Is she there with you now?" Branigan asks.

"Hang up now," I shout.

Kurt remains in his car, looking at me while talking on his phone.

"No," Rachel says. She's clearly distracted, so it doesn't sound convincing. "Can I speak with Nico?" she asks.

"Why don't you have Jill call us," Branigan says.

"He doesn't have the balls to speak to me, does he?"

"Weren't you listening to Dr. Decker?" Branigan asks. "Having a friend call into your boyfriend's radio show is a form of stalking."

"Let me talk to him," Rachel repeats.

"If Jill has something to say to Nico, she can call the show herself," Branigan says. "We'd love to have her as a guest."

"Nico, I just can't believe you're doing this to Jill," Rachel yells. "After everything she did for you!"

"What exactly is he doing?" Branigan asks. "She's the one following him around."

"You don't date someone for six years and then dump them less than a month after proposing."

I bury my face in my hands. She just told the whole world that I waited six long years for a proposal that lasted all of three weeks.

"Well," Branigan says, "the fact that it took him six years to pop the question—"

"It took him that long because he's a—"

Whatever she says next is beeped out. Smyth and Branigan are laughing too hard to speak. The station breaks for commercial.

I kill the ignition. The radio goes silent. "NO!" I scream as I pound my steering wheel. The horn gets stuck, sending one long continuous beep through the parking garage. Kurt steps out of his car and stares into my window as he walks by. I imagine he's thinking *Unstable employee in the parking lot. Get security.*

⚜ ⚜ ⚜

As I step off the elevator, the sales team files through the vestibule, heading for their weekly meeting. Ryan whispers something to Tyler. They both look back at me and laugh. If I didn't have so much work to do, I would turn around and go home. Instead, I continue walking toward my cube. The smell of maple syrup gets stronger as I make my way down the hall. I turn into my aisle. Renee is on the phone yelling at the printer for some kind of printing error. Ben is at his desk, eating pancakes and reading the news online. As always, his radio is on. He spins in his chair as I pass by. "You okay?"

"Yup." I don't stop.

He follows me into my cube. "Did you listen today?"

I nod.

He picks up a Snoopy figurine I have on my desk and winds it up. "Maybe you should go on the show. Give your side of the story." He sets the toy down on my desk and Snoopy walks across it.

"You can't be serious. Branigan will eat me alive."

Snoopy stops moving, so Ben winds him up again. "You need to stand up for yourself. Maybe if you do, it will end all this." He puts Snoopy down again.

"Going on the show would only make things worse."

"You don't know that," he says as Snoopy steps too close to the edge of my desk and tumbles to the floor. Ben bends down to pick up the toy.

"I do."

My phone rings. Stacy's name flashes across the console. "I need to see you. Now." She speaks loud enough for Ben to hear her even though the receiver is pressed against my ear.

"That doesn't sound good," he says. "Good luck." He pats me on the back.

As I make my way down the hallway toward Stacy's office, I see Kurt from HR is sitting at the round table in front of Stacy's desk. She's summoning me to a meeting with human resources. *This can't be good!*

I pause in the doorway. There's a small stack of papers in front of Kurt. The paperwork for my termination?

Stacy motions at me with her hand. "Come in. Take a seat."

Kurt nods. "Jillian."

As I sit down across from him, he gets up to shut the door. I swallow hard and look out the window. There's a flock of turkeys marching through the snow along the side of the building. It always amazes me that so much wildlife exists just minutes from the congested highway.

Kurt returns to his chair. He and Stacy stare at each other across her desk. "This is your meeting, Kurt," Stacy says. "Lead it." She pulls out a tube of hand cream from her desk drawer and squeezes some on the backs of her hands. Its strong floral scent reminds me of a funeral home.

"We're wondering how you're doing," Kurt says.

I glance at Stacy. She's wringing her hands to rub in the moisturizer.

"I'm fine."

"I saw you outside in the parking lot. You looked upset."

Stacy turns toward her computer as her email pings.

"I'm fine," I repeat.

"I listen to *BS Morning Sports Talk*, so I know what's going on," Kurt says.

Outside, the turkeys are headed into the woods. I wish I were with them.

"Your fiancé leaving and having the breakup discussed on air, that's a lot to deal with," Kurt says.

Stacy's phone rings. She reaches for it, but Kurt shoots her a nasty look. "For Pete's sake. Stop beating around the bush and get to the point," she says.

Kurt slowly exhales. I imagine he's trying to control his temper.

Stacy's clearly run out of patience because she pulls out her stress ball and squeezes the bejesus out of it. "We have resources available that can help you," she says. She points to the stack of papers in front of Kurt. "Give her those, and let's be done with this. I have work to do."

He hands me a flyer with the words *Employee Assistance Program* centered across the top of the page in big bold letters. Under that headline in smaller italics letters it says: *Whatever you're going through, we can help.* Following that is a list of services available through the program.

I stare at the flyer in disbelief. The vice president of human resources is recommending I speak with a psychiatrist. Have I been acting that crazy? I think of Nina catching me driving through her neighborhood; my considering sleeping with Ben as a way to move past Nico; the police officer who saw me giving the radio the finger; and Kurt, who watched me screaming in my car and pounding my steering wheel.

"Talking to someone might help," Kurt says.

"I can talk to my friends." I'm too embarrassed to meet his eye so I'm looking down at the floor. *When was the last time Stacy's rug was vacuumed?*

"Like the friend who called into the show today."

I'm pretty sure Mr. Human Resources is using sarcasm. Surely there are rules against that.

"It might help to talk to a professional," he continues. "And if you need to take some time off to get yourself together, we'll supp—"

"No time off until we finish with our new branding," Stacy interrupts.

Get myself together? An image of Humpty Dumpty falling off the wall pops into my head. "I'll think about it." *Please let this meeting be over.*

"EAP is a wonderful benefit. I really encourage you to take advantage of it," Kurt says.

I look up at Stacy. She's grimacing, like this conversation is hurting her as much as it is me.

"There's no shame in talking to a professional," Kurt goes on.

"I have a nine thirty," Stacy interrupts.

It's 9:29. I stand. "I'll think about what you said," I say, doing my best to sound sincere.

Renee and Ben are on me as soon as I return to my desk, demanding to know what Stacy wanted. I hold up the flyer for the Employee Assistance Program. "HR was there. They want me to talk to someone about what has been going on with the radio show."

"They're sending you to a shrink," Renee bellows.

I wince, hoping the sales team is still in their meeting. "They just suggested that I talk to a professional."

Ben takes the flyer from me and reads it. When he's done, he crumples it into a ball and tosses it into the garbage. "If you need to talk to someone, you can talk to me, us. Renee and me."

Chapter 18

Just before noon, my phone rings. "There's someone here to see you," says Barbara, the receptionist. In the background, several other lines are ringing, and she immediately clicks off. The only person who's ever surprised me at work is Nico, but there's no way he'd show up here today out of the blue. Or is there?

Instead of waiting for the elevator, I race down the four flights of stairs to reception. My brother, Christian, is sitting on the edge of the sofa drumming his fingers on the table housing all the company's marketing literature. I freeze. My heartbeat becomes erratic. I can't swallow. What is he doing here? Did something happen to my parents?

The door bangs shut behind me. He turns his head toward it. When he sees me, he doesn't smile. Something is definitely wrong. Someone must have died. Why else would he come all this way without letting me know?

He stands. "Hey, Jillian."

He never calls me by my full name; usually it's *Jill the pill*.

"What's wrong?" I ask. The constant ringing of the phone in this room is driving me crazy. Barbara answers each call the same way: "Cyber Security Consultants, please hold." It's like a verse playing over and over again on an endless loop. I press my hands to my temples and massage them.

Christian has crossed the room and is right in front of me. He wraps me in a tight embrace. "How you doing?" he asks.

His hug and question heighten my anxiety. His usual greeting is a slug in the arm while asking *Keeping out of trouble?*

"Are Mom and Dad okay?"

"They're fine."

I sigh. "Why are you here?"

He tugs at his tie. "I've been in New York on business and decided to take the shuttle up to Boston to see you."

He travels to Manhattan at least once a month and has never come to see me before.

"Why?"

He stares at a spot above my head. "I've been streaming Nico's show all week."

I picture him sitting in a hotel room staring out at the New York skyline while Branigan interviewed Dr. Decker. He probably called my parents and told them to tune in. I'm surprised I haven't heard from my mother. "I haven't been stalking Nico," I say.

He looks me in the eye again. "I didn't think you were. I just wanted to make sure you're okay."

He flew all the way to Boston because he's worried about me. I blink back tears and embrace him again, realizing how much I miss having my family nearby.

"You were always way too good for that jerk," he says.

⚜ ⚜ ⚜

Christian and I carry our lunch trays from the cashier to the seating area and look for a place to sit. At just a few minutes past noon, most of the company's employees are here in the cafeteria eating, and there are no empty tables. Off to the side by the windows, I see a group of coworkers from accounting leaving. Christian and I rush toward their abandoned four-top.

"So how did things get so nasty with Nico that they're ripping you on the radio?" he asks.

I'm definitely not confessing to my brother that my coworkers hacked the radio station's website or that I purposely made a bad call during a tennis match to ignite the hostilities. He'd give me that big brother disappointed look he mastered during high school and try to convince me to apologize to that bastard Branigan. No way. "I don't want to talk about that. Tell me what's going on with Molly."

I bite into my slice of pizza while he pulls out his phone to show me the latest pictures of my niece. My heart breaks seeing how much she's grown and realizing how little I know her. They moved away before her second birthday.

"She's taking tennis lessons so she can play with you on your next visit," Christian says. "She's not too bad either." He tells me stories about her on the court and shows me videos he's recorded of her.

I get misty eyed, thinking I would like to play with her and take her to movies and shopping. Get to know her as well as I know Rachel's kids. *Why did they have to leave Boston?*

When I look up from his phone, Lucas and Ben are heading for our table with lunch trays. "Can we join you?" Ben asks, giving my brother the once-over. Christian studies him as well.

I motion for Ben and Lucas to sit and introduce my brother. Ben shakes Christian's hand while Lucas nods.

"I can see the family resemblance," Ben says.

With his thick, wavy blond hair, light skin and dark eyes, Christian takes after my father while I inherited my mother's dark, straight hair, light eyes, and dark complexion. No one ever thinks we look alike. I give Ben a skeptical look.

"I can," he insists. "From the nose down." He twirls his index finger into my cheek like he drilling a hole. "Same dimple and everything."

Christian raises an eyebrow. *Why is he touching you like that?* practically scrolling above his head.

"I don't see it," Lucas says.

Ben rolls his eyes at him. "What brings you to Boston?" he asks Christian.

My brother looks at me before answering. "Just making sure Jillian's okay."

Ben nods. I look at my watch because I have a twelve-thirty meeting with Stacy and Renee. I'm five minutes late. Christian has been so busy telling me stories and showing me pictures that he hasn't touched his buffalo-chicken sandwich. "Sorry, I have to run, but finish your lunch." I hug him goodbye.

"Excellent. Now you can tell us embarrassing stories about Jill," Ben says as I walk away.

At the exit, I turn around to wave, but my brother doesn't notice because he's too busy laughing at something Ben says.

⚜ ⚜ ⚜

My meeting with Stacy and Renee lasts over ninety minutes. When I get back to my desk, Ben is just returning from lunch. He comes straight to my cube and plops down in the guest chair. "Your brother's a good guy."

"Yeah, he is," I say, wondering what they were talking about for all that time.

"He thinks you blame him because your parents moved."

I didn't know Christian was aware of this. "I do," I admit.

"Well, he didn't take them at gunpoint," Ben says.

He may as well have. I think about all the times he called them, whining, *Molly misses her grandparents. When are you coming to visit?* The way he barraged them with irresistible pictures of her angelic face. *She changes so much every day!* he'd say. *You better come see her soon.*

"He brainwashed them into moving."

"He said he never expected them to leave Massachusetts," Ben says.

"What else did he say?"

A big goofy smile breaks out on Ben's face. "You slept with the light on until you left for college because you were afraid of the dark."

Of course Christian would tell him embarrassing stories about me. "It was only until I was ten," I correct.

"You cried for weeks when he broke your Little Mermaid water globe," Ben says. "He thinks you still haven't forgiven him for it."

"I haven't!" The statue was a gift from my grandmother on my ninth birthday, the last present she gave me before she died. We had seen the movie together. Ariel was swimming around the globe in a purple bikini top with a greenish-blue fin, like she was under the sea. The base was purple with fishes and shells glued to it. It sat on my nightstand and was my most treasured possession, until Christian hit it with a baseball, cracking it in half. "I loved that thing. My mother and I searched all over for a replacement, but they stopped making it." Even thinking about it now makes me sad. "I can't believe he told you about that."

Ben shrugs. "Someday I'll introduce you to my sisters," he says. "The stories they tell you about me will be much more embarrassing."

I try to picture him as a kid. I see a tall, skinny boy with unruly curls being chased on the playground by a bunch of girls with huge crushes.

"Your brother is really worried about you," Ben says. "I promised him I'd keep an eye on you, make sure you have some fun, and don't spend all your time sulking about Nico." He taps me on the knee. "So you have to go to Renee's party with me."

Chapter 19

Branigan's black Porsche is parked diagonally across two spaces when I pull into the parking lot of the tennis club. It's my first time back since the doubles tournament. I was apprehensive about coming, and now that I know that Branigan is here, I think about throwing my car in reverse and driving home.

Inside, there's a long line at the reception desk. I take my position at the end to get my court assignment. As each person reaches the front, they sign some type of document. "What's going on?" I ask the woman standing ahead of me.

"There's a petition for a rematch of the mixed doubles final," she explains.

"You're kidding me?"

"Nope. I guess whoever was the linesman purposely made a bad call."

The man on the other side of the woman squints at me. I don't know his name, but I often see him around the club with Branigan. "Weren't you the one calling that game?"

The crowd turns toward me like they want to tar and feather me. "The ball was out. Branigan lost. The Longs won. You can't make them play again." It's the helium-injected version of my voice.

"The ball was on the line," the man says. Some in the crowd behind him nod.

"I had the best view," I say.

"I was watching from the café window," the woman in front of me says. "Looked in from there."

"You blame Sean for your boyfriend dumping you. That's why you called it out," the man says.

I swallow hard because what he's saying is close to the truth. The bell rings, and the crowd disperses. David gives me my court assignment. "I might have to do it, you know. Have a rematch," he says.

⚜ ⚜ ⚜

Down in the narrow tunnel that winds under the parking lot to the back courts, I see Sean and Tammy Branigan approaching from the opposite direction. Sean is bragging about a great shot he made in the match he just played and doesn't notice me right away. When he does see me, all the muscles in his body tense. He stalks up the musty corridor toward me. I am certain he's fantasizing about choking the life out of me. I can practically see images of his hands around my neck dancing through his head as he gets closer. He stops directly in front of me, so close to me that the tips of our sneakers touch. I can smell on his breath the banana he eats after each match. He extends his racquet toward the concrete wall, blocking my path.

Tammy races up to him. "Keep moving, Sean," she urges.

"Jillian," he spits. "You are persona non grata here. Most members agree you stole the match from me."

I swallow and step backward. "The ball was out."

Branigan leans forward, the vein in his forehead pulsates, and his bulbous nose glows redder than usual. "It wasn't!"

"Sean, you need to calm down," Tammy says.

He clenches and unclenches his fist. "I want you to come on the air and admit what you did."

I think he's kidding, but no, he's just lost his mind. "I won't do that."

"Well, I'll find a reason to keep talking about you until you do."

The second bell rings. "Let me by, please."

"You still have the ring, don't you?" He smiles. "We'll see what our listeners have to say about that."

❧   ❧   ❧

After seeing Branigan at the club, *BS Morning Sports Talk* becomes an addiction again. I know it's bad for me, but I can't stop listening. I set my alarm so that every weekday I wake up to the sound of his pompous voice. I jack up the volume of my radio so I can hear the show over the shower. I wait for a commercial before dashing out of my apartment into my car or from my car into the office, as though if I miss one word they say about me, I'll be putting my life in grave danger.

This morning as I get dressed, Branigan and Smyth are talking to Nico. "How many dates has it been now?" Branigan asks.

"I lost count," Nico says, his voice steadier than the first few times he spoke on air.

"Well, how long has it been? Five weeks, six?" Smyth asks.

"Our nine-week anniversary is Saturday," Nico answers.

I'm stepping into my tights, so his response literally catches me off balance. I stumble forward. In six years, he never once remembered our anniversary, but he has no trouble recollecting his first date with the Namaste Nitwit. Jerk!

"So things are getting serious?" Branigan asks.

"I like her," Nico answers. "Really, really like her."

And I really, really hate you.

"We've talked about her moving in," Nico continues.

"Sounds like things are heating up fast," Smyth says. "Will you have to make another call to our friends at Kaufman's Jewelers?"

"It's crossed my mind," Nico says.

I pull out the leg that was in my tights and sink to the floor. *Crossed his mind. It hasn't even been three months. Why did it take six years before it crossed his mind when he was dating me?*

I remember a few days after my thirtieth birthday, Rachel asked me to watch Sophie. She was seven months pregnant with Laurence and was having an ultrasound that day. We were in her living room looking at the images when she got back from her appointment. Sophie was sitting on my lap. Rachel turned to me, her expression reminding me of the one she had when we were fifteen and she was comforting me after my dog Pete Sampras died. "At your party, I asked Nico when he was going to propose," she began, putting her hand on my shoulder before continuing. "He said it's much too soon to be thinking about that." Nico and I had been dating for just about two years then.

"Well, he's not going to tell you when he's going to do it," I said, sure he didn't mean it. I even laughed.

"I don't know," Rachel said. "You might want to cut your losses." Sophie reached for her mother. Rachel took her from my arms. "We're not getting any younger, you know."

I considered her advice and thought about breaking up with Nico, but a few days later my parents announced they were moving to Georgia. Nico was the closest I had to family in Boston. I couldn't cut him loose and lose everyone at once. Then, over the years, maybe I just became too dependent on him to part ways.

On the radio now, I hear Branigan say my name and something about how the time might be right to return the ring. The show breaks for a commercial. I force myself to stand. Instead of dressing in the cute dress I planned to wear today, I slip back into my pajamas, suddenly feeling too exhausted to work. The little men are back in my head, jackhammering away. I go to the kitchen, where my phone is, so that I can call Stacy to tell her I won't be coming in today. Nico's jacket hanging on the back of the chair stops me in my tracks.

Get rid of it.

He'll be back for it.

The competing thoughts make my head hurt worse. I need a pill but still haven't bought more. Before Nico left, I didn't get headaches. That was his thing. They were so bad that he had to have his head scanned. Everything checked out. The doctor said they were most likely stress induced. "It's the damn job," Nico told me, like he was an emergency room physician or a soldier deployed in Iraq or Afghanistan instead of a producer for a stupid sports talk radio show.

Outside, Mr. O'Brien's car pulls into the driveway. I watch him plod up the driveway and across the walkway. The cup of coffee he's holding still steams. When he makes it to the front porch, I open my door and call out to him, "Do you have any aspirin?"

He passes by his side of the house and comes to mine. "What's wrong?"

"Just not feeling well."

He stares at me through the storm door. "You don't look sick."

A FedEx truck rumbles down the street.

"Well, then I look better than I feel."

"Did it come on suddenly?"

For crying out loud. What was I thinking, calling out to him?

He sips his coffee, waiting for me to answer. Water drips from the icicles hanging off the roof. A drop lands on Mr. O'Brien's shoulder. He wipes it off.

"I had a headache when I woke up. It got worse as I got ready for work."

"Were you listening to the radio?" he asks. Another drop splashes on the bill of his baseball cap. He glances up. "I'll be right back."

He returns a few minutes later with the biggest bottle of ibuprofen I have ever seen and a shovel. "Return it when you feel better," he says, handing me the pills. After I close the storm door, he extends the shovel high into the air and swipes it to the right. The icicles that have reformed since he last whacked them off fall from the roof, shattering on the porch. "Sometimes there are easy solutions to things that bother you," he says.

"Thanks for these," I say, shaking the bottle and closing the door. Back in my bedroom, Branigan and Smyth are talking about diamonds. "Don't you think some men feel the need to buy big ones to compensate for, um, some of their smaller body parts?" Branigan asks.

I kill the radio's power and go back to bed.

Chapter 20

Rachel almost sideswipes my passenger side as she pulls into the spot next to me. She's been driving that minivan for almost five years, but still can't remember it's double the size of the tiny Toyota she drove before Sophie was born. I get out of my car and make my way to her driver's-side rear door, expecting to see a backseat full of kids, but it's empty.

"Where is everyone?" I ask.

"With Mark. I have exactly forty-five minutes to find what I need and get home." She races for the mall's entrance before all the words are out of her mouth. I hustle to keep up with her as she makes a beeline for Lord and Taylor. She needs a dress for a party she's going to tonight and a gift for a birthday party Sophie's attending tomorrow. I agreed to meet her here to keep an eye on the kids while she did her errands, because Mark was supposed to go to the office to prepare for a big trial that starts Monday.

In the store, Rachel blazes through the women's clothing section, ripping dresses off racks. I stop to pick up the ones she's knocked off the hangers. When I catch up to her, her arms are full. "Here," she says, thrusting two identical dresses in different sizes at me.

A saleswoman who looks old enough to be Mr. O'Brien's mother approaches us. "Do you want me to take those to a dressing room for you?" she asks in a weak voice.

Rachel shakes her head but hands the woman half of her pile. "You can start ringing these up. Keep them all on the hangers and in different bags so they don't get wrinkled, please."

"Don't you want to try them on?" the saleswoman asks. I reach for the clothes Rachel gave her, because honestly they look too heavy for her to carry. I'm pretty sure her knees buckled when Rachel piled them on top of her.

"No time," Rachel says as she continues to ransack the racks. She ends up with six different dresses, each in two sizes. As the saleswoman rings up the twelve items, Rachel taps her credit card on the counter. Finally, she lays it down on the register. "Sign my name and meet me at the toy store." She dashes off before I can respond.

The saleswoman frowns. "She'll be back later this week, making more work for me when she returns all the ones that don't fit."

I don't say anything because the woman is right.

Weighed down with a dozen large bags across my arms, I plod through the mall toward the toy store. I curse Rachel under my breath for leaving me with all these dresses to carry. Other shoppers brush my shoulder on their way past me without saying excuse me. I walk by a store with an overpowering smell of flowery perfume coming out its door and try not to breathe in the scent. A little later, rap music blasting from a teenage clothing shop assaults my eardrums. I quicken my step and pass a window with posters of ridiculously young models dressed in sexy lingerie. A woman looking down at her phone rushes out of the store and crashes into me hard, knocking all my bags to the floor.

"So sorry, my bad," she says, finally looking up from her screen.

Something about her heart-shaped face is familiar. I stare, trying to figure out where I've seen her before.

She bends to help me pick up the dresses. "Looks like someone went on a shopping spree." She makes a noise that sounds like hiccups. It takes me a moment to realize she's laughing. "Did you buy out the entire store or what?" She laughs again. I want to offer her a glass of water or suggest she hold her breath and count to ten.

She hands me the bags. "Do you need help getting these to your car?"

I tilt my head in the direction of the toy store. "I'm meeting my friend over there."

The woman says something else, but I don't hear her words because I'm distracted by the man approaching from behind. It can't be. My underarms get sticky as he gets closer. It is. What is he doing at the mall? He would never go with me. It's like he was afraid shopping would cause his testosterone levels to plummet. I can tell by the way his familiar slanted dark eyes blink repeatedly that he has just noticed me as well.

I expect him to pretend he doesn't see me and keep walking, turn around, or duck into a store. Instead, he heads directly for me, stopping so close to the woman who crashed into me that their shoulders touch.

"Jill," he says.

"Nico." It comes out as barely a whisper. His usual five o'clock shadow is gone. In its place is a full mustache and goatee. They make him look older because several gray hairs are mixed among the black.

He places his hand on the small of the woman's back. My knees buckle as I study her face. Bonnie, the Namaste Nitwit. It's just my freaking luck that the idiot who smashes into me is her. I look back toward Nico. He's wearing a dark blue ski coat with the Ralph Lauren Polo logo that I have never seen before and is most definitely not his style. Nitwit here must have picked it out for him. Holy hell! What's that in his hand? It's a small pink bag from Victoria's Secret. Why did I have to see that?

"You two know each other?" Bonnie, the brain surgeon, asks.

"This is Jillian," Nico says. He makes a soft clicking noise with his tongue. It's a tic he has the rare times he loses his composure. I doubt anyone else has ever noticed it.

Bonnie swipes a piece of blond hair away from her eye. "Oh!"

Oh? What does that mean? What did he tell her about me?

"I'm Bonnie," she says. "Nice to meet you."

No! It's not nice to meet you. "The contest winner," I say.

"Nico's girlfriend," she corrects.

Nico stares down at the floor of the mall. It occurs to me that if I say anything else, it will somehow be a subject of discussion on Monday's talk show. Heck, if Nico tells Branigan he saw me, Branigan will spin it as evidence of stalking, even though we're less than ten minutes from where I live and almost thirty minutes from Nico's new apartment. I have to get out of here. "I have to run," I say.

Nico's standing directly in front of me, blocking my path. "Excuse me," I say, trying to sound confident as I step around him.

"Well, that was awkward," I hear Bonnie say with her hiccup-like laugh.

By the time I make it to the other end of the mall, I'm shaking. I plop down on a bench next to the toy store and wait for Rachel. I'm keeping an eye on the direction I came from to make sure Nico and Bonnie aren't coming my way, so I miss Rachel exiting the store. "Who are you looking for?" she asks.

"Nico and his new girlfriend. I just ran into them. Literally."

"Nico's here? At the mall?"

I nod. "Shopping at Victoria's Secret." My voice breaks as I say it.

"Oh, Jillian," Rachel says. She slides the bags of dresses to the end of the bench and sits next to me. "Are you okay?"

"He has a goatee. God, did it look bad."

We sit quietly. The smell of pretzels floats in the air. Rachel stares at the stand across the way. "She was beautiful," I say. "Scarlett Freaking Johansson beautiful."

Rachel stands and walks away. A few minutes later she brings back two pretzels with caramel dipping sauce. "He's getting on with his life, Jill. You should too."

"I'm trying."

Rachel drags a piece of her pretzel around the plastic container of caramel. "You're not. You need to start dating again."

I watch the crowd rushing by us. Couples, friends, families. No one is alone. "Who am I supposed to date?"

"You need to take a chance," Rachel says. "Do online dating. Make something happen instead of waiting for something to happen."

⚜ ⚜ ⚜

Sunday is the kind of late-winter day that is a coming attraction for summer. The temperature soars to sixty-four degrees, which feels more like a hundred after suffering through single digits for the past three months. Dressed in shorts and a T-shirt, I lace up my sneakers and head outside for my first outdoor run of the year.

Mr. O'Brien stands at the top of a ladder, raking the remaining snow off the roof. Zachary waits on the ground below him, looking up with his hand tented across his forehead.

"Is it safe for him to be up there?" I ask, looking up at Mr. O'Brien. I have to shield my eyes from the bright rays of sunshine reflecting off the ladder.

"It's fine," Zac says.

"It's more dangerous for you to be standing there," Mr. O'Brien calls down. A moment later a pile of slush falls from above and lands next to me. "Move before you get hurt," he yells.

I wave goodbye and jog down the driveway, out onto the wet street. After being cooped up all winter, it feels great to be outside with the wind at my back. Clearly I'm not the only one who thinks so, because when I turn onto Commonwealth Avenue, there's a large group of runners on the other side of the street, a club getting ready for the Boston Marathon, which is less than a month away. Nico and I often talked about training for it, but neither one of us was willing to commit—the story of us, I guess.

A feeling of malaise has settled over me since bumping into him yesterday. I'm hoping running will shake it off, but I can't stop thinking about him as my sneakers pound the pavement. I wonder if seeing me has made him regret leaving, or after I walked away, did he wipe the sweat from his brow, kiss Bonnie, and laugh, saying, *Dodged a bullet there!*

This thought causes me to quicken my pace. Sweat drips down my face. The sound of my heavy breathing drowns out the music on my iPod, so I crank the volume. The song is about a woman who has just gone through a break up and is fighting to take back her life. I sing along. The lyrics make me think about Rachel's lecture. She's right. I just can't hide away in my apartment. I need to get out and meet people. I'm going to do it, starting with going to Renee's party with Ben and then activating my profile on the online dating site.

Three miles later, exhausted and sweaty, I turn back into my driveway. The ladder is gone, the icicles have all been knocked off the house, and the roof is snow-free. Old man winter might finally be releasing his grip on us.

Inside my apartment, I head straight to my phone to text Ben: *Do you still need a date for Renee's party?*

His response is immediate: *No, I'm taking you.*

⚜ ⚜ ⚜

Before I go to bed that night, my phone rings and Nico's name flashes across the screen. I blink hard and read it again, just to be sure I'm not imagining it. I'm not. He's really calling. Maybe seeing me made him realize how much he misses me. *God, Jill. I should never have let you go*, I imagine him saying. *Can we go to dinner, talk?*

You had your chance. You blew it, I'll say, and I'll laugh.

You won't! says my know-it-all voice. *You'll welcome him back with open arms.*

I swipe my screen horizontally to answer the call.

"It's me," Nico begins.

Me who? I want to ask to show him he's not first in my thoughts anymore.

"It was weird seeing you yesterday." The way his voice breaks catches me off guard.

"You too." I sit on my bed. The image of the Victoria's Secret bag in his hand flashes through my mind. "So Bonnie is pretty, but boy that laugh must be tough to take."

"When did you get so nasty, Jill?"

The day I came home to find the back of your pickup truck loaded with all your belongings. "What are you talking about?"

"Hacking the website and writing horrible things about me, replacing Bonnie's picture with Miss Piggy, calling her the contest winner, making fun of her laugh. That's not you, Jillian."

"I had nothing to do with the hack, and you have to admit, she sounds like she has a bad case of the hiccups when she laughs."

He sighs. "I don't want to fight."

"Why did you call?"

"Sean told me he hasn't seen you at the tennis club for a while."

Was he asking Branigan about me? "Yeah, well, I'm public enemy number one around there after the mixed doubles tournament."

"That's what I wanted to talk to you about."

"You want to talk about the tennis club?"

"Sort of." He pauses. "I want you to come on the air and apologize for your bad call in the tournament."

His request leaves me speechless.

"Branigan will leave you alone if you do," Nico says.

"You want me to apologize to him?"

"It's the only way all this will end."

"I have to go."

"I'm trying to help you, Jillian," Nico says.

"Why?"

"Why? Just because we're not together doesn't mean I don't still care for you."

"Yeah, I can tell how much you care by all the stuff they've been saying about me on your show."

He sighs again. "Branigan is unreasonable. We both know that. You're going to have to be the bigger person to end this."

"I'm not apologizing to him. He hit the ball out."

"Did he really?" Nico asks.

I see the ball bouncing, just catching the line. If I had to do it all again, I wouldn't, but there's no going back now. "Even if he didn't, it's no excuse for what he's said about me."

"Jill, I'm giving you a way to end this. Don't you want to put it all behind you?"

"Not if it means I have to apologize."

"Will you at least think about it?" Nico asks.

"He should apologize to me," I say before hitting the end button.

Chapter 21

Monday morning I'm stopped at a malfunctioning traffic light that stays red for three minutes but remains green for only fifteen seconds. I know this because I've been stuck here for six cycles and timed it on the fourth. The song I was singing along to ends. I change the station back to *BS Morning Sports Talk*. For the entire commute, I've been punching the radio's buttons, alternating between music and the sports station. Talking to Nico yesterday has put me on edge. Branigan is up to something. Otherwise, Nico wouldn't have called. So far, though, they have been talking about nothing but baseball on the show.

"We're going to switch gears for the third hour of the program," Branigan announces. "Nico's ex-fiancée hasn't returned the ring to Nico." My grip on the steering wheel tightens. "We want to hear from you. Does she have the right to keep it, or should she give it back?"

The first caller is Kevin from Ayer. "Hell yeah, she should return it," he says. "If she won't give it back willingly, take it forcefully, man. Finger and all."

The driver in the car next to mine laughs. I hope he's listening to something else.

The light turns green. I accelerate through the intersection, barely making it through before the signal goes back to red. Smyth takes another call: Susan from Somerville. "Hasn't the poor girl had enough heartache?" she asks. "Let her keep the ring."

Thank you, Susan.

A long line of slow-moving vehicles coming from the opposite direction prevents me from turning left. I edge out, hoping someone will stop. A woman in a CR-V blasts her horn, almost clipping my front bumper as she creeps by. Like it would have killed her to stop? Honestly. A man in a pickup motions for me to go. I wave as I cross in front of him.

Natasha, an attorney from Framingham, is next on the show. She has this to offer: "The engagement ring is a conditional gift—the condition being that a marriage will take place. If it doesn't, the agreement is null and void."

As I pull into the parking garage at work, Branigan takes a call from Frank from South Boston, but it's definitely my landlord's voice that comes over the airwaves. I sit in my car listening to what he has to say. "When did this show turn into a soap opera?" Mr. O'Brien asks. "Aren't you fools supposed to be talking about sports?"

"Okay, Frank," Branigan says. "We'll talk about sports right after the break. For you callers we didn't get to, cast a vote on our website."

Cast a vote on the website? I walk into the building outraged by how far Branigan is taking his revenge. In my aisle, Ben and Renee are sitting in his cube drinking coffee. "There's my date to your party," Ben says as I join them.

"I'm glad you're coming, sweetie," Renee says as she stands to return to her desk.

"What made you change your mind?" Ben asks.

"I need to get out and have fun."

He cocks his head. "I'll be sure you have fun," he says in flirty voice. "I'll make it a night you can't forget."

"That's what I'm counting on." I wink at him.

⚜ ⚜ ⚜

It's like picking a scab, causing it to bleed again, the way I keep visiting the radio station's website to check on the survey results, feeling more disappointed each time I do. More than 95 percent of respondents think I should return the ring, 2 percent say I should keep it, and the rest don't care.

"How many times are you going to look at that?" Ben asks. It's the fourth time he's caught me on the site today. He places the printout of the new brochure he's designing on the desk beside me. "All the text doesn't fit. Can you cut some out?"

I look through the copy while he leans over my shoulder reading my computer screen. After going through the brochure a few times, I strike out a paragraph. As I'm reviewing the copy again to ensure everything still makes sense, Ben asks, "Why don't you return the ring to Nico?"

I add two new sentences before responding. "He's never asked for it."

Ben rolls his eyes and points toward my monitor. "This is his passive-aggressive way of asking."

"Yeah, well, he's going to have to man up."

Ben shrugs. "If you want to show him that you're over him and have moved on, you should give it back."

I hand the brochure to him without saying anything.

"Maybe you're not over him," Ben says.

After he leaves, I look at the survey results again. The percentage of respondents saying I should return the ring has jumped to 97. I tell myself that I'm keeping it because after everything Nico's done, he doesn't deserve it back. In the back of my mind though, the tiny voice that doesn't let me get away with anything whispers, *You're keeping it because you think you'll wear it again someday.*

⚜ ⚜ ⚜

All twenty-seven members of sales and marketing are sitting around the conference room table waiting for Brian from IT to connect Stacy's laptop to a projector. She's previewing our new website to the team today. A bright light shines on the ceiling as the IT guy fiddles with the projector. He adjusts its height and the light moves off the ceiling down the wall. After he presses a few buttons on Stacy's computer, the image of the new home page fills the white screen.

The conversations around the table end. A few people gasp. "Wow."

"This is the beta version of our new website," Stacy announces. She highlights the company's name, Cyber Security Consultants, and points to the logo, a lock with the acronym CSC written out in what looks like a string of binary numbers. She toggles to another screen to compare the new image with the old CyberCrimeBusters logo, a cartoon of a burglar typing on a keyboard. "Much more professional, wouldn't you say?"

She previews the site page by page, starting with the About Us section. She clicks on an employee profile that focuses on Lucas and enlarges his picture. No one recognizes him because he's wearing a dress shirt and tie instead of his usual flannel shirt and skull cap. "Highlighting a staff member is a great new feature," Stacy says.

Everyone around the table nods in agreement.

As Stacy shares the site, she occasionally looks at Renee, Ben, or me and smiles. Each time she does, Ben nudges my foot with his while Renee elbows me.

"What did you think?" Stacy asks after showing the last page. "Did you see anything that you'd change?"

Ryan raises his hand, which isn't at all surprising. He has to talk during every meeting to show how smart he is. Usually, he proves the opposite. "The graphics in the banner should have more variety."

Ben folds his arms across his chest. "They need consistency to tie the site together."

"It's all the same. It's boring," Ryan says.

"There are subtle differences," Ben counters.

"Give me an example of a site you like," Stacy says to Ryan.

The room is quiet while Ryan tries to think of one. Of course he didn't have anything in mind. He just spoke to hear himself talk.

Renee sneezes. We all say "Bless you." The silence returns.

"You can't give us an example?" Stacy asks.

"One," Ryan finally says. He glances at me. "www.wspr.com."

My muscles stiffen as Stacy types the URL into the browser. The radio station's home page appears. The banner displaying logos of all Boston's sports teams comes up first. Then the menu listing each of the station's shows across the top of the screen appears. "Click on any of those," Ryan instructs. "You'll see the pages that come up are different."

Stacy moves her cursor to the first link, which of course is the one for the morning show. She clicks her mouse. *BS Morning Sports Talk*'s page fills the screen. In big bold letters, the headline across the top of the page screams: **SHOULD**

JILLIAN RETURN THE RING? There are two radio buttons, one labeled *Yes*, the other with *No*. The survey's up-to-the-minute results appear below, showing that 97.8 percent of listeners think I should give the diamond back.

I push my chair away from the table. I eye the door, thinking about running out of the room. Would that make me look more or less pathetic? More. Definitely more.

Stacy frowns as her mouse moves across the copy. My coworkers stare at me. I look down at the table, refusing to make eye contact with anyone.

Stacy removes her glasses and taps them against the edge of the table while she studies me.

For the love of God, click off the page.

She turns her attention to Ryan. "I like our treatment of the images better." She looks at me with what I think is a smile and drags her mouse to the No radio button and clicks on it. Renee and some of the other woman in the room clap. Stacy shuts down her laptop and the screen on the wall goes blank. *Thank God!* "We'll do some minor modifications and be ready to go live in three weeks," she says.

The meeting ends. Ben quickly stands. "If you would just return the ring, you could end all this." He rushes out of the room without waiting for Renee or me.

Chapter 22

Ben, Renee, and I are at Donovan's, a restaurant down the street from the office. Stacy let us go early after demo-ing the website. It was Renee's idea to come here. I hate this place. There are banks of televisions tuned to sports channels on each wall and above the bar. Whenever Nico and I came here, he'd spend more time paying attention to the games than to me.

"Did I tell you Lenny hired the band that played at our wedding for the party next week?" Renee asks.

"Will you have to check them out of the nursing home for the night?" Ben asks.

Renee swallows the last of her wine. "They're only in their fifties, wise guy."

"Only," Ben says, reaching for a nacho. "By the way, what do I wear to this shindig?"

"The suit you wore to the holiday party," Renee answers. "With a different shirt and tie."

An image of Ben in his charcoal gray suit and red shirt, the night of the Christmas party, flashes through my mind. He's holding me tight during the last dance of the night, our bodies practically melded together. *This is dangerous, Jill. I wish I were the one going upstairs with you.* I push my empty glass to the side and cast a sideways glance at him, wondering if we'll pick up where we left off that night.

The waitress arrives at our table. "Another round," Ben says.

Renee shakes her head. "Not for me. Gotta get to Joel's hockey game."

"Jill, you'll have one more with me?" Ben asks.

Renee and the waitress walk away from the booth together, leaving Ben and me alone.

"What are you wearing to the party?" he asks. "I'll coordinate my shirt to your dress color."

Leave it to a graphic artist to worry about that detail. I think of Nico with the one suit, white dress shirt, and tie he owns. In a million years, he would never have thought to match his shirt to my dress.

I shrug. "Haven't thought about it yet."

"How about that blue strapless number you wore to your father's retirement party." He whistles.

My hand freezes over the plate of nachos. My father retired over four years ago. If Ben hadn't reminded me, I might not have remembered what I wore to the party. "How do you know what I wore?"

"You showed us pictures."

Bringing in photos of myself to show to my coworkers doesn't sound like something I would do, especially because when my father retired I was new to the company. "I don't remember." I struggle to pull a nacho out of the pile because the melted cheese is causing all the chips to stick together.

Ben pushes the plate closer to me. "Probably saw them on Facebook then."

Now I remember. Christian posted pictures from that night and tagged me and Nico. Nico had been elbowed in the face during a basketball game a few days before and had a black eye. He was mad my brother put the pictures on social media. "Oh yeah, Nico's eye was messed up in that picture."

Ben shrugs. "Don't remember."

"You remember my dress but not his mangled eye? There were close to two hundred comments on the picture and they were all about Nico's face."

Ben starts to say something, but the waitress returns with our drinks, a beer for him and a glass of wine for me. As she places them in front of us, I notice a group of women at the bar are checking him out. "I think they're into you," I say, dipping my head in their direction.

He turns toward them. One of them waves. He looks back at me. "She's not bad," he says. "Let's find someone for you." We both search the room. Even though we're in a sports bar, there are definitely more women than men here, probably about four to one. "How about him?" he asks, pointing to a scraggly looking man with greasy blond hair and a long, unkempt beard. The guy's shirt and pants are stained. "Filthy, just like you like them."

"Oh yeah, the dirtier, the better."

"I can get pretty dirty," Ben says in a flirty tone.

"Mmm," I say, sipping my drink. "You are downright nasty in your color-coordinated outfits."

Ben looks around the room. "There isn't anyone here who does it for you?"

A bunch of high school boys to our right are shooting spitballs at each other, two old men to our left are staring up at the television, and a really cute boy about eight years old is having dinner with his mother in front of us. "Nope."

He leans across the table toward me. "Not even me?"

I try to answer in a joking manner, but the look of fear that crossed my face may have already outed me. "Well, that goes without saying. Too bad you don't plug it in at work." I wink at him.

"I'd make an exception for you." He sloshes his beer around his glass. "Have you ever thought about us together?"

My face burns as I remember Nico lowering me to the bed in the hotel room after the holiday party, Ben's face popping into my mind, and how I pretended it was Ben in bed with me. He continues to stare at me like he expects an answer. "Nope." If I could regularly hit notes that high, I might have a career as a lead soprano.

My hand is splayed out on the table. He reaches across and covers it with his, slowly moving his finger back and forth over my wrist. My muscles tighten. "Not even when we were dancing together at the holiday party?" It's a rhetorical question, the way he asks it.

Maybe I should be truthful. Tell him that I fantasized about him. Take Ellie's advice. Invite him back to my apartment. Make the fantasies reality and move on with my life. I take a deep breath in and slowly exhale. "Not even then." I pull my hand out from under his.

"You're lying," he says. "And I'm looking forward to dancing with you again at Renee's party."

⚜ ⚜ ⚜

In the middle of the night I get up for a glass of water. I make my way downstairs through my dark apartment. A loud thump comes from the kitchen. I freeze in the living room, holding my breath while my heart beats wildly in my chest. I stand that way for several seconds, listening, but there is no other sound. I continue on my way. The light above the stove is on, casting large shadows on the wall. There's another thump. I quickly turn my head in its direction and jump, seeing what I think is a man sitting at the table. When the figure doesn't move, I realize it's not a person at all. It's

Nico's jacket. I hear the noise again. This time I know it's the ice maker. I let out the breath I was holding.

Sipping my glass of water, I rest my hand on the back of Nico's coat. The soft leather is cool to my touch. He was wearing this jacket the day I met him. We were sitting next to each other at a Red Sox game. I was there with my brother and sister-in-law, and Nico was with one of his friends. It was early in the season, so when the game started it was warm. By the eighth inning, the temperature had plummeted more than thirty degrees. Although I was wearing a sweatshirt, I was freezing and decided to take the train back to Newton.

"You're leaving with the score tied?" Nico asked. I knew enough about baseball and the Red Sox to have a conversation about the game, and we had spent most of the night talking. "I thought you were a real fan, not a pink hat." That's what he called people, women especially, who came to the game to socialize instead of watch it.

"It's freezing."

He slipped off his jacket and handed it to me. "I don't want you to miss Big Papi's walk-off." He said it like he was absolutely certain David Ortiz would hit a game-winning home run. A few innings later, when he did, Nico pulled me into a tight embrace. After I agreed to have dinner with him the following night, he said I could wear his coat home. "This way I'm sure you won't back out and I get to see you again," he said. It wasn't until we'd been dating for a year that I realized how much he loved this stupid jacket and what a risk he had taken by letting me leave with it.

He's coming back for it. He has to.

Chapter 23

Ellie's been traveling for business, but today she is back in the office. At lunch, she asks me to walk to the sandwich shop around the corner so we can catch up. An inch of slush coats the sidewalk from the melting snow and ice, so we walk single file in the narrow road, stepping around deep puddles every few feet. Halfway there, she shouts something over her shoulder. The only word I can make out is *Nico* because a delivery truck rumbles by at the same time, making it impossible to hear.

I wait until we reach the sub shop's parking lot to speak. "What about Nico?" A cold gust of wind kicks up from seemingly nowhere, reminding me that in March and sometimes in April, winter likes to sucker punch us. Just when we think we've moved on to sunshine, blue skies, and warm temperatures, BAM! Bad weather returns.

Ellie and I are side-by-side now. She grabs hold of my wrist with her gloved hand. "I saw the survey on the show's website. It's time to give back the ring and forget about Nico."

"I'm trying."

"You're not trying hard enough." She opens the door to the restaurant and waits for me to pass through. There's a long line snaking from the front counter around the tables to the back wall. We take our place at the end. "Tomorrow night with Ben," she says, "make it happen."

"I'm thinking about it," I admit, remembering the pink Victoria's Secret bag dangling from Nico's fingertips.

"We know what the pros are. What are the cons?" she asks. It's the same question she asks in most of our work meetings.

"It could ruin our friendship."

"Or it could take it to the next level."

I tell her about the night at Donovan's. How Ben was flirty and brought up our dancing together at the holiday party. "He said he was looking forward to doing it again."

"So, he's definitely up for it," she says. "You just have to show him that you are too."

"How am I going to do that?" I ask as we reach the counter.

Before she places her order, she gives me a look similar to the one Mr. O'Brien often gives me that makes me feel like the stupidest person in the world.

Once we're seated with our food, she offers advice. "Be flirty. Make subtle innuendos. Touch him. Dance with him the way you did at the Christmas party." Her suggestions remind me of the articles in *Seventeen* magazine that Rachel and I used to read out loud to each other when we were in our early teens. It's what we did all summer sitting by her pool.

I bite into my veggie pocket. A nasty earthy flavor fills my mouth. *Damn! I told them no mushrooms!* I gulp down my soda to wash away the taste. "Isn't it bad that I'd be using him to get over Nico?"

Ellie laughs. "He won't mind."

I inspect my sandwich for more fungus.

"Just don't expect more," Ellie says.

"What do you mean?"

She puts down her chicken Caesar wrap. "Sleeping with him doesn't mean the two of you will be in a relationship." She picks up her sandwich again. "Don't think of it as anything but a night of fun."

Rachel always teases me because I've never had sex outside a serious relationship. She says I should have been born before the sexual revolution of the 1960s. Well, it's time to prove that post-Nico Jillian is different. If I'm going to have a one-night stand, Ben's the best person to have it with because we're friends and I care about him.

"I will think of it as nothing more than moving on from Nico," I say.

Chapter 24

Late Saturday morning, I carry my overflowing laundry basket down the steep stairway to the basement. The musty smell hits me as soon as I hit the bottom step. I try not to breathe in the scent. Stupid, I realize, because it's not like I can hold my breath the entire time I'm down here.

The lights are on in the back corner where Mr. O'Brien let me set up my washing machine and dryer. For a second, I think I forgot to shut them off when I was here last, but then I see the old man hunched over his workbench.

"Hello," I yell while I'm still several feet away so that I don't frighten him.

Startled, he jumps and turns in my direction. "What are you doing sneaking up on me like that?"

"Just came down to do my laundry."

"You scared me half to death," he says. Several broken pieces from what looks like an old coffee mug are scattered on the workbench in front of him. He slides them around, trying to fit them together as though he's doing a puzzle. The man hates to throw anything away, as evidenced by the stacks of plastic bins piled from the floor to the ceiling four rows deep along every grungy concrete wall of the cellar. Each of the containers is carefully labeled to identify its contents: Colleen's artwork, Colleen's baby pictures, 1996 Christmas cards, Playbills—That's the one that got me, because I can't see the old man spending an evening in the theater.

As I sort through my dirty clothes, tossing bras and panties into the washer, I occasionally glance over at Mr. O'Brien because I'm embarrassed to be handling them in front of him. He's too busy rummaging through a drawer of his red tool chest to pay any attention to me though. He pulls out Elmer's glue, rubber cement, a glue stick, Gorilla Glue wood adhesive, and finally clear epoxy, which apparently is what he's looking for because he returns everything else to the drawer. He lowers his head toward the workbench and squirts the epoxy onto a thin wooden stick and then carefully transfers the adhesive to a broken piece of the mug. It seems like an awful lot of work to repair an old coffee cup.

When I finish loading my dirty clothes into the machine, he's still painstakingly gluing the pieces back together. "Goodbye," I say quietly so that I don't scare him again.

He doesn't even look up. I make my way toward the stairs but stop when I walk into a spiderweb stretching from a piece of lumber resting against the wall to the metal shelves housing more of Mr. O'Brien's tools. I cringe as I brush it aside.

Mr. O'Brien clears his throat. "Zac knocked it off the table this morning," he says. "Caught him throwing it in the trash. Don't even know why he had to touch it." He looks up now, his blue eyes watering more than usual. "It was Carol's. Drank her coffee from it every single morning."

Now I feel my eyes misting up as well. "I'm sorry."

"What are you sorry for?" he asks. "Zac's the one who broke it."

I climb back up the stairs with my empty laundry basket. Somehow, it seems heavier than it did on the way down.

After my laundry is done, I spend the rest of the day getting ready for Renee's party. I go to the nail salon around the corner from my apartment and get a French manicure and pedicure. From there, I drive across town to see Karen, my hairdresser, to have her style my hair because I can never get it to hold a curl the way she can.

Karen was cutting my hair long before I ever met Nico. Her husband, Phil, is a huge sports fan who regularly listens to *BS Morning Sports Talk*, so she knows all about Nico's and my split. She even sent an email to tell me how sorry she was. "I was so excited when I saw you on the books for a blow dry," she says as soon as I walk in. "Does this mean you have a special date tonight?"

How can I possibly explain what tonight is? "Kind of."

She hands me a cape and leads me to the sink for a wash. "So, who is he? How did you meet?"

"I've known him for a long time," I answer. "We work together."

"Ohhh, an office romance. How scandalous. Are you keeping it on the down low?"

Jeez, I hadn't thought about that. If Ben and I sleep together, I don't want anyone at the office but Ellie knowing, especially not Renee, who gets her hair cut at this same salon. I better squelch this right now so that rumors don't start. "It's not really a romance. One of our other coworkers is celebrating her twenty-fifth anniversary by renewing her vows, and we're going to the party together."

The water she's spraying over my head is much too hot. I jerk upright.

"Sorry," she says. She adjusts the temperature and is quiet while she pumps the shampoo into her palm.

"You must be into him if you're getting your hair done though."

"We're friends. I guess he's my work husband." I feel all the tension leaving my muscles as she massages my scalp with her fingertips.

Jason, another hairdresser who's washing one of his clients' hair at the sink next to ours, chimes in. "Karen's going to have you looking so hot when you leave here that your work husband will be asking for conjugal privileges tonight."

Chapter 25

Back at home, I have less than an hour to get dressed. Instead of picking underwear from my usual drawer, I go to the nightstand where I keep my special lingerie and select a red lacy brassiere and panty set that Nico gave me for Valentine's Day last year. I swear I feel like a porn star whenever I wear them, which, okay, was just one time—the night Nico gave them to me, because he insisted I try them on. I look in the mirror now and admire myself in them. Not too bad. I fantasize about taking a selfie and firing it off to Nico. *Going out with Ben tonight and look what I'm wearing*. No doubt the picture would end up on *BS Morning Talk Show*'s website.

I slip on a dress I took from Rachel. It's short-sleeved and green, or as Ralph Lauren likes to call the color, malachite. When I tried it on earlier, I thought it made me look skinny because of the way it twists and gathers at the waist. Looking in the mirror now though, I decide it makes me look matronly. I take it off and instead put on the blue dress that I wore to my father's retirement party.

Just as I finish changing, the bell rings. Ben is twenty minutes early picking me up. My breath catches in my throat when I open the door and see him standing there. Dressed in a charcoal gray suit with a light blue shirt and solid dark blue tie, he's holding a bouquet of flowers. He always looks handsome at work, but tonight on my front step, he is disturbingly good-looking.

"Hi," I say, trying to play it cool and ignoring the pounding in my chest.

He stares at me, grinning through the storm door.

Mr. O'Brien's station wagon pulls into the driveway. I hurriedly usher Ben into the house before the old man gets out of his car. I don't want to introduce them. When Nico and I first started going out, Mr. O'Brien would wait up for me. After a few dates, when it became clear Nico would be sticking around for a while, my landlord made a point of knocking on my door to introduce himself, stopping just short of asking Nico his intentions. Later Mr. O'Brien mentioned that Nico didn't look him in the eye when the two shook hands, something my landlord apparently never got over.

"Your hair. It's different," Ben says.

Does he hate it? "Same hair I've always had." I attempt to smile, but now I wonder if Karen overdid it with the curls.

"It's not usually curly," he says. *Damn. I should have styled it myself instead of shelling out forty bucks plus a tip.* He grins. "It looks amazing."

That Karen! She knows exactly what she's doing! Worth every penny!

Ben eyes me appreciatively. "Did you wear that dress for me?" he asks in a low voice.

"Maybe."

"Well, you look really hot." He steps toward me. I think he's going to kiss me, but he hands me the flowers.

"These make tonight seem like an official date," I say, laughing to make it seem like I don't really think it's a date.

"It is, isn't it?" Ben asks with a cocky grin.

I remember Ellie's instructions to be flirty. "It can be anything you want." I was going for coy. Judging from Ben's confused expression, I didn't pull it off. I should have made my voice breathy. I repeat it in my head that way. It definitely sounds more flirty. I decide to use a breathy voice the rest of the night.

We stand awkwardly in the foyer, staring at each other. "How about a glass of wine before we go?" If I'm going to go through with what I have in mind tonight, I'll need alcohol, lots of alcohol.

With his hand on my lower back, Ben escorts me down the hall. "I have a good feeling about tonight," he says.

"Me too."

In the doorframe between my living room and kitchen, Ben comes to an abrupt stop. I follow his eyes right to Nico's jacket, still hanging over the back of the chair. "You still have that?"

"I just—" *I just what? I'm just waiting for him to come back?* "I haven't had a chance to return it to him yet."

Ben frowns. "It makes it look like he still lives here or that you're expecting him back at any time."

"It's one coat," I say.

"You could throw it away." He gives me a challenging look, like he expects me to take it to the trash now.

I hand him the bottle of cabernet and a corkscrew. "Can you open this while I dig out the wine glasses?"

"Sure," he says, but he's still frowning.

After I pour our drinks, I ask him to make a toast. He thinks for a minute, staring at Nico's leather coat. "To you getting on with your life."

I move my glass before he can touch it with his. "And to us having a good time together." This time I use a breathy voice and narrow my eyes, trying to look seductive.

"Are your contacts bothering you?" he asks before clanking my glass.

Mixed Signals

⚜ ⚜ ⚜

All the guests are sitting in chairs arranged in a semicircle around a fireplace on the far wall of the dining room. Ben and I scurry across the dark hardwood to the only empty seats at the end of the last row. He stretches his long legs sideways and extends one arm over the back of my chair. I move all the way back so that my shoulders brush up against his forearm. Any type of physical contact is good, according to Ellie's instructions—and those old *Seventeen* magazine articles, if I remember right.

Dressed in a long off-white gown, Renee stands in the center of the circle, beaming at a tuxedo-clad, grinning Lenny. Their daughter, Cheryl, stands in front of them with a leather-bound notepad in her hand. She has the same hooded eyes as her father, as well as an identical bump in her nose. I haven't seen her since her high school graduation two years ago. Back then, she didn't wear makeup. It was a form of rebellion against her mother, who wouldn't be caught dead without lipstick and mascara. The rebellion is clearly over. Tonight, Cheryl's made up like she's about to do a photo shoot for Cover Girl.

Renee's son, Joel, slumps against the brick wall behind his sister, staring at the floor. At sixteen, he is tall and lanky, clearly still growing into his body. Nico and I took him to a hockey game last season. He's grown half a foot since then.

Lenny nods at Cheryl. She takes a deep breath and opens her notebook. "Good evening and thank you for coming." She reads in a slow and deliberate manner.

Ben leans toward me. "She should have guzzled down wine to loosen up." He doesn't say it, but I hear the word *too* at the end of his sentence, and I feel like he's passing judgment on me. I slugged down two big pours before we left my apartment. Meanwhile, Ben didn't finish his first glass.

Cheryl continues. "Twenty-five years ago, my mother and father joined their hearts and hands and vowed to love, honor, and cherish each other." She finally looks up from her notes. "My dad also swears that my mom promised to obey, but she denies that."

The guests laugh. Renee shakes her head.

Cheryl consults her notes again. "Throughout the years, life has brought my parents some wonderful blessings." She looks up and grins. "Me, for example, and some challenges as well." She looks at Joel, whose cheeks turn ruddy.

"Through it all, they fulfilled the promises they made to each other. Today, they want everyone to know, knowing everything they do, they would do it all again." She pauses, scans the crowd, and then turns back to her parents. "Do you want to renew your vows?"

"We do," Renee and Lenny say together.

Lenny reaches for Renee's hand. "All these years later," he says, "I still can't believe that you picked me. You're my best friend. You know me better than anyone else does, and still you want to be with me." He sounds incredulous. "You are my one and only, my soul mate. It is a privilege to recommit myself to you and our marriage today."

I glance at Ben, expecting him to be scrolling through his phone, checking scores or messages, because that's what Nico would be doing. Instead, Ben is leaning forward in his seat, paying such close attention to the vow renewal that he's not even aware I'm looking at him.

I refocus my attention on Renee and Lenny, noticing the way Lenny's voice breaks as he recites his vows, the mist in Renee's eyes as she smiles up at him, the way their fingers are entwined. If I reached out into the air in front of me, I swear I could grab hold of a piece of their love. It's that palpable. I think of Mr. O'Brien earlier in the day, gluing his dead wife's mug back together. Nico and I didn't love each other like that, I realize. We would have swept up the broken pieces and deposited them in the trash without a second thought. I want someone to love me enough to renew vows with me on our twenty-fifth anniversary and glue my coffee cup back together.

When the ceremony is over, I remain seated as everyone around me rises and rushes to the bar in the other room. Noticing that I haven't moved, Ben returns to his chair. "You okay?" he asks.

"Sure," I say, forcing a smile because I don't want to be Debbie Downer.

"Someday we're going to do this too," he says.

I shoot him a questioning look.

"I don't mean together," he hurriedly adds, getting back to his feet. "But we're each going to find that right person to make vows to. I'm sure of it."

I tilt my head and smile up at him. "You had me so excited when I thought you meant we'd be reciting vows to one another," I tease. This time my flirting is not premeditated.

"I wouldn't necessarily rule it out." He flashes me his lady-killer grin. It's the first time he has smiled since we were standing in my foyer.

⚜ ⚜ ⚜

Ben and I are seated with two of Renee's college friends, Darlene and Jennifer, and their husbands. Darlene looks like a blond version of Renee, with the same short, spiky haircut, wide forehead, prominent cheekbones, and inflated lips. I'd bet my life they went to the same plastic surgeon.

"You could be her sister," Ben says.

"If you mean the much younger, prettier sister, then yes." Darlene touches Ben's arm as she speaks.

Jennifer has salt-and-pepper hair and a full, round face. I'm pretty sure she's never had work done and can picture her teasing Renee and Darlene about theirs. She hasn't spoken a word but her name, but I like her already.

After we all introduce ourselves, I expect Ben to escape to the bar to watch the Celtics game until dinner is served, because that's what Nico would do. Instead, Ben has the table in stitches with his impersonations of Renee and her hot flashes at work. When he's done with his stories, he says, "Give us the goods on her college years. Stuff we can use to blackmail her."

Darlene and Jennifer talk over each other filling us in on Renee's days at the University of Massachusetts.

As the salad is being served, a hefty man with curly dark hair joins our table. He introduces himself as Tommy Mackay and tells us he's Lenny's cousin. "Looks like I timed it perfectly and missed the vow renewal. What a crock of shit that is." He reaches over me to grab a roll. "You married?" he asks, looking at Ben.

Ben shakes his head. "Smart man," Tommy says.

"Or an unlucky one," Ben mumbles.

His remark surprises me. I look up at him and notice a twinge of hurt in his expression.

Between large bites of his chicken saltimbocca, Tommy tells us about the night Renee and Lenny met. "She was dancing with me first," he says. "We didn't even make it through an entire song. Can't believe Len's put up with her for twenty-five years." He laughs, opening his mouth filled with half-chewed food. "I'm kidding. I love Renee."

Ben elbows me. "Renee wanted to set you up with Tommy," he whispers.

I think he's kidding, but then I remember Renee telling me about Lenny's single cousin. Why in the world would she think this buffoon is a good match for me? *Because he's over thirty and he's single.* Damn. I pick up the glass of red wine the waitress has already refilled two times and take a large sip.

Tommy stares at me like he might have heard what Ben said about Renee wanting to set us up. "Jillian," he says. "That name is familiar. How do you know Renee and Lenny?"

"I work with Renee," I answer. "The both of us do," I say, pointing at Ben.

"That's right," Tommy says. "You're the one who was dating the producer of the morning sports radio show."

Jennifer's husband's head snaps in my direction. "You're Jill from *BS Morning Sports Talk?*"

I reach for my wine again.

"Branigan sure is gunning for you," he says. "What did you do to the guy?"

He and Tommy stare, waiting for me to answer. I take another sip of wine. They don't turn away from me. "I called his ball out," I say. They look at me blankly. "During a tennis match. It was near the line. I said it was out, and he lost because of that."

"Was it out?" Tommy asks.

Ben cocks his head in my direction.

"It was really close. Probably could have gone either way."

Tommy laughs. "Bet you wish you had called it the other way now."

I reach for my glass again, but it's empty. "Excuse me." I bolt for the bar, where I order a rum and Coke.

A few minutes later Ben joins me. "You okay?"

"The ball was on the line," I admit. "I should have called it in."

Lenny and a group of men approach the bar, slapping each other on the back and laughing. Lenny winks at me.

"I know that," Ben says. "It wouldn't make sense for Branigan to go on this vendetta against you if the ball was out." He flags down the bartender and asks for a scotch and soda.

"He was already talking about me before the tennis match."

"No," Ben says. "He arranged a contest for Nico and mentioned that you used to date him."

The anger in his voice surprises and confuses me. "I can't change what I did." I stir the ice in my drink with the swizzle stick.

Lenny and his friends at the bar count backward, shouting, "Three, two, one." They all throw back a shot.

"No, but you can apologize," Ben says. "End this whole thing."

"Why do you sound so mad at me?"

"It's been almost four months, Jill. You should be ready to move on with your life."

I read somewhere that the time it takes to get over someone is two weeks for every year you spent together, which I guess means that Ben is right and I should be over Nico by now.

I drop my hand to Ben's leg and take a deep breath. "I was hoping you could help me move on tonight?" I'm deviating from Ellie's plan; she told me I should wait for Ben to come on to me, but things are spiraling out of control.

He glances down at my hand. "What are you talking about?"

I muster my best seductive look while I slide my hand up his thigh. Just as I reach my intended destination, he jerks away from me.

"Jill, what the hell are you doing?"

"You don't like it?"

He narrows his eyes. "Are you actually trying to get me to sleep with you as a way to get over Nico?"

"I'm ready to move on," I say defiantly.

"Yeah, well, I'm not going to be your rebound guy."

"I promise you'd have a good time." I reach for him again.

He stands. "I was really looking forward to tonight. I used to have the biggest crush on you," he says while shaking his head. "You really need to get yourself together."

I order another drink, thinking I may have just reached rock bottom. Damn, I played that wrong.

Back at the table, the waitstaff is serving strawberry cheesecake. Jennifer leans over to me. "Sorry that all came up," she says. "It must be hard."

I nod.

"It looks like you've moved on just fine." She smiles appreciatively at Ben, who folds his arms over his chest.

"We're not together," I clarify. "We're friends." Or we used to be.

As we eat dessert, the band changes the background music from soft instrumentals to a rendition of Taylor Dayne's "I'll Always Love You," which the lead singer announces was Renee and Lenny's wedding song back in 1991. The guests all watch while Renee and Lenny dance.

When the song ends, the music gets faster. Several people get up to dance, but Ben and I remain sitting.

"Do you mind if I borrow him?" Darlene asks, pulling Ben by the arm. She drags him out to the dance floor.

I slump in my chair as I sit at the table alone. Ben and Darlene laugh as they try to outdo one another with crazy moves. I pull my phone out of my purse to text Ellie for an emergency consultation: "Not going well." Ben glances over at me. He takes Darlene's hand and spins her around in circles. My message doesn't go through because there is no signal.

When the song ends, the music gets slower. Ben and Darlene leave the dance floor. Darlene heads for the bar where her husband is, and Ben returns to his seat next to me. "Who are you texting?" he asks.

"No one."

His jaw tightens.

"Ben, Jillian," Renee calls from the dance floor. "Get out here."

Neither of us moves.

"Don't make me come over there and get you," Renee yells.

"We better," Ben says. He stands and heads toward her without waiting for me.

When I catch up to him, he places one hand on my hip and the other on my shoulder and holds me loosely. Remembering the last time we slow-danced together, I step closer to him, trying to spark something. He immediately steps backward, taking another piece of my self-esteem with him. What was I thinking?

⚜ ⚜ ⚜

Ben and I don't say much to each other on the drive back to my apartment. He stares through the windshield at the road in front of him with a clenched jaw, while I look out the passenger window at the dark houses we pass. The silence in the car screams at me, so I switch on the radio. He has it tuned to the sports station, which is airing a promotion for Monday's morning show. I immediately change the station, flipping until I come to Beyoncé singing about being a boy. I sing along.

Ben glances at me. I can tell he's trying to fight it, but he smiles. "God, you're awful." He takes his hands off the steering wheel to cover his ears. "Please stop," he says. "You're tone deaf and you don't know the words."

In response, I sing louder.

"Seriously, Jillian, stop."

"Let me hear you do better."

He shakes his head.

"I'm going to keep singing until you do." I belt out the chorus.

"Okay," Ben says. "You win." He clears his throat and sings the chorus with me.

We both laugh because he's worse than me. He turns onto my street and pulls into my driveway. The motion lights snap on. The curtains in Mr. O'Brien's living room window move. The old man is probably surprised to see me home so early. It's just after ten. Renee's party was still raging when we left.

Ben's seat belt clicks, surprising me. I turn toward him. "Are you going to come in?" I hate how hopeful I sound.

"I'm going to walk you to the door," he says.

"I'm all set," I say. "I've made it across the porch plenty of times before."

He ignores me and steps out of the car, leaving it running. He silently follows me up the walkway. As we get closer to the house, I see a shock of Mr. O'Brien's white hair in the window. By the time we pass it, he's no longer standing there. On my side of the duplex, Ben holds the storm door open while I turn my key in the lock.

Before I step inside, I turn to face him. "I'm sorry about earlier. It was a bad idea."

"I can't even believe you thought I'd go along with it."

"Ellie said you would."

"Ellie," he mutters.

I think about bringing up the dance at the holiday party and what he said to me, but he'd probably tell me I misunderstood him. I've had enough humiliation tonight. "Good night."

I turn away from him, but he grabs my shoulder and spins me back toward him. "It's not that I don't want to, but the time is definitely not right." He leans toward me, his lips heading for mine. Wrong. He kisses my cheek. "Good night," he whispers, and hurries back across the porch.

I wait in the doorway until he gets back to his car. He gives me a small wave before driving off.

I touch my face where his lips brushed against it, thinking *I wore the uncomfortable underwear for that?*

Chapter 26

My phone rings at eight o'clock the next morning, waking me from a restless sleep. I reach toward the nightstand to grab it, knocking over my bottle of water. I curse under my breath as I say hello.

"Did you have a good time last night?" Ellie asks. I imagine she's been up for hours, staring at the clock waiting for a time she thought wasn't too early to call me.

I try to think about how to answer, the best way to describe the colossal failure that last night was.

"Oh my God," Ellie says, rushing to fill the silence. "Are you still with him?"

"No!"

"Oh." The two-letter word is punctuated with disappointment. I don't know who feels it more, me or her.

"Well, you sound distracted."

"You woke me up!"

"Fine. Go back to sleep."

⚜ ⚜ ⚜

I've been waiting for close to fifteen minutes when I receive Ellie's text telling me she's on her way. We're meeting to walk around the pond. Snowbanks still flank the paved path that winds around it, making it narrower than usual. Runners and walkers dodge a large puddle of melting snow as they pass me. I turn my face toward the sky and revel in the feel of the sun on my face. A jogger pauses and raises her foot up onto the bench next to me to tie her sneaker. "It's like a summer day," she says before taking off again.

Bored from waiting, I pull out my phone again. I take my turn in the latest game of Words with Friends I'm playing with my brother, scroll through Twitter, and then check Facebook. Renee wasted no time posting pictures from last night. She even tagged Ben and me in one. It was taken before I suggested he sleep with me to help me get over Nico. We're sitting at the table and he's smiling at me, not aware that we're being photographed. I, on the other hand, am looking straight into the camera with a huge grin.

The picture has 147 likes and two comments. The first is from Ellie: *Looking good, you two.* The second is from my mother: *Handsome. Is he the "friend" Christian told us about?* Her use of quotation marks makes me want to die.

In the distance, a group of kids on scooters make their way toward me. Ellie is behind them. She sees me and waves, a huge grin on her face as if I invited her here to share good news. When she reaches me, she squeezes my wrist, a playful light in her eyes. "Tell me everything that happened."

"There's nothing to tell. It was a disaster."

Her eyes dim like the lights in a movie theater just before the show starts. "What happened?"

As we walk, I explain how things got off to a good start with Ben bringing me flowers, but then steadily declined with the first glass of wine in my apartment.

"By the time the band was playing, he didn't even want to dance with me."

"It makes no sense," Ellie says. "I saw a picture Renee posted. He looks so into you."

"He was really insulted." I kick a rock and watch it skid across the pavement, bouncing off the shoe of a man walking a few feet in front of us. He turns to look at me, so I mutter an apology.

"What do you mean, he was insulted? I would think he would have been flattered."

"He said he used to have a crush on me, but now he basically thinks I'm pathetic."

Ellie stops to unzip her sweatshirt and tie it around her waist. "What exactly did you say to him?"

"He was giving me a hard time for not being over Nico, so I suggested he help me move on."

"By having sex with you?"

The man in front of us looks back at us over his shoulder. Ellie and I both glare at him until he turns away from us.

"Well, I didn't come right out and say it, but he got my gist."

"Oh, Jillian. You weren't supposed to tell him the reason you wanted to sleep with him. You were supposed to have fun, flirt with him. One thing would lead to the other."

My face burns in embarrassment. "When he dropped me off he said it's not that he didn't want to, but that the timing wasn't right. What does that mean?"

"It means he was trying to let you down easy."

We walk in silence as we pass a group of children feeding the geese in the pond. Once we get by them, Ellie asks, "Were you drunk?"

"I'm done talking about this. Time to move to plan B."

"What's that?" Ellie asks. "Or should I say, who's that? Lucas?"

"Very funny, wise guy. Sleeping with Ben was your idea," I remind her.

"That's because I was secretly hoping something would come of it."

Her words cause a sinking feeling in the pit of my stomach. I'm not sure why.

Chapter 27

Plan B is online dating, and I can't believe I'm resorting to it. The whole drive home I had to talk myself into it. I finally convinced myself it's no different than shopping on Zappos, Rue La La, or Amazon. Instead of buying shoes, clothes, or books, I'm looking for a boyfriend, or at least a date—or someone to help me move on with my life.

Back in my apartment, I log in to the site and guide my cursor to the activate profile button. My finger hovers over the mouse. I count backward from three and click. My profile goes live. I stare at the computer, waiting for something to happen. Nothing does. Well, what did I expect, a bunch of hunky men to burst through my screen?

A button at the top of the screen that says Design Your Ideal Mate catches my attention. Who wouldn't be intrigued by that? I click on it. *Answer these questions to describe the person you most want to date.* Two radio buttons appear under the text: *Male* or *Female*. I click on male. A long questionnaire appears, beginning with *Choose an age range for your ideal mate.* While the directive seems harmless enough, it depresses the hell out of me because it reminds me of how old I am. In less than a month, I'll be closer to fifty than twenty. How can that be? I select thirty-five to forty-four, only because there isn't an option that allows me to choose thirty-five to thirty-nine. I don't want to date a forty-year-old.

Before I move on to the next question, my computer dings. A picture of a man with chubby cheeks and a dark crew cut pops up, filling half my screen. Next to it, an instant message appears: *You have beautiful eyes.*

Whoa! Can he see me? I roll my chair away from the computer. *Relax, Jillian. He's looking at your picture.* Still, I'm creeped out and leave the room. Thirty minutes later when I return, the message is still there, but now under it in smaller text it says Passion Pete has signed off. Passion Pete. Who's going to contact me next, Horny Hank? Maybe this isn't such a good idea.

More wary now, I resume creating my ideal mate. I answer a dozen questions about physical appearance. As I review my answers—light brown hair, green eyes, taller than five ten—I start to feel twitchy, realizing the ideal mate I'm creating looks nothing like Nico but exactly like Ben. I get the same sinking feeling in my stomach that I had at the pond with Ellie this morning and wonder if the reason I want to sleep with Ben has more to do with the fact that I'm attracted to him than getting over Nico.

I go downstairs for an ice-cold glass of water to help me clear my mind. Over the past few months, Nico's coat hanging over the back of the chair has become as familiar a sight as the gray vinyl tile on my kitchen floor. I don't even notice it anymore. Today it jumps out at me the same way a broken egg on the tiles would. I think about how Ben reacted when he saw it last night, how that stupid jacket ruined the good vibe we had going when he first arrived. Perhaps it is time to get rid of it. I can't throw it away though. It's a perfectly good jacket. I promise myself I will donate it to a charity's coat drive. In the meantime, I hang it in the back of the hallway closet.

I return to my desk, ready to move on. Twenty minutes later, I have completed all the preferences for my ideal mate. If only I could press a button and have him shoot out of my printer. Now that would be something. Instead I press *Search* and a list of the closest matches appears.

Before I can read through it, my doorbell rings. By the time I make it downstairs, I hear footsteps outside walking away. I throw open the door. Mr. O'Brien is halfway across the porch to his place. He walks back to my side of the house.

"What took you so long?" he asks.

I was soliciting strangers on the Internet for a date. "I was upstairs."

"I have to get in there," he says. He pulls the storm door open and steps forward.

I block his path because I hate that he never gives me any notice before doing work on my apartment. When Nico lived here, Mr. O'Brien always called before coming over. "Why?"

He clears his throat and points up. "The ice dams. I have to make sure they didn't do any damage, check for leaks."

"There aren't any."

"Are you sure?"

"Well, I haven't noticed any."

"I'm coming in," he says, brushing past me and heading for the stairway.

"You don't have to go up there." I exhale loudly as he traipses through my apartment, leaving his usual trail of sandy wet footsteps behind him. "I would have noticed if the ceiling is leaking."

He pauses on the third step, turns around, and looks at me through narrowed eyes. He clears his throat again. "Am I interrupting something? Is there someone up there?"

"What? No!" *I wish!*

He eyes the top of the stairs suspiciously.

"There's no one up there." For crying out loud, he saw Ben drive away last night.

I follow him up the stairs, noticing the brown age spots on the back of his hand sliding along the railing as he slowly makes his ascent. At the top of the staircase, he pauses to look upward. Nothing there but a pristine white ceiling. He proceeds down the hall to my bedroom. I cringe as he enters because it's a mess. The dress, nylons, and shoes I wore to Renee's party are piled in a heap at the foot of my unmade bed, along with the dress I didn't wear. A laundry basket overflowing with clothes that need to be folded or ironed sits in the middle of the room. A collection of half-empty water bottles lines my nightstand, and the curtains are still closed tight. "Cleaning lady's day off?" he asks.

"There are no stains," I say.

"What are those?" he asks, pointing to the smattering of glow-in-the-dark star decals stuck to the ceiling.

Nico put them there to surprise me. We had planned a week away, camping in Acadia National Park, but I got sick, the flu. In July. Even my doctor couldn't believe it. *It's not something we usually see this time of year,* she said. So while I was sacked out on the couch huddled under an electric blanket to fight off the chills while spiking a fever with a 102 temperature, he was upstairs turning our bedroom ceiling into a night sky so I could pretend I was sleeping outdoors. The memory makes me smile.

"I like to sleep under the stars," I say.

Mr. O'Brien shakes his head. "Then sleep outside. Don't destroy my ceilings."

As we make our way down the hall, he keeps his eyes up, but there is no water damage. I wait in the hallway while he checks the bathroom. "What stinks in here?" he asks.

For the love of God. I lean into the room. "Nothing!"

"It's this!" He picks up my mulberry and thyme diffuser.

"It's an air freshener. It smells good."

He returns it to the vanity. "I prefer to light a match."

Great. Now an image of him sitting on the toilet pops into my head. His tan pants are bunched around his ankles, exposing his skinny pale legs and thick black socks. He's reading a newspaper, and there's a book of matches on the hopper's tank, waiting to be lit.

He follows me to my office. From the doorway, I see the IdealMate website filling up the twenty-seven inches of my iMac's screen. I freeze. Mr. O'Brien bumps into me. "What are you doing stopping like that," he grumbles.

"Nothing to see in here either," I say.

He nudges his way past me. Of course, he heads straight for my desk. His eyes narrow as he looks toward the computer. I think about diving across the room and ripping the plug out of the outlet.

Mr. O'Brien leans closer to the screen. The website's slogan, *Meet Your Ideal Mate*, fills the top half. "What's this?" he asks.

There's no way I'm explaining this to him.

He clears his throat. "Are you doing Internet dating?"

"What's wrong with that?" I ask, surprised he knows about it. "It's how single people meet other single people these days." I hate that I feel the need to defend myself.

"I've heard about these sites on the news," he says. "It's how young women get themselves killed." His mouth twists. "Meeting strangers on the computer, getting in the car with them or going to their houses. Why do you want to do something like that?" He's still facing my monitor, his eyes traveling up and down, looking at the pictures of my ideal matches.

"How else am I going to meet someone?"

"Meet them in real life. Like we did before these new-fangled devices became so popular." He motions with his hand like he's trying to shoo away my computer. "Grocery stores, church, the laundry mat."

My seventy-four-year-old landlord is giving me dating advice. Perfect.

"The key is that you have to keep your eyes open," he says.

I step around him and minimize the screen. "Where did you meet Carol?"

He flinches at the mention of his dead wife's name. "At work. She was the boss's daughter. Came in to help with the phones one day when the regular girl was out sick." He actually smiles as he speaks. I picture him younger, chatting up a secretary while she ignores the ringing telephone behind her. It's one of those old-fashioned ones with the rotary dial. "There must be single men in your office," he says.

Ben's face flashes through my mind. "No one I can date," I say. "That was risky, asking out the boss's daughter."

"Pshh. Dating someone you meet on the computer is risky," he says. "Especially when you're too distracted to notice what's right in front of you." He points to a large yellow stain on the ceiling above my desk. "It's practically dripping on your head. I don't know how you missed it."

Chapter 28

There is no traffic on Monday morning as I drive to work. In fact, there isn't even another car on the highway with me, making me wonder if I missed a detour that bypasses this road.

On the radio Branigan is taking calls. "And on line two we have a caller who claims to work with Jillian," he says.

Here we go again. With the lack of traffic, I thought I might be headed for a good day, but no. I wonder which of my coworkers is selling me out and quickly settle on Ryan. I turn up my radio, waiting to hear what he'll say.

"So how long have you worked with Jill?" Branigan asks.

"Four years." I almost drive off the road when I hear the caller's voice because it is most definitely not Ryan's. It's Ben's. "Guess what she asked me to do to help her get over Nico?"

Maybe I should drive off the road? Why is he doing this to me?

"Why don't you tell us," Branigan says.

Behind me, someone honks. I look in the rearview mirror, surprised to see bumper-to-bumper traffic. Where did it come from so suddenly?

"She solicited me," Ben says.

I feel like he punched me in the gut. Why would he call the show to tell the world that?

"She did the same thing the night of the company holiday party too," he says. "Which was the night after she got engaged."

I might hate Ben more than Nico right now.

Behind me there's beeping again. I glance in my rearview mirror. It's Mr. O'Brien driving an eighteen-wheeler that is bearing down on me.

The honking gets louder as the truck rear-ends me. I hit my head on the steering wheel and black out. I wake up in my bed with my alarm clock blasting and Mr. O'Brien banging on the wall.

It's Monday morning. Time to go back to work and face Ben again. Clearly, I'm dreading it.

⚜ ⚜ ⚜

Neither Renee nor Ben is at the office yet when I arrive. I breathe a sigh of relief and hope that Ben has decided to take the day off. In my cube, I log into the radio station's website to see if the stupid survey is still active. I find that it is—sort of. There is a survey, but it now reads, *Did Nico make a mistake breaking up with Jill?* I don't believe for a second that the radio station posted this question. More likely, Lucas and Ben are at it again. They must have hacked the site before Renee's party, because Ben wouldn't have wanted to help me after it. The headline is the only thing they messed with because *Yes* still accounts for more than 98 percent of the responses, but because of the way the question is worded, those respondents are now on my side.

I turn on my radio to hear what Branigan is saying about the survey. "Whoever is messing with our website scored big this weekend," he says. "Nico and Bonnie had a falling out this weekend and decided to call it quits. Today, Nico would probably be part of the majority of respondents who think he made a mistake breaking up with Jillian."

"Jill never tried to change me," Nico whines.

Nico and Bonnie broke up. I thought when I heard that news my spirits would soar like a helium balloon released from a child's hand. Instead, I feel nothing, except curiosity about what they fought about. Did he leave his jacket hanging over the back of his chair? Pile his dirty dishes and glasses by the sink, expecting her to wash them, or was it something more serious?

My thoughts are interrupted by footsteps and voices in the aisle. I didn't hear the door open so am surprised by the sound of them. "Did you have a good time?" Renee asks.

"Sure," Ben answers. "I enjoyed meeting your friends."

"Did you have fun with Jill?" She says it in a teasing voice.

I remain perfectly still, waiting for his response. There's a long pause. "I hate seeing her so hung up on Nico still," he finally says.

A few seconds later, he enters his cube and looks over the wall into mine. "You're here already?" he asks.

I nod but keep typing and don't turn to face him, hoping he'll think I'm busy and leave me alone.

"Do you want to go to the cafeteria and grab a coffee?" he asks.

"I have to finish this," I say, my fingers dashing across the keyboard.

"Jill, we should talk."

"Later. I have to get this to Stacy."

He stands where he is, watching me, until his phone rings.

❦ ❦ ❦

I successfully avoid Ben all morning. At lunch, he leaves the building with Lucas while Renee and I eat in my cube, reviewing the profiles of the few men who contacted me on the online dating site. The picture we're looking at now is of a pudgy blond man with deep dimples.

"He's absolutely adorable. I want to eat him up," Renee says, taking a bite of her tuna sandwich.

"I don't know. He doesn't seem too smart." I point to the last line of his message. *Lets meat. You definately won't be sorry.*

"Oh, honey," Renee says. "At your age, you can't be ruling out potential dates because of their spelling."

I flinch at her words. When I was a teenager imagining my life in my midthirties, I assumed I'd have a handsome husband; two beautiful children, Amanda and Trevor; and a golden retriever named Agassi. We'd go for nice long walks through our tony neighborhood, my husband holding Agassi's leash with one hand and mine with his other. Our dark-haired kids would be riding their bikes in front of us, Amanda arguing that she was ready for the training wheels to come off and Trevor wanting to stop the ice cream truck. It never occurred to me that I'd be searching a website, looking for a man who is husband material.

"How about him?" Renee asks, using the mouse to click on a user named Doug1234. She studies his picture. "He's not too bad."

"Yeah, that's exactly where I set the bar: not too bad." I stare out the window. It's good to see grass instead of the mounds of snow out there.

"It's hard to reach the bar when you get older, sweetie, so you have to lower it."

"We're done here." I reach for the mouse so I can click off the site.

She moves it away from me. "Not until you respond to someone." She settles back in her chair and crunches on her smelly sour-cream-and-onion potato chips.

I read through Doug's message again. It's perfectly nice. I study his picture. His average-looking face stares back at me. He looks like a typical Bostonian male from Irish descent with his pale skin, light eyes, and receding hairline. I bet when people meet him, they're convinced they've seen him before. *I know you from somewhere,* they probably say. He nods knowingly. *I get that a lot.*

So he's not handsome, but he's not ugly either. Maybe Renee's right. I am being too picky. After all, who do I think I'm going to date?

The Bradley Cooper look-alike who you work with. The thought takes me by surprise, and I get that same sinking feeling in my stomach I had at the pond and when I was creating my ideal match. Do I want more from Ben than one fun night? No! I don't want anything from him. I hit the reply button and type a message to Doug.

"Good girl," Renee says.

The door at the end of the hall buzzes open. Ben's coming down the aisle. I recognize the sound of his walk. He takes larger and therefore fewer strides than anyone else.

He peeks into my cube. "You two look guilty of something." He steps behind me as my message disappears into cyberspace. "What are you doing?"

"Trying to find Princess Picky over here a date," Renee answers.

"You're doing online dating." There's a hostility in his voice that makes me feel like he slapped me across the face. Even Renee flinches.

"What's wrong with that?" I ask.

He folds his arms across his chest. "N-nothing," he stammers. He leans closer to my monitor. "Can I see your profile?"

I bring it up on my screen. He and Renee exchange a look. Until now, she has seen the profiles of the men who contacted me, but not mine. "Oh, honey," she says. "You need a better picture."

It's true. Rachel didn't use the best photograph when she created the profile, and I didn't bother to replace it. In it, I'm sitting at a picnic table in her backyard drinking sangria. My hair is tied back in a ponytail, and my cheeks are flushed. It's probably the only picture she has of me without Nico. It's not the best shot of me, but I don't think it's as bad as Renee suggests.

Ben stares at my screen. "That picture is perfect," he says in a tone I can't read.

Renee elbows him. "I have one from the party you can use," she says. "Ben, I'll send it to you so you can cut yourself out of it."

⚜ ⚜ ⚜

Ben and I don't talk about anything other than work for the rest of the day. Before he leaves for the night, he sends me an email with the subject line "Your Photo." I don't open it until he's gone. His message says *Good luck with online dating.* I blink as I stare at the image. Ben cropped himself out of the picture, but he's also made other changes. He altered my appearance, making me look twice my size. He added deep lines around my eyes and mouth, and sprinkled gray streaks through my dark hair. *What the hell?*

Doug and I exchange several emails throughout the week and agree to meet for a drink on Friday night. When I tell my coworkers, Renee bounces in her seat. "That's exciting," she says.

"You never spoke with him on the phone?" Ben asks. "That's a red flag." He's in his cube, shouting over the wall, but he's sitting so I can't see him. Things have been strained between us all week. I'm not sure if it's because of Saturday night or because I'm doing online dating.

"You're acting like an overprotective father," Renee says.

"Or a jealous ex-lover," Ellie adds. She's leaning against the support pole in Renee's cube.

"I didn't want to talk on the phone. I thought it would be awkward."

"Talking on the phone is awkward but meeting in person isn't?" Ben asks.

"It's easier if I can see his facial expressions and read his body language," I explain, wishing I could see Ben right now so that I could better understand what his objection is and why he's not supporting me in this. Wasn't he just complaining he hates seeing me so hung up on Nico?

"What do you even know about this guy?" he asks. Ellie, Renee, and I all exchange a look because the irritation in Ben's voice is impossible to miss.

"The point of meeting him is to get to know him," I say.

Chapter 29

On Friday night, I sit at a table in the bar facing the entrance, watching for Doug. He's almost ten minutes late. Every time the door opens, my entire body tenses. I hope he doesn't show. I'd rather be curled up on my couch alone with a bowl of popcorn, watching a good movie, than here waiting for him and wondering what he's going to be like. Nico and I had spent more than five hours sitting beside each other, talking and rooting for the Red Sox, so I knew what I was getting on our first date.

In college we had an unwritten rule that we would only wait fifteen minutes for late professors. I'm applying the same principle to online dating, staring at my watch eagerly. Doug has one minute and forty seconds. With less than twenty seconds to go, the door swings open and a man of about fifty steps inside. It doesn't occur to me that he might be my date until he waves. He is at least a decade older than the man I saw in the picture.

"Jillian?" he asks as he approaches my table.

Sorry, no. The words are on the tip of my tongue.

He extends his hand. "I'm Doug. Sorry I'm late. Just as I was leaving, my son called to let me know he got accepted to MIT."

"Wow, he must be bright," I say. What I mean is *wow, you have a kid old enough to go to college.* His profile says he has two kids, but I pictured them being the same age as Rachel's, not a few years younger than me. Okay, that's an exaggeration, but I could probably relate better to his son than to him.

He sits across from me and stares. "You need to get a better picture for the dating site," he says. "The one you have up looks nothing like you."

Because of the ridiculous changes Ben made to Renee's photo, I kept the one that Rachel used. Still, Doug has some nerve. He has black hair in his photograph. In person, it's salt-and-pepper, mostly salt, and there is even less of it than there is in his online image. "My picture doesn't look like me?"

He smiles. It's a nice smile that takes about ten years off his face, making him look about forty-five. "You're much more beautiful in person," he says.

Well, now I feel bad. "Thanks."

A waitress greets us. I order a glass of wine. As Doug asks about beers on tap, I see Lucas's familiar blue cap bobbing through the door. Ben is right behind him. I nervously tap my foot against the leg of the table. *What are they doing here?* They both scan the room, stopping when they see me. Ben flashes me a coy smile. He knows I was coming here tonight, so why would he show up here? He and Lucas make their way across the restaurant to the bar and choose a table facing me. I want to run out the door because the last thing I need is Ben watching my clumsy reentry into the dating world. Wasn't last week's try with him bad enough?

The waitress leaves. I drag my eyes off Ben and Lucas, back to Doug. "So tell me about yourself," he says.

God, I hate that question during job interviews, but it's even worse on a date. I shut my eyes and then slowly open them. "What would you like to know?"

"What do you do for work?"

"I'm in marketing for a company that does cyber security," I answer, realizing I'm doing a horrible job promoting myself. "What about you?"

"I'm an engineer. My company designs robots."

He continues talking about his job while I glance over at Ben. He's leaning back on his stool, exaggerating a yawn and looking at his watch. *Sorry my dates aren't as exciting as yours!*

Doug turns to see what I'm looking at. Ben and Lucas both wave. He nods. "Do you know them?"

"I work with them. I'm sorry. Just ignore them."

"Did you know they were going to be here?"

I shake my head, but I can tell by the look he gives me that he doesn't believe me.

The waitress returns with our drinks. We sip in silence for the most uncomfortable minute of my life. At the table behind Doug, Ben scribbles on a napkin.

"How's online dating working out for you?" Doug asks.

Ben holds up the napkin. In his beautiful penmanship, he's written, "Lose him. Join us."

Why is he even here? "You're the first person I've met."

Following my eyes, Doug looks over his shoulder. Ben drops the napkin to his lap. "Ahh, your first online date. That explains why you brought backup."

I shake my head to reiterate that I didn't know they would be here.

"Don't worry. You'll get used to it," he says.

"How many people have you met?"

"You're the twenty-second."

I almost spit out my wine. "Twenty-second!" He's suffered through this twenty-two times. Kill me now!

"I'd like to figure out what I'm doing wrong." He looks at me eagerly.

I want to cry for him. Honestly, I do. "Well, you know. It's a numbers game. Keep trying and eventually you'll meet her."

"What did you think when you first saw me?"

Oh boy! Why is he putting me on the spot like this? I glance at Ben and Lucas, hoping they'll somehow help me answer this question, but they're talking to their waitress and not paying attention to me. "You're fine."

"No, I saw your face drop when I first came over," Doug says.

Did my face drop? It probably did. I've never been good at hiding what I'm thinking. How can I politely tell him he looks much older than his picture? I look away from him and blurt it out. "I was expecting someone younger." I am the worst person in the world. A woman who discriminates based on age, that's who I am.

"Didn't you see my age in my profile?"

I might as well finish what I started. "You look older than forty-four. Sorry."

"Forty-four," he repeats. "You must be mixing up my profile with someone else's. I'm fifty-five."

I shake my head. "You're the only person I responded to."

He pulls his phone from his coat pocket and busies himself pecking and swiping at it. Finally, his hand freezes. He pulls the screen closer to his face, squinting. "Well, that was a typo," he says. Instead of fixing it, he slides his phone back into his pocket.

I stare at him without saying anything, trying to figure out if his virtual lie was an honest mistake.

"You think I did it intentionally?"

"Your picture is outdated too."

"My daughter picked it out. She said I look handsome in it."

"Well, you do look great for fifty-five." That sounded better in my head.

He winces. "Yes, because men as old as me are usually decrepit."

"I'm sorry. That came out wrong."

The waitress has left Ben's table. He stares at me with a concerned expression, like he can sense the tension over here.

Doug and I sit awkwardly, not speaking. He signals for the check. We've been together for less than fifteen minutes, I have had two sips of my wine, and the date is ending. I am terrible at this.

"I'm sorry I didn't meet you a decade earlier," Doug says. He puts money in the billfold and walks away before I can thank him for the drink or say goodbye.

By the time he reaches the door, Ben has taken his seat. "What happened?" he asks.

"What are you doing here?"

Lucas sidles over to the table and hands Ben his jacket and beer. "I'm taking off," he says.

"Not so fast. Why were you here in the first place?" I ask. "To spy on me?"

"Spy? That makes it sound bad. We came here to keep an eye on you."

"Why?"

Lucas shrugs and points to Ben. "His idea." He pats Ben on the back. "See you Monday, Bro."

Ben and I stare at each other across the table. "Why are you here?" I ask.

He lifts his mug. "To make sure you didn't do anything stupid."

I watch his Adam's apple bob up and down as he sips his beer. "Like what?"

He returns his glass to the table and raises an eyebrow. "Seriously, what did you think I would do?"

"I didn't want you to make the same suggestion to him that you made to me last week."

"You suck!" People at nearby tables turn to look at us. I lower my voice. "You think I would ask just anyone that?"

"I don't know where your head's at."

I reach behind me for my coat. "You, Ben. You're the only one I would ask."

As I slide my hand into the sleeve of my jacket, he reaches for my arm. "Please don't go."

I shake free of his touch and stand. "Why do you care anyway?"

"Because I care about you!" He grabs my arm again. "Please, sit back down."

I let out a deep breath and return to my chair.

"If we hadn't started talking about Nico that night, you wouldn't have had to ask me," he says. "When I saw you in that dress, I didn't even want to go to Renee's party, but then I saw that stupid jacket in the kitchen. Like you're just waiting for him to come back."

My eyes get misty because Ben's right. I have been waiting. I look away from him.

"He doesn't deserve you, Jill."

"Over the past few years, he's been the one constant in my life. My brother moved. My parents left. Rachel started her own family. He was the only one who was always there for me."

"Things change. People leave. That's life," Ben says. He motions for the waitress and orders us both another drink.

As we wait, he looks around the bar. "Table to the right of the emergency exit," he says. "They're on a blind date."

"How's it going?" I ask.

"A lot better than yours did."

I smile, happy to have things back to normal between us. "I don't know. I think mine has turned out all right."

The waitress returns with our drinks. "To us having a good time together," Ben says, clanking his beer mug against my wine glass.

"So why no date tonight?" I ask.

He tilts his head and studies me. "There's this girl I've been wanting to ask out, but the timing has never been right."

"Why not?"

"Jillian? Is that you?" I turn. Tania from my tennis club is standing behind me. "Haven't seen you since the tournament," she says while she hugs me. "Are you injured?"

"No, I, I've been busy."

I introduce her to Ben. Despite Tania's protests, he stands to shake her hand. I imagine that if I were here with Nico, he'd look back at her over his shoulder, nod, and then immediately return his attention to the television above the bar.

Tania turns to me. "With his height, he'd make a great partner," she says. I raise an eyebrow at her. "Nothing would get by him at the net." *A tennis partner, of course.* She addresses Ben. "You should do the mixed doubles tournament with Jill next year."

He nods. "I'd love to. Jill and I make a great team."

"Are you any good?" Tania asks Ben.

"At tennis?"

She nods. "I can hold my own," he says.

An image of us giving Branigan a smackdown in the final flashes through my mind, Ben hugging me by the net after the winning point. We should do it.

A woman sitting at a table in the dining room motions to Tania. "Hope to see you at the club soon," she says before leaving to join her friend.

"So why haven't you been playing?" Ben asks.

"The members want to tar and feather me."

"You can't let them scare you off."

"I'm not going back there."

"You are and you're taking me," he says.

Chapter 30

Ben's car rumbles into the driveway right on time on Saturday morning, but I'm not ready. The red wine I drank last night has left me moving in slow motion today. I peek out the window. Mr. O'Brien, Zachary, and Ben are admiring Ben's vehicle, a black Dodge Charger with a Hemi engine that emits testosterone from the exhaust pipe. Ben must be introducing himself, because he shakes Zac's and Mr. O'Brien's hands.

I rush to finish getting dressed. When I finally make it outside, Zachary and Ben are laughing at something Mr. O'Brien is saying. My landlord gestures wildly with his hands as he speaks.

I edge my way into their circle. "Walter had a sixty-three Dodge Charger," Ben tells me.

It takes me a minute to realize that he's talking about my landlord. First, I'm used to thinking that his first name is Frank, the fake name he gives on the radio. Second, in all the time I've lived here, I've always called him Mr. O'Brien. Never once has he said *call me Walter*, but in two minutes of meeting him, Ben's already on a first-name basis. I guess I shouldn't be surprised.

"Best car I ever owned," Mr. O'Brien says. "I'll dig out some pictures. Show you them the next time you're here."

Mixed Signals

"Looking forward to it," Ben says.

I raise an eyebrow at him, wondering what he told Mr. O'Brien about who he is.

Ben walks around to the passenger door of his car and holds it open while I climb in. As I wait for him to circle back to the driver's side, I look up at Mr. O'Brien. He's standing at the end of the walkway watching me. He nods before turning around and making his way back inside.

"You sure made fast friends with him," I say, trying to remember an amicable conversation Nico ever had with my landlord. Mostly all I remember is Mr. O'Brien growling at Nico and Nico complaining that Mr. O'Brien was senile.

"I love talking to old people," Ben says. "They have so many great stories. He told me about every car he's ever owned. That ninety-six Buick he drives now belonged to his late wife. He hates it but can't stand the thought of getting rid of it."

"Sweet," I say, realizing that's not generally a word that comes to mind when I think about Mr. O'Brien, but then I remember the coffee cup. He keeps surprising me with his sentimentality.

"I think he really wanted to take my car for a spin. See how it compares to the one he had fifty years ago."

I imagine Mr. O'Brien behind the wheel of Ben's car. The sunroof is open, and all the windows are down. Mr. O'Brien's baseball cap flies off. His snow-white hair blows in the wind, that one dark piece sticking straight up. The old man can't stop laughing as he drives faster and faster. It's the best time he's had since the station wagon became his. "You should let him," I say.

❖ ❖ ❖

Sean's black Porsche is in the parking lot when we arrive at the tennis club. "Branigan is here," I say, pointing at his expensive sports car.

Ben whistles. "Sweet wheels."

Perhaps he didn't notice the apprehension in my voice. I brace myself for an encounter with Branigan as Ben and I cut across the pavement to the entrance.

I check in and get our court assignment while Ben wanders around looking at the pictures on the wall. At the front desk, there's a flyer announcing a rematch of the mixed doubles tournament. A feeling of relief washes over me as I read it. Maybe if Branigan wins, he'll leave me alone.

I find Ben standing in front of a picture of Branigan and Tammy receiving the runner-up trophy after last month's doubles tournament. "He looks like he wants to kill someone," Ben says.

"Yeah, me."

The bell rings, and we head downstairs and through the tunnel to our court.

As I push aside the curtain leading into the bubble, I hear a ball bouncing. Branigan is part of a foursome playing on the court next to ours. I stop to wait for their point to be over before we cross through their court. Ben wasn't expecting me to stop and crashes into me, pushing me forward so that I trip over the rope that ties the curtain down. I end up with my face planted in the clay.

Ben scrambles to my side to help me up. "Are you okay?"

I reach for his extended hands. He pulls me to my feet. I'm still holding them when Branigan notices us. "Well, well," he says. "Who do we have here?" He walks toward us from the baseline. I let go of Ben's hands. Branigan's eyes run up and down Ben's body. "Are you a new member?"

"A friend of Jill's," Ben answers.

I smile, stupidly happy that he didn't say coworker.

"A friend of Jill's," Branigan repeats. He turns toward me. "Good for you, Jillian." He places a hand on Ben's arm like they're old friends. "Just to warn you, she goes a little crazy after a breakup."

Ben starts to say something, but I grab him by the elbow, leading him through the opening in the curtain, to our court. I can tell by the white-knuckle grip he has on his tennis racquet that he's as annoyed by Branigan as I am. "You okay?" he asks.

"I'm fine."

He watches me strip off my sweatpants and jacket, revealing my white tennis skirt and tank top. A huge grin breaks out across his face.

"What?" I ask.

"That's what you wear?" He stares at my legs.

One of the benefits of the jogging I do and the tennis I play is that they are super toned. Nico used to love running his hand along my thigh. He'd pay more attention to it than my breasts, which is probably a good thing because they're virtually nonexistent. Just in case Ben's a leg guy too, I tense my muscles so that they look more defined. "We should start," I say.

"Right," he says, finally raising his eyes to my face.

We warm up by tapping the ball back and forth to each other. Ben lets it bounce before returning it, but I take it in the air, trying to improve my net game. When he tries to imitate what I'm doing, the ball skids off his racquet to the right, landing out of bounds. "You make it look so easy," he says.

"Keep your wrist still and use your shoulder as the hinge," I call. "The racquet's path should be high to low."

He tries again. This time the ball shoots high in the air and almost comes down on his head. "Forget it," he says.

"You need to be able to do this if we're going to take him on." I use my thumb to point to Branigan, who is pounding a forehand at his female opponent.

I walk around to Ben's side of the court, where I stand behind him and place my hand over his on the racquet. His immediately tenses. I squeeze it. "Relax. I'm just showing you how to volley." I wrap my other arm around his waist and guide his swing. "Go down on the ball. Almost a gentle rub with the edge of your racquet." His motion is jerky, and he hits up on the invisible ball instead of down. "Are you even listening to me?"

He looks at me over his shoulder with a sheepish grin. "You smell really good. It's distracting me." He bends toward me, almost burrowing his face in my neck, and inhales sharply before moving away. "Vanilla," he says.

My neck tingles, and I feel woozy. "It's my shower gel."

I return to my side of the net, and we start our first game. Deep in the court, we slide and shuffle from side to side, pounding the ball back and forth. When I'm trying to add power to my swing, I grunt. As our rally goes on, my grunting gets louder.

Finally I pound the ball into the back right corner. Ben is all the way over on the left side of the court and scrambles to get to the other side, reaching with his long arm and swinging wildly. He misses the ball. "Yes!" I scream, pumping my fist.

"Sounds like you're having an orgasm over there, Jillian," Branigan says. He's standing by the opening in the curtain, watching us. He winks at Ben. "Was it as good for you?"

"Come on, Sean," Tammy calls.

He turns for the exit but stops. "Did you hear, there's going to be a rematch of the finals?"

"Good luck," I say.

"I don't need luck, just an honest linesman." He steps toward the exit but stops to turn back to me. "After I win, you can come on the show and apologize for stealing the first match from me. Then we can get back to being friends like we used to be."

Instead of answering, I serve the ball to Ben. We begin our next point. "Think about it," Branigan calls out.

After four games, I have a four–love lead on Ben. In the fifth game, I jump to a thirty–love lead. On the next point, Ben whacks the ball so hard that it flies over the baseline and bounces off the wall behind me. I walk over to where it lands, bend over and pick it up. "Sorry," he says, but his eyes twinkle with mischief.

We start the next point, and the same thing happens. He shrugs when I look at him. After the third time, I know he's doing it on purpose. "What gives?" I ask.

He tilts his head and gives me a sheepish grin. "Kind of enjoying watching you bend over to pick up the ball in that short little skirt."

I feel myself blushing and get that same fluttery feeling I've had around him since Nico left.

Chapter 31

I hear the jingle for *BS Morning Sports Talk* as soon as I walk through the door to my area. When I get to my row, Ben's leaning back in his chair with his hands laced behind his head and his feet kicked up on his desk. "They're going to talk about the new guy in your life," he calls out as I walk by, stopping me in my tracks.

"What new guy?" Renee asks. Holding a bowl of yogurt overflowing with strawberries and blueberries, she rolls her chair out of her cube into the aisle.

"Apparently Jillian played tennis over the weekend with an extremely handsome man." Ben uses air quotes so I know the description is not his own.

Renee's eyes grow to twice their normal size. "So things went well with your online date and you saw him again." She nods as she says it.

She's so excited that I feel bad telling her. "Not quite."

"Well, then who did you play with?"

"Yours truly," Ben answers.

"Oh." The disappointed look on Renee's face says so much more than the one word she utters.

The advertisement ends. Branigan comes back on the air. "For those of you upset that we've been too hard on Nico's ex, there's no need to worry about her. I saw Jillian at the tennis club this weekend with her new love interest."

"Ben, your love interest," Renee repeats, as though she finds the idea ridiculous.

Meanwhile, my face feels like it's on fire. *Is that what Ben has become?*

"Jill and Ben," Ryan screams from his row. "I knew it!"

Branigan continues. "I'm comfortable enough in my manhood that I can say this. He's a good-looking young man."

"How good-looking?" Smyth asks.

"Well, when Jillian was with Nico, she was definitely the better-looking part of the duo. With her new guy though, she's dating up. Way up. He looks like the American Sniper—not the real one, but the actor who played him in the movie."

Dating up? What the hell?

"Bradley Cooper," Zachary chimes in. "I met him at my granddad's this weekend. Ben, not Bradley Cooper."

Ben has a dopey smile on his face, clearly enjoying being talked about on the radio. He points to himself with his thumb. "Movie-star handsome." He chuckles, almost as if he doesn't know it's true.

"So, Nico," Branigan asks, "how do you feel about Jill moving on?"

The radio is silent for several seconds. I swear I hear that weird clicking sound Nico makes with his tongue when he's stressed. Finally, his voice comes over the airwaves. "All I've ever wanted is for Jill to be happy." His tone is eerily reminiscent of the time he told my mother he loved the sweater she gave him for Christmas minutes after he came back from returning it.

⚜ ⚜ ⚜

Rachel has a doctor's appointment near my building. Her mom is watching Sophie, Laurence, and Jacob, and Rachel's not ready to give up her kid-free time, so when the appointment ends, she calls me to go to lunch. I have a meeting at one and can't be gone for long, so instead of going to eat we decide to take a quick walk around my office park.

As I wait for her in the visitor parking lot, I see her green minivan chugging up the hill. It's covered in a grimy coat of salt and dust. She pulls into a spot in front of me, straddling the line separating it from the next. She throws open her door, and it scrapes against the car parked to the left. Oblivious, she steps onto the sidewalk, greeting me with a hug.

She looks me up and down. "You look great, Jill." I'm wearing my favorite outfit, the short black skirt, blue sweater, and tall boots.

"Why do you sound so surprised?"

She laughs. "No offense, but you've been miserable the last few times I've seen you."

We set off in the direction Rachel came from. While the snow has all melted, the stakes marking the road for the plow remain, warning us not to get too optimistic about spring's arrival, because Mother Nature could make another sneak attack at any time.

"So what is this about you playing tennis with Ben?" Rachel asks. "What's going on?"

"You listened to the show this morning?"

"Mark did. He said they called Ben your new love interest." Her face is pinched. "Why do I have to hear these things secondhand?"

"It's not true."

Her expression relaxes. "Thank God!"

The sun, which has been hiding behind the one puffy white cloud in the bright blue sky, pops out. "He's actually a good guy."

Rachel inches toward the trees lining the edge of the sidewalk so that she can be in the shade. "From everything you've told me about him, he's a player, and the last thing you need is to be played again."

"How did Nico play me? We were together for six years."

"And that entire time he made you believe he would marry you."

A car approaches from behind, beeping. Lucas's Jeep pulls up next to us. The roof is off, and Ben is riding shotgun. "We're going to Dom's for lunch. Can I bring you something back?" he asks. His hair is already windblown from the brief ride from the parking garage to the spot on the hill where we are standing. I resist the temptation to reach out and smooth down his curls.

He looks past me to Rachel. "Hello," he says.

I introduce him and Lucas. She moves to the edge of the sidewalk, next to Lucas's vehicle. "I've heard a lot about you," she says as she pushes her sunglasses back into her mass of black curly hair.

Ben eyes me. "I'm probably not as bad as she makes me seem."

Lucas revs the engine.

"I'll have a—"

Ben cuts me off. "I know. The caprese."

The Jeep continues its descent toward the main road. Rachel waits until it's out of sight before speaking. "Does he always look at you that way?" she asks.

"What way?"

She wraps an arm around my shoulder. "Oh, Jill, you always miss what's so obvious to everyone else."

⚜ ⚜ ⚜

When I get home from work, I rummage around the refrigerator, looking for something to eat. As usual there is no food except for two eggs and a little bit of milk. I hate grocery shopping. Nico used to do it all. I search through the cabinets. They are as barren as the fridge, though.

With few other options, I decide to make scrambled eggs for dinner. I crack one against the side of the counter and empty it into the mixing bowl. A piece of shell floats on top. I try to scoop it out with a spoon but can't separate it from the slimy, stretchy goo, so I dip my finger into the mess to extract it. Nico used to laugh watching me cook the few times I tried. *Good thing I'm around or you'd be five hundred pounds from all the fast-food takeout you'd be eating.* He'd kiss the top of my head. *Go relax, and I'll finish this.* He'd take over dinner preparations while I caught up on what he used to call my girly shows, *The Good Wife* or *The Affair*.

Since I heard him on the radio this morning, I haven't been able to forget what he said on the air or how he said it. *All I've ever wanted is for Jill to be happy.* As I beat the eggs and milk, I think about his jacket, wondering why he hasn't come back for it. The butter heating up in the frying pan sizzles, so I turn down the burner. The fire extinguisher resting in the brackets mounted to the wall next to the stove catches my eye. Nico is fastidious about planning for worst-case scenarios and installed it there the day he moved in.

I pour the contents from the mixing bowl into the skillet. As I wait for the eggs to begin to set, I think about how he always has contingency plans. If we were spending a day at the beach, he'd have a list of ideas of what we could do if it rained. If we went out to dinner without a reservation, on the drive to the restaurant he'd list his second and third options in case the wait was too long. If we were going to see a movie, he'd have second and third choices in case his first was sold out.

The eggs have finally begun to set, so I pull the mixture around the skillet with my spatula, moving the cooked pieces away from the bottom and bringing the remaining liquid closer to the flame. As I stare down at the large, soft curds of egg, it occurs to me that I am Nico's plan B. He left his jacket here and hasn't asked for the ring back in case things don't work out for him. He knows me well enough to know that as long as I think there's a chance he'll return, I'll wait. After all, how many other women would wait six long years for a proposal? Agitated, I whisk the eggs around the pan, sending some flying over the top onto the stove. It's time to show Nico that I've changed. I'm not the same girl he left.

⚜ ⚜ ⚜

The following evening when I get home from work, Zac's Civic is parked in the driveway behind his grandfather's station wagon. As I walk by Mr. O'Brien's living room window, I see the two of them sitting on the couch watching a baseball game.

Inside my apartment, I head straight upstairs to my bedroom, to the bureau with the ring. I pull open the drawer and find it at the back. The diamond still sparkles, like it's full of hope and promise for the future. I slip it back on my finger, struggling to get it over my knuckle, which is weird because I never had a problem with that before. I look down at my hand. The ring, which I always thought was so perfect for me, doesn't look like it belongs there, especially because my nails are a mess, uneven in length and some with ragged edges. It's definitely time for a manicure, which I used to get once a week when I was wearing the diamond. The ring slides off easier than it went on. I place it in the small blue box it was in when Nico gave it to me and head downstairs to the closet for his leather coat.

Mr. O'Brien and Zac are both cheering wildly when I ring the bell. My landlord opens the door with a huge smile, which must mean the Red Sox are winning. It's the beginning of April. The season started a few days ago, and already the old man has his hopes up.

"Can I talk to Zac for a minute?" I ask.

If Mr. O'Brien is surprised to see me standing on his welcome mat with a jewelry box and Nico's coat, he doesn't show it. He pushes open the screen door and motions for me to come in. Even though I've lived next door for more than eight years, I can count on one hand the number of times he's invited me in. Like the few other times I was in my landlord's house, the collage of photographs of his wife at different stages of her life captures my attention. There's a picture of her as a beautiful twenty-something bride with a young, smiling Mr. O'Brien standing beside her; as a new parent with a baby Colleen cradled in her arms; as the mother of a teenage daughter with a laughing Colleen standing next to a bicentennial sign with tall ships in the harbor behind her. The one that really gets me is the image of her as a frail older woman, resting all her weight on Mr. O'Brien, whose smile doesn't reach his eyes, as though he knows their time together is almost over.

Mr. O'Brien catches me staring at the collage. "My Carol. It's like it all happened yesterday," he says. "You think you have all this time, but it goes by in the blink of an eye."

Zac rises from the couch. He places a comforting hand on his grandfather's shoulder. "What's up?" he asks.

"Can you do me a favor and give these back to Nico?" I extend the ring box and coat toward him.

"Is that what I think it is?" he asks, pointing to the box.

"Probably. Can you make sure he gets it?"

"Sure," Zac says.

As I hand over Nico's belongings to Zac, Mr. O'Brien removes his hat, like he's witnessing a solemn event.

Chapter 32

On Wednesday night, Ben and I are sitting at the bar at Donovan's. This morning when I told him that I returned the coat and ring to Nico, he insisted on taking me out for a drink to celebrate. "So when's your next online date?" he asks.

"There's no way I'm telling you."

The bartender slides a glass of wine in front of me and a beer to Ben.

"So you have one?"

"Maybe."

Ben raises his mug for a toast. "To it going as well as your last one."

"My last one was a disaster."

"Exactly," he teases.

I spin my bar spool so that I'm looking at his profile. "Why are you so opposed to me doing online dating?"

He turns his chair toward me as well. "Jillian." He says my name in a low, quiet voice that sends chills down my spine. He looks into my eyes hard, like he's considering whether he should share the secret of life with me. After several seconds, he turns away and picks up his beer again. "Because there are a lot of freaks on those sites. They're dangerous."

A blanket of disappointment covers me. What did I expect him to say? *Because I want to date you.* Fat chance. "I can weed them out."

Two women plant themselves on the stools next to Ben. He doesn't notice them. "What happened with the guy from Friday?"

"He lied about his age and used an old picture."

He pokes my arm. "Proving that you can't weed them out."

"Next time I'll be sure the profile has a bunch of pictures, not just one."

Ben reaches into the bowl of peanuts on the bar and tosses a handful into his mouth.

"You shouldn't eat those." I slide the dish closer to me.

"Why not?"

"You don't know who's had their hands in there or what they were doing with those hands."

He pulls the nuts back toward him and scoops up another handful. When he's done chewing, he says, "You need to lighten up, Jillian Atwood." He picks out one peanut and extends it toward me. "Eat it," he commands. "I dare you." He wiggles it in front of my mouth.

I lean away from his outstretched arm. "No way!"

Ben summons the bartender. "Two shots of tequila."

"What? No!"

"I'm going to teach you how to lighten up."

"I'm not doing shots."

"Fair enough." He picks a peanut out of the bowl and holds it between his thumb and index finger. He reaches toward my face and traces my lips with it. His finger grazes the tip of my tongue, and just for a second I taste his skin. I swallow hard. "Peanut or a shot. The choice is yours," he says.

"Neither."

He nudges my chair with his foot. "That wasn't a choice."

He makes a show of eating peanuts until the bartender returns and places the shot glasses in front of us.

"What's it going to be?" Ben asks, rolling another peanut over his finger.

I glance at the bowl and then around the room. A man on the other side of the bar swipes the inside of his ear with his finger and then reaches into the bowl of peanuts in front of him. I pick up the shot glass. "Bottoms up." I shoot down the tequila in one large swallow. YUCK! It burns going down and the taste makes me want to vomit. I frantically reach for my wine, gulping it down to wash away the nastiness of the tequila.

Ben doubles over, laughing. "You should see your face," he says. "I wish I had recorded that."

"Your turn." I point to the second shot glass.

He slides it toward me. "That's for you too. If you want me to drink it, you know what to do." He pops another nut into his mouth and chomps down on it. He swivels in his bar stool and rests his feet on the bottom of mine, grazing my leg with his and sending sparks all the way up my body. *Why does he have this effect on me after all these years of knowing him?*

I pick up the glass. Ben's eyes widen. "Seriously? You'd rather do another shot than eat one lousy peanut?"

He reaches into his coat pocket for his phone. I slam down the contents of the glass before he can video me. This time I make a noise to go with my twisted expression. Several people around the room turn to look. I ignore them and guzzle down my remaining wine.

Ben smiles. "Didn't think you had it in you, Jillian. I'm impressed."

The tequila and the wine must be working their magic because I'm feeling wonderfully buzzed. "I am impressive." Salt from the peanuts dots his navy oxford. I reach out to wipe it away, letting my hand linger on his chest, my fingers drifting to the hair exposed by his open buttons.

He stares down, then slowly lifts his eyes to mine. "Jillian." He says my name the same way my mother used to when she was losing patience with me and I was about to get in big trouble.

I drop my hand to my lap. Damn. How many times does he need to reject me before I take the hint. I swivel my chair so that I'm not facing him. He grabs the backrest and spins me toward him. His expression reminds me of a sympathetic doctor about to break bad news to a favorite patient. I can see the excuses going through his mind like the news ticker on the bottom of a television screen as he thinks of a way to let me down gently: *You're not over Nico yet. It would ruin our friendship. You're like a sister to me.*

No matter which one he chooses, I'll know what he really means: *I'm not attracted to you.*

What he says is, "Not while we're working together."

Chapter 33

As Ellie and I look through the shelves of nail polish, picking out colors for our manicures, her stomach grumbles. "I need to get something to eat after this," she says. It was my idea to come here at lunch. She wanted to go to the sandwich shop.

She chooses a shade of red called Size Matters while I select my usual light pink to go with my standard French manicure.

"Do something different," Ellie encourages. She hands me a bottle. I laugh as I read the name: Get to Bed Red.

We take seats in side-by-side stations. My manicurist inspects my nails and says something to Ellie's manicurist in what I think is Vietnamese. They both laugh. Every time I get my nails done, the person doing them speaks to another salon employee in a language I can't understand. I always think they're talking about me, saying something like *her fingers are fat* or *how is it possible to chip your nails like that*. They go on for so long though, that their conversation can't be about only my hands, so I worry that they're critiquing my entire appearance. *Have you ever seen hair so limp? She's too old for acne, don't you think? What was she thinking when she got dressed this morning?*

Ellie, of course, is not bothered by her manicurist speaking a language she can't understand. She scrolls through her BlackBerry with the hand the manicurist isn't working on, paying no attention to the foreign dialogue. It has probably never occurred to her that they might be talking about her. If it did, she would assume they were complimenting her. *Her hair is so pretty. Have you ever seen eyes so blue. She must work out eight hours a day to get a body like that.*

"What's your name?" I ask the woman working on me.

"Kimberly," she answers.

"I'm Jillian. Nice to meet you."

Ellie's manicurist says something, and they burst out laughing again. I raise an eyebrow at Ellie, who only shrugs as she drops her phone into her purse. Kimberly removes the old polish from my left hand and points to the small bowl of soapy water for me to soak it in while she works on the right one.

Just as Ellie is about to dunk her fingers, her phone rings. Instead of ignoring it, she pulls it out again. "It's a client," she says to her manicurist by way of an apology. She doesn't want to miss any opportunities, because Ryan is threatening to overtake her as the top salesperson this quarter. Last week, he closed a big deal with the sports radio station. They were an obvious target, the way Lucas and Ben have been hacking their website, and Ellie is furious with herself for not cold-calling them herself.

"Ellie Gardner," she says cheerfully into her phone. A second later, she mouths to me, "Candace from SharkBytes." They are by far our top client, outspending our second and third clients combined. Landing that account was Ellie's biggest coup.

The two manicurists talk among themselves, occasionally glancing at Ellie, who smiles at them.

"Ben Colby," Ellie says. My head snaps toward her. "Sure, I know him." She widens her eyes at me. "About four years."

Kimberly lightly slaps my hand to get my attention. "Switch," she says, pointing to the hand that's soaking. I take it out of the bowl and dunk the other. She drips oil on the nails of the hand that just came out of the bowl and pushes back my cuticles.

Ellie changes the hand she's holding the phone with so that her manicurist can begin working on it. "He's extremely creative," she says. "He recently redesigned our website."

A feeling of dread overtakes me. "Why are they asking about Ben?"

Ellie holds her finger to her lips and turns her back to me.

Kimberly taps my knuckle. "Relax your hand," she says.

"I'd hate to see him go, but yes, I think he'd be a great addition to your team."

An addition to your team.

"So tense," says Kimberly, who's now massaging moisturizer into the back of my hand.

Ellie returns her phone to her purse.

"Did you just give a reference for Ben?"

She nods. "They're hiring a new creative director for their in-house agency. Ben interviewed."

"He's getting a new job," I say in a panicked voice, trying to imagine work without him. It would be miserable.

"I guess so," Ellie says. "I wish he had given me a heads-up on needing a reference so I would have been better prepared."

How could he be interviewing without telling me? And then it hits me. Maybe he did tell me last week when we went out for drinks. I replay his words in my head: *Not while we work together.* Maybe he wasn't letting me down gently like I thought. Maybe he was telling me to be patient.

❦ ❦ ❦

Back at the office, Ben is at his desk working on an image that's enlarged on his monitor. The tip of his tongue is folded over his top lip as he maneuvers his mouse, dropping and dragging letters and shapes in different spots on the screen. He's focusing so hard on what he's doing that he doesn't notice me standing in his cube entrance, watching him. He loves this job and he's good at it. Why would he want to leave?

"Is that for the brochure?" I ask.

His hand jerks so that the mouse skids off its pad. "I had no idea you were there."

As I step into his office, he moves a bag off his guest chair so I can sit. "I was just with Ellie." I pause.

Ben turns back to his computer. "Okay."

"SharkBytes called. About you."

"Oh." He spins his chair so that he's facing me again. "They weren't supposed to do that."

"What's going on?"

His cell phone rings. He reaches across his desk to silence it. "This isn't how I wanted you to find out."

"So you are leaving?" I whisper.

He bends toward me and answers in a low voice. "If I get the job."

"Why?"

He gives me the same look he gave me at Donovan's last week, like he's weighing the weight of the world. "It's been eight years. It's time," he finally says.

Renee calls out to us, "Hey, guys. Time for our meeting with Stacy."

I stand. "It won't be the same here without you."

He reaches for my arm as I turn to leave. "Jill, there are other reasons."

His intense expression causes my knees to buckle.

"We should talk, but this isn't the time or place," he says.

Chapter 34

Thursday night I'm in the kitchen pouring my bowl of Rice Krispies for dinner when someone tries to open the front door. At first I think it might be Mr. O'Brien, but he always rings the bell. When whoever is at the door can't get in, they fiddle with the lock. My entire body stiffens. I scramble for my phone and punch in 9-1. I leave my finger hovering over the 1 as I tiptoe toward the hallway. Before I reach it, the person gives up trying to unlock the door and knocks.

"Jill?"

I recognize Nico's voice immediately and move my hand away from the phone's number pad. What's he doing here? For months I was sure his leather coat would lead him back. Now that he has it, he decides to come over?

"Hey," he says when I pull the door open. We stare at each other for a few seconds. The first thing I notice is that even though it's about sixty degrees and there's no need for it, he's wearing the stupid jacket. The next thing I realize is that he looks better than he did when I saw him at the mall. His Greek skin is darker than usual, and his chocolate brown hair has streaks of gold, like he's been out in the sun. The mustache and goatee are gone, replaced by his usual light beard this time of night.

He pulls open the storm door. I quickly step in front of him, blocking his path so that he can't get in. "What are you doing here?" I ask.

There's a loud slapping sound. Mr. O'Brien hovers nearby on the porch, banging his doormat over the railing, something I've never seen him do before.

"Can we talk?" Nico asks.

Mr. O'Brien clears his throat. I glance over at him. He tugs on the bill of his baseball cap, scratches his nose, and then wipes his mouth. I wonder if he's trying to give me signs like a third-base coach.

"I have nothing to say to you."

Mr. O'Brien nods.

Nico turns toward him and back to me. "All you have to do is listen."

Mr. O'Brien shakes his head. I wish he would go inside. I'm not sure I'm comfortable with him here listening to me and Nico.

"Can I come in?" Nico asks.

Okay, I'm definitely more comfortable with Mr. O'Brien eavesdropping than Nico coming inside. "You can say whatever it is you need to say right there."

"Please, Jill. Give me a chance to explain."

Most of me is outraged that he would show up here and expect me to talk to him after everything he has put me through the past few months. Still, there's a tiny piece of my heart that wants to hear him say he's sorry, that he misses me, and wants to try again—even if it's just so I can shoot him down. "Months ago when I wanted you to explain, you wanted no part of it." I'm trying to sound confident but even to me, my voice sounds shaky. Why do I always have to get so emotional?

Mr. O'Brien, still banging the mat over the railing, shuffles down the porch closer to us.

"You shouldn't have come here," I add in a steadier voice.

"I get that you're mad, Jill. I don't blame you, but please—"

"You get that I'm mad! You have no idea!" I try to slam the door, but Nico uses his foot to hold it in place.

"Please, Jillian. Just hear me out." It's the same desperate tone he uses when praying to the television during the tense parts of a big game. *Please, Big Papi. Knock it out of the park. Come on, Tom. Put it in the end zone. Let's go, Bergeron, score.*

"It's too late. I don't want to hear anything you have to say."

He starts to speak again, but I cut him off. "You should leave."

"Not until you hear what I have to say." He puts his hands on his hips and widens his stance.

Mr. O'Brien throws the mat to the ground. It lands with a thud. The old man's shuffle turns into a deliberate stride as he makes his way toward my side of the house. When he reaches my door, he grabs Nico's shoulder with one of his large, age-spotted hands. "She asked you to leave."

Oh boy! There's going to be a fight. I can imagine that Mr. O'Brien has wanted to slug Nico for a long time. Would Nico hit him back?

"Mr. O'Brien, it's okay."

"I'm just trying to talk to her," Nico says. He jerks his arm forward trying to free himself, but Mr. O'Brien has a firm grip on him.

"She's made it clear she doesn't want to hear anything you have to say."

Mr. O'Brien's face is bright red. The squiggly vein running from his forehead to his right ear is bulging so much that I'm afraid it might burst or he'll have a heart attack right here at my front door. "Please, Nico, just leave."

"Okay, okay." He raises his arm as he says this, inadvertently bumping Mr. O'Brien's hat off his head.

Murder flashes through the old man's eyes as he shoves Nico against the clapboard. "Don't give me a reason to hit you." His spittle lands on Nico's leather jacket. He pulls Nico toward him and then flings him back against the wall.

I rush out the door, grabbing my landlord by his shoulder. "Stop!"

"It was an accident," Nico shouts, lifting both hands above his head.

Mr. O'Brien releases him. "Get the hell off my property."

We watch Nico stagger to the driveway with his head down. When he reaches his car, he looks up at me. "Jill, we need to talk. Call me."

⚜ ⚜ ⚜

Mr. O'Brien is raking the flower beds when I leave for work the following morning, his jacket tossed on the grass beside him and his cup of coffee sitting on the walkway. At eight o'clock, it's already above sixty degrees. The meteorologist on the early news said today Boston has a chance of beating the record high of ninety-four degrees set for this mid-April day back in 1976.

I approach him with trepidation. "How are you today?" Even after Nico left last night, I worried about my landlord, sure I was going to wake from a deep sleep to the sound of sirens blasting and a red strobe light flashing on my bedroom walls as an ambulance roared into our driveway. It can't be good for an elderly person to get as upset as Mr. O'Brien did. It can't be good for anyone to get that upset.

He leans on his rake. "You let me know if he bothers you again."

I smile, touched by his concern, but it also makes me miss my dad, who should be here watching over me instead of my landlord. "I appreciate you looking out for me, but I can handle Nico."

"If I see him here again," Mr. O'Brien says, "I'm calling the cops."

"I don't think you need to do that."

He scratches at the grass with the rake. "Do you want him coming around?"

I hesitate before responding. Mr. O'Brien holds up his hand. "None of my business."

"He won't be back."

Mr. O'Brien resumes cleaning the flower bed, gathering a large pile of decomposed leaves. It doesn't seem like that long ago they were alive and vibrant with color, hanging from all the trees. I think about how much has changed since the fall. Nico and I got engaged, we broke up, and he moved out. I should have thrown my ring at him as he walked out the door. Maybe if I had, I would have moved on by now.

"Wish I had picked these up when they first came down," Mr. O'Brien mutters. "I wouldn't have to deal with the mess now."

⚜ ⚜ ⚜

In my car, as I do every morning, I press my preset for WSPR and check in on *BS Morning Sports Talk* to see if their discussion involves me.

Branigan is speaking. "How old is your grandfather?" he asks.

Zac's deep voice comes through my speakers. "He's seventy-four."

"Nico, why did you hit an old man?" Branigan asks.

Mr. O'Brien must have told Zac what happened, and now Branigan's busting Nico's chops about it. Good!

"I didn't hit him," Nico snaps.

"For those of you just waking up, let's get you up-to-date," Branigan says. "Nico realized he made a mistake breaking up with Jillian and is trying to get her back."

For months, this is exactly what I've been wishing for, what I thought I wanted. But Branigan's words bring me no joy today.

"He went to talk to her last night, but she kicked him out. Let's go to the phones and see if our callers have any suggestions on how you can win her back."

Steve from Douglas is the first to offer Nico advice. "That ship has sailed, Brother. Once you break up, you need to keep moving forward."

Caren from Foxboro has a different perspective. "Inundate her with gifts. Flowers, chocolate, jewelry, and if that doesn't work, give me a call." She cackles.

A minute later, Branigan announces that Frank from South Boston is on the line. I expect Mr. O'Brien to direct the conversation back to sports. "That girl has always been too good for that louse. Tell him to leave her alone." There's a loud click. I imagine Mr. O'Brien slamming down his landline and heading back outside to rake.

⚜ ⚜ ⚜

As I enter the door to my floor at the office, Ben approaches from the opposite end of the hallway. The smile he gives me causes my heart to flutter. When we meet, he stops. "SharkBytes made me a great offer."

Boo, I thought the smile was for me. "So you're taking the job?"

"I'm on my way to tell Stacy."

My heart sinks. I've been in the building less than a minute, and it's already a bad day. "Are you sure you want to do this?"

He places his hand on my shoulder. "This will be good for us."

Us? Does that mean there could be such a thing? I practically skip to my cube.

Renee is waiting for me there. "Did Ben tell you his news?" She slouches into my guest chair.

"I saw him on my way in."

"I can't believe he's leaving us." She mindlessly stirs her yogurt, mixing in blueberries and granola.

"He's been here a long time. It was time for him to pursue other opportunities." Could dating me be considered an opportunity?

Renee's head snaps up. "I expected you to be down about this. You hate change more than anyone I know."

"I don't hate change."

Renee's eyes widen. "Please," she says. "Your parents moved over four years ago and you still haven't gotten over it. And you still haven't tried to move on from Nico."

"That's not because I hate change." I turn my back to her to open the blinds. The sunlight brightens my cube.

"Then why is it?"

"I don't know, Renee."

She leaves me alone in my cube, wondering if the reason I stayed with Nico for six years is because I don't like change.

⚜ ⚜ ⚜

Ben and I run out at lunch to pick up sandwiches. He starts his car, and the sports station comes on. "Did you listen today?" I ask. I don't think he did because he hasn't said a word about Nico stopping by my apartment.

He backs out of his parking space and turns the radio to music. "I did."

As we wind down the hill, I lower my window so I can breathe in the warm spring air. It would seem like a summer day, except the trees we pass are all still bare. "When do you think the leaves will grow back?" I ask.

"May seventeenth at 2:00 p.m." Ben pokes my leg as he says it. "I don't know."

"Some of them are starting to bud." I point to a large maple whose branches are showing signs of life. "I love this time of year because everything gets a chance to start over."

Ben lowers the radio's volume, silencing Selena Gomez, who is singing about being sick of the same old love. "Speaking about starting over, I've been waiting for you to tell me what happened with Nico." He stops at the bottom of the hill before turning right onto the main road.

"There isn't much to say. He came over to explain why he left."

"What did he say?"

"I didn't give him a chance to say anything. I told him to leave, and my landlord made sure he did."

We stop at a red light. Ben turns to look at me. "So how did you feel about him showing up?"

"I was mad, but I was also curious about what he would say. Part of me wants to hear his explanation."

"Why?"

"Closure, I guess."

Ben frowns. "You get closure when you decide he doesn't matter anymore, not because of something he says."

"That sounds like something I might have heard at EAP if I had taken HR's advice." I laugh.

Ben remains serious. "He'll try again, you know." The light turns green. He steps on the gas so hard that I am thrown backward in my seat. He pats my knee. "Sorry."

"He already has," I admit. "He called this morning after his show."

"And?"

"I didn't pick up."

"Why now?" Ben asks as he turns into the parking lot.

I shrug. "I think he's afraid I'm moving on. I gave him back the ring. Branigan saw me at the club with you."

"He thinks we're together?" Ben circles around looking for an empty space.

"Who knows, but he's always had a thing about you."

"What kind of thing?"

"Jealousy, I guess."

Ben smiles at me. "You used to talk about me all the time, didn't you?"

I blush because what he's saying has some truth. "It's because of what happened at the Christmas party."

"He saw us dancing together?"

"No, I'm talking about the first party I went to." I poke his arm. "He heard you tell me that I looked smoking hot."

"Well, you did." Ben has circled around the lot three times, but there are no free spots, so he pulls up to the curb. "You pretty much always do." He dashes out of the car to get our sandwiches, leaving me alone, giddy about what he just said.

We make small talk on the ride back until we reach the office park.

"My last day is Friday," he says as we start up the hill.

"I know. I saw Stacy's email."

He eases up on the gas. The car slows. "So as of Friday night, we'll no longer be coworkers." He shoots me a look that sends chills up and down my spine. "I was thinking it would be a good night to go to dinner together."

"Like a date?" I'm sure there's a stupid grin on my face.

"No," he says. "Not like a date. An actual date."

Chapter 35

A few hours after I say goodbye to Ben for the last time at the office, he's standing on my doorstep holding a small gift-wrapped box in one hand and a bottle of wine in the other. My heart beats wildly as I let him in. *I'm going on a date with Ben!*

"Hi," I say shyly.

He gives me a quick hug. "Hi, yourself." He extends the box to me. "I was going to bring flowers or chocolate, but this is much better." He holds up the Malbec. "We can have a drink before we go, and you can open it."

"Sure."

He follows me to the kitchen, where I rummage through the drawer for a corkscrew. Usually I have no problem opening a bottle of wine, but tonight I can't even remove the foil covering the cork because my hands shake so much. "Let me do that," Ben says, taking the bottle and corkscrew from me. I reach into the cabinet for two glasses. One slips from my hand, shattering on the countertop. Ben and I both jump.

"Are you okay?" he asks.

"I'm fine. Just clumsy." *Relax. It's only Ben.*

"Be careful you don't cut yourself," he says, helping me clean up the broken glass.

When it's all picked up, he corners me against the counter. "Are you nervous?"

"I guess so. I don't know why."

"I'm nervous too." He smiles as he places a hand on my shoulder. "So maybe we should get this out of the way." He leans down to kiss me, his lips soft and gentle on mine. As I respond, his kiss becomes more demanding and his hands drop to my waist. He pulls me against him so that are bodies are melded together as his tongue slips into my mouth. My eyes are closed, but I see an explosion of colors over the darkness, red, orange, and yellow, a fire burning out of control. I run my fingers through his wavy hair. God, I have wanted to do that for so long! His breath quickens and his hold on me tightens.

As the kiss continues, all my senses are heightened. I'm aware of the faint taste of peppermint on his tongue, the spicy scent of his cologne, and the hardness of his thighs pinning me in place. Nico was never all that interested in kissing. He seemed to think of it as something he had to endure to get to the good part, like a kid eating his vegetables so he can have dessert. Ben, on the other hand, clearly views making out as an enticing appetizer, fresh bread dipped in oil, and cheese that you overindulge in before the main course.

Neither one of us wants to be the first to pull away, and the kiss goes on and on. Outside a car door slams. Ben lifts his mouth from mine and steps backward. Woozy, I stumble toward him, and he reaches out to steady me.

"Not too bad for a first kiss," he teases.

"Not too bad at all," I agree.

After he pours us each a glass of wine, we settle in the living room so that I can open the gift. It's wrapped in shiny paper that is the exact same shade of green as Ben's oxford. "You coordinated the gift wrap to your shirt," I joke.

"Actually, I wrapped this weeks ago. I was waiting for a good time to give it to you."

Why would he get me a gift weeks ago? Usually I take my time opening a present, trying to preserve the paper, but tonight, once I loosen the gold ribbon that he tied around the package, I tear off the wrapping in one fell swoop. He bites down on his lip watching me.

My hands tremble and my eyes fill with tears when I realize what the gift is: a replica of the Little Mermaid globe that my grandmother gave me and Christian broke all those years ago. "Where did you find this?"

"On eBay," he says. "Started looking for it the day you told me about it."

I picture him pouring over the eBay site day after day to find this for me. The image makes me think of Mr. O'Brien gluing his wife's mug back together. "That's incredibly sweet." I wipe away a tear that's rolling down my face and lean toward him so that I can hug him. As our heads come closer together, he moves in to kiss me again. There is nothing gentle about this one. It's hungry and suggestive. As it intensifies, there's no doubt what it's leading to. He lifts my sweater as I work on the buttons of his shirt and his belt buckle. He tugs down my skirt as he pushes me backward. At some point we roll off the couch onto the floor, both of us crying out as we go over the edge. Later we move to my room, where we make love again under the glow-in-the-dark stars Nico pasted to the ceiling in what seems like another lifetime.

⚜ ⚜ ⚜

The next morning I wake up sated and sore—but in a good way. *The best sex I ever had.* Did I really say that to him? I flip over, expecting to see him sleeping soundly. The other side of the bed is empty. I lie still and listen for him in the bathroom or downstairs. The house is silent. I get out of bed and peek out the window. His car is gone. My stomach flips.

He must have left a note, I think, and race downstairs. On the way to the kitchen, I pass my clothes from last night, scattered on the living room floor along with the wine glasses and a large red stain from when we tumbled off the couch onto the floor, knocking over my glass.

I search the counters and the table, but there is no note. Damn. I imagine him doing the walk of shame across the porch and down the driveway, and I experience the same rage I get when listening to *BS Morning Sports Talk*.

How could I have been so dumb? I am just another of his conquests. Serves me right for coming on to him the way I did.

By the time I get back to my bedroom, the pain I'm feeling is no longer good. I have rug burn. My lips feel swollen and bruised, and my inner thighs ache. I fling open the windows and rip the rumpled sheets from the mattress.

I feel like such an idiot. For crying out loud, what did I think would happen? I'd sleep with Ben and he'd declare his never-ending love for me? *Yeah, you did think that. Idiot!*

The doorbell rings. Ben returning? I rush to the door. Mr. O'Brien stands there carrying a ladder. Holding a large plastic container by a bright blue handle, Zachary stands next to his grandfather. "We're fixing the ceiling. Told you yesterday," Mr. O'Brien says. "Did you forget?"

"No." *Yeah, I did!* I hold the door open. He and Zachary come in and head toward the stairway. The old man pauses on the third step, glancing into the living room. I swear he's looking right at my discarded bra. I wonder if he saw Ben sneaking off in the early morning hours.

While Mr. O'Brien and Zac work upstairs, I clean the living room. Before I get far, the doorbell rings again. *Thank God*, I think, hurrying to answer it.

"Surprise!" my mother yells. She opens the storm door, steps inside and hugs me. My father trails behind her. He too embraces me. I want to dissolve into tears in his arms.

I try to compose myself. "What are you doing here?"

"We had nothing going on this weekend, so we thought we'd take a quick trip up to see you."

"Why didn't you call?" I guess it's a good thing that Ben left.

"It was a last-minute decision," my father says.

I usher them to the living room, frantically surveying the area to be sure there are no telltale signs of what went on here last night. My mother immediately hones in on the dark red stain on the carpet. "Did you spill wine?"

"I knocked over a glass."

She goes to the sink and runs water over a paper towel. "Did you even try to clean it?"

"I just spilled it and was about to do that."

"You were already drinking this morning?" my father asks.

My mother blots the spot with water. "No, the spot is dry. It didn't just happen." She returns to the kitchen for the saltshaker.

"Marianne, why are you pouring salt on the carpet?" my father asks.

"It will help draw out the wine. How long has it been here?" she asks.

"It happened last night."

She shakes her head. "And you didn't try to clean it up."

I was busy! I shout inside my head.

"We only just got here. Let's not annoy her already." My father winks at me.

There's loud pounding from upstairs. My parents look up at the ceiling. "My landlord is doing work," I explain.

My mother continues her inspection of the living room. She bends over and reaches for something beside the couch. I can't see what's captured her attention. My heart beats faster. *I took the bra upstairs, but what about my panties?*

"Where did you get this?" She's holding the Little Mermaid globe.

How could he give me such a sweet gift and then sneak off in the morning?

"A friend found it for me."

She bends down again. This time she comes up holding the wrapping paper. Her eyes go to the dark red stain in the carpet. I can see her doing the math. "A friend as in a boyfriend?"

"He's no one," I answer. I think of Ben skulking out of my apartment before I woke up this morning. *Clearly I'm no one to him.*

There's another large bang from upstairs, and then the sound of tiny pieces of plaster hitting the floor, like the world is coming down on me.

⚜ ⚜ ⚜

"Who are you expecting to call?" my mother asks. It's Saturday evening. We're eating at a tapas restaurant in my neighborhood. After dinner, we're heading to Boston to see a musical. Earlier, we went shopping at the outlets in New Hampshire. My parents are wearing me out.

I drop my phone back into my purse. I haven't missed any calls or texts. I didn't need to pull it out to find that out. The volume is on high. If it had rung, I would have heard it. "No one."

"You've been checking that thing all day."

It's true. I've convinced myself that there is a reason Ben left, and he'll call to explain. "Bad habit."

"It's rude," my mother says.

She's right. They came all this way to see me, and I'm paying more attention to an electronic device than them. "Sorry."

She pushes the plate of goat cheese croquette toward me. "Have you heard anything from Nico?"

I sip on my sangria before responding. "He came by a couple of weeks ago. He's been calling too, but I don't want to listen to anything he has to say."

"You might want to hear him out," my father says.

Clearly he has no idea that I've been a victim of radio bullying over the last few months. "We never told you kids this, but your mother got a case of cold feet a few weeks before our wedding."

I drop my fork and turn to my mother. "You did?"

Her cheeks turn red and she glares at my father. "Andrew," she snaps.

"I'm just saying it happens. At this point, you've invested six years; what's another few minutes to hear what he has to say? If I hadn't heard your mother out, you wouldn't be here."

That's the last type of advice I expected from my father.

⚜ ⚜ ⚜

By the time I get home from dropping off my parents at the airport on Sunday evening, I still haven't heard from Ben. I think about calling him, but decide that I will not humiliate myself chasing after him, the way I did Nico.

Right before I go to bed, my phone rings. It's not Ben, though. It's Nico. Instead of ignoring his call as I have for the past three weeks, I decide to talk to him.

He sounds stunned that I answered. "You picked up."

"You caught me at a weak moment." I lie down on my bed, looking up at the stars he pasted there.

"I'm sorry I've been pestering you," Nico says. "But we really need to talk."

I resist the urge to remind him of Dr. Decker and the show on stalking. "So talk."

"I'd rather do it face-to-face," Nico says.

"You can't come over. Mr. O'Brien will kill you."

"I wish I knew why he doesn't like me," Nico mutters "We can meet someplace. Grab a drink or dinner."

I should be thrilled by his offer. A few weeks ago, all I wanted was the chance to talk to him, but now I can't imagine there is anything he could say that would make me want to forgive him or understand.

"At the very least, we can clear the air," Nico says.

For the past six years, he's been the person I have relied on most. We should end things amicably. "I'll meet you for dinner."

Chapter 36

Monday, my first day at work without Ben, does not start well. Just as the elevator doors begin to slide shut, Ryan waves his arm between them and boards. We are the only two on it. It jerks upward, and I reach for the railing behind me.

"Morning," he says with his usual lecherous stare.

I nod and look down at my phone, pretending to be interested in something on its screen.

"So you and Nico are getting back together," he says.

"No." I swipe at my screen to discourage further conversation.

"Come on now. He said on air that you have a date tonight."

Now I look up.

"I understand why you would want to keep it on the down low." The elevator beeps as we reach the fourth floor. "Sort of makes you look like a doormat, going back to him."

"It's really none of your business."

As we get to the door to our area, Stacy approaches from the other side with a balding man, whose suit pants are too short and jacket too tight. She shakes his hand, thanks him for coming in, and promises to be in touch.

I stop to wait for her so that I don't have to walk with Ryan. "You're interviewing for Ben's position already?"

"No time to lose. We have a lot of work to do."

I look back through the window at the first candidate, who's waiting for the elevator.

Stacy follows my gaze. "Not quite the eye candy that Ben was, but his work is quite impressive."

My first thought—that I can't wait to tell Ben what she called him—causes a pang in my heart. My second thought is that she sounds like she's already made up her mind. "I'm sure there are lots of talented people looking for work."

"I hate interviewing," she says before turning left for her office.

"Hey, sweetie," Renee calls as I walk down our aisle.

I step into her cube. "Stacy already started interviewing for Ben's position."

"I know. We saw him this morning. Ben said he looks like John Candy."

"How did Ben see him? Did you send him a picture?" I try to imagine Renee covertly snapping a picture of the guy as Stacy led him to her office. There's no way she could pull that off.

"Ben was here this morning. Forgot his phone on Friday. Poor guy couldn't get in the building all weekend because he doesn't have an access badge anymore."

He didn't have his phone. He couldn't call me! "What did he have to say?" *That doesn't explain why he left in the first place.*

"Not much. He was in a hurry because he didn't want to be late on his first day."

Back at my desk, I'm tempted to text Ben, but I convince myself that now that he has his phone, he will definitely get in touch with me. I'm wrong though. When I leave to meet Nico that night, he still hasn't called.

Chapter 37

My eyes take a moment to adjust to the interior of the dimly lit pub where I'm meeting Nico. Even though smoking hasn't been allowed here for more than ten years, the place still reeks of cigarettes. I'm not sure if the stench is ingrained in the old red vinyl booths or if it's coming off the patrons, most of whom have a hand wrapped around a short glass filled with hard alcohol and their eyes glued to the computer screen showing the winning Keno numbers.

Nico is sitting at a table facing the door, but he's turned sideways so that he can see the baseball game on the television in the bar. He doesn't notice me until I arrive at the booth. "Jill." He sounds surprised, like he forgot I was coming. I can tell, though, that he's made an effort for tonight, because he's wearing a button-down shirt instead of one of his many Boston sports teams' jerseys and isn't wearing a baseball hat. "I wasn't sure you were going to show."

"Neither was I," I admit. From the street I saw his truck in the parking lot and drove past the restaurant, intending to go home. At the light a mile up the road, I changed my mind again, made an illegal U-turn, and circled back.

Nico stands and steps toward me like he's going to hug me. I move sideways, evading his outstretched arms. He drops his hands back to his sides. "Thanks for coming," he mutters.

He waits for me to slide into the booth before sitting again. We stare across the table at each other for a few seconds without speaking. I can feel my heart beating. I'm not sure why I'm so nervous. I only came here so that I can understand why he left and get closure.

"You look good." I think he says it to end the awkward silence, because it comes out sounding like a prerecorded message. *Thank you for calling our hotline for people who have nothing to say to each other. Press one for insincere compliments, two for humorless jokes, and three for meaningless small talk.*

A waitress in a short-sleeved shirt arrives with menus. Her arms are covered in tattoos. I can't stop staring at them. I spot a snake and a monkey below her right elbow, and a dragon above it.

"Are you here for drinks or food?" she asks.

"Both," Nico answers.

"Drinks," I say and ask for a rum and Coke because they don't serve good wine at a place like this.

"Give us a minute," Nico says after ordering his beer.

"I think I saw Waldo's red-and-white striped hat on her arm," I say after she leaves.

He narrows his eyes. "What are you talking about?"

"Her tattoos."

He looks at me blankly.

How could he not notice them? "Never mind." Ben would have understood. When the waitress returns, he would stealthily touch a spot on his own arm. *Snake*, he would mouth.

Rabbit, I would counter, pretending to scratch an itch. The entire time we were here, we'd play a secret game of I Spy.

Nico glances toward the television. "No hits through four."

Whoop de doo.

He opens his menu. "Did you already eat?"

"I'm not hungry." I haven't had an appetite since I woke up alone on Saturday.

"You love the chicken teriyaki sandwich and onion rings here. It's why I picked this place."

"I love the filet at the Capital Grille too, and the ambiance is much better."

"Can't watch the Sox there," he says, glancing toward the television.

"Yes, because we came here to talk about the game and not us."

He makes the clicking sound with his tongue. "Sorry."

The waitress returns with our drinks. This time, I study the artwork on her left arm, noticing a spider and what I think are Chinese letters. "What did you decide about food?" she asks.

"None for me."

"Chicken teriyaki sandwich and the onion rings," Nico says. "We'll split them."

Onion rings. I would never eat them on a date now. I'd be too worried about my breath, not to mention what the fried batter would do to my weight. Did I just not care when I was with Nico? Did I eat them in front of him when we first started dating, or sometime in our six years together did I become complacent? "I'm not going to have any."

"You might change your mind."

"You're the one famous for that."

He winces, making me feel a tiny bit bad. "What happened with Bonnie?"

He exhales loudly. "Look, Jill. The radio station. The ratings were lousy. We were trying to attract female listeners.

Branigan suggested the contest. I told him I'd think about it. The next thing I know, he's moving ahead with the idea. I'm sorry."

"Why did you leave?"

He fiddles with his silverware. "Once I gave you the ring, everything felt different. I couldn't stop thinking of the notion of forever. It scared me."

"Why didn't you talk to me about it?"

He sighs. "Look, Jill, I made a mistake." He makes a point of looking in my eyes. "I want to correct it. Give me another chance. Please."

I wait to feel elated. Isn't this what I have been dreaming about since the day he left? All I feel is sad. I slump against the backrest and study his face. The dark, slanted eyes, his straight nose with the narrow nostrils and pointed tip, the five o'clock shadow that I used to find sexy. Renee's right. He does look dirty.

"I know I hurt you," he says. "Give me another chance. I'll make it up to you."

"How can we go back to what we used to be when I can't trust you?"

"I don't want to be what we were. I want to be better." He reaches across the table for my hand. I let him take it, wishing I could find a way to forgive him and forget the last four months ever happened. Get back to planning our wedding instead of to online dating.

I hear an all-too-familiar clearing of the throat and look up. Mr. O'Brien is walking up the aisle toward us; his eyes zero in on my and Nico's entwined hands in the center of the table. As he gets closer, his gaze meets mine. He doesn't say a word, but the disappointed look on his face shames me. I pull my hand out of Nico's as Mr. O'Brien turns to the right to pick up another Keno card.

Nico glances over his shoulder to see what I'm looking at. "Oh man," he whines.

I think of how Mr. O'Brien took an immediate liking to Ben, but never warmed up to Nico. "What's your problem with him?" I ask.

"I didn't like that he was all up in our business all the time. And that BS about raising your rent when I moved in. Did he decrease it after I left?"

"As a matter of fact, he did." Nico doesn't have to know the decrease was about one-tenth of the increase.

The waitress drops off Nico's meal. He cuts the sandwich in half and transfers it and a handful of onion rings onto a smaller plate, which he slides across to me. He's sharing them with me to be nice, but his gesture annoys me. Even though the food looks and smells delicious, I resist the temptation to reach for it because I don't want Nico thinking he knows better than I do.

"We can't live at your place. You'll have to move in with me," he says.

I push the food back at him. "I'm not moving in with you."

"We'll find a new place then."

"You don't get it. I'm not living with you anywhere." It's just like him to assume I'd take him back, no questions asked. He might be more arrogant than Branigan.

"Okay, we'll take it slow," Nico says. "See what happens." He bites into his sandwich like everything's been settled.

"Why didn't you try to stop Branigan?"

"I tried, but you brought that on yourself. All you had to do was apologize to him."

I fold my arms across my chest.

"Sorry. Look, Jill, I want to focus on moving on and not replaying everything that happened."

"Funny, you're usually a big fan of replay."

He smirks. "I'll let you get away with these jabs for a little while, but eventually you have to forgive me."

I feel a weird sensation under the skin on my arms and imagine my blood is boiling. "I have to forgive you? I don't think so."

He reaches for my hand again, but I jerk it away. "Jillian, we went through a rough patch. All couples do."

"A rough patch? Is that what you call it? You made my life a living hell. Humiliated me on air. I was the laughing stock of my office."

"Things got out of hand because you picked a fight with Branigan."

"And you did nothing to stop him!"

"I tried." He stuffs an onion ring into his mouth.

"Well, you didn't try hard enough."

He looks down at his lap.

"Why do you want to get back together?"

"Because I miss you."

"What exactly do you miss about me?"

He sighs. "Why are you making this so hard, Jillian?"

"What did you think would happen? You'd say sorry and everything would be fine?"

He pushes his mostly uneaten sandwich to the side of the table. "I was hoping you'd want to work things out and not just throw away the six years we spent together."

"You're the one who did that." I stand.

He grabs me by my wrist. "So that it's? You're not going to give me another chance?"

I shake my arm free. "You don't deserve another chance. You don't deserve me." I take a deep breath, straighten my shoulders, and head for the door.

"Jill. Jillian," Nico calls out.

I keep walking and don't look back.

Chapter 38

Tuesday morning when I wake up, I decide that Ben owes me an explanation so I will send him a text. I type *Why did you leave on Saturday?* I delete it because the tone is combative. I lighten it up. *Hey, where did you run off to Saturday morning?* Yes, that sounds friendly and doesn't make me seem like a crazy stalker. I fire it off.

His response is fast, brief, and cold. *Had someplace to be.*

Bastard! Now I wish I had never sent the text because not knowing why he left was actually better than knowing. Damn.

My phone pings again. *How was your date with Nico last night?*

Screw you, Ben. *Perfect!*

I flip on the radio, hoping Nico isn't talking about what happened. Fortunately, Branigan and Smyth are talking about baseball. I keep the radio tuned to their show and get ready for work. As I'm drying my hair, a commercial for Kaufman Jewelers comes on, making me wonder what Nico will do with the ring. Someday down the road, will he present it to a woman he's dating and try to pass it off as something he picked out especially for her? She'll believe him because she won't have a reason not to. She'll love it until Branigan sees it on her finger. *You're wearing a recycled ring*, I imagine him telling her, and she'll demand a different one.

Mixed Signals

The jewelry advertisement ends. "How was your date with Jill last night? Did you give her back the ring?" Branigan asks. I'll say this for the guy, he's smooth with his transitions from commercial breaks back to the show.

There's a long silence before Nico answers. "Not yet."

"But you think you will?"

"We agreed to take things slow. When I earn her trust again, she'll slide the ring back on, and we'll get back to planning our wedding."

He is such a liar. I have a white-knuckle grip on my hairbrush. I place it down on the vanity and stretch my hand. On the bright side, his lie backs up what I said to Ben. *Had someplace to be.* What a big jerk.

"Frankly, I'm surprised she's giving you another chance," Branigan says. "We put her through the ringer these past months."

"You did that," Nico says. "Last night was a good start for us. And that's all I want to say. From now on, we're not going to talk about my personal life or mention Jill again. Agreed?"

"I don't know about that," Branigan says. "I'm still waiting for my apology."

After another commercial break, Branigan goes to the phones, where everyone who calls in lambastes me for giving Nico another chance. "Does she have no self-respect?" Eric from Burlington asks.

I snap off my radio and finish getting ready for work. As usual, Mr. O'Brien pulls in as I'm leaving my apartment, and he's listening to the radio. He climbs out of his car as I stomp across the driveway to mine. He gives me the same disappointed look he did last night.

"It's not true," I blurt out.

"What's not true?"

"What Nico said on the radio, about us working it out. We're not." I open my car door.

He sips his coffee. "There are a lot of listeners who think it is."

"Well, there's nothing I can do about that."

"Why can't you?" he asks. "Don't you have a phone?"

I slam the door shut. I could go on the radio and call out Nico on air. Sure, if Ben's listening, he'll find out I misled him about my meeting with Nico, but the rest of the listeners won't think I'm a doormat. "I need the number for the caller line."

He waves at me to follow him and leads me through his front door to his kitchen. I'm surprised to see he has a state-of-the-art pod coffeemaker.

He catches me staring at it. "Do you want a cup?"

"No. I'm just wondering why you go to Dunkin' Donuts every day if you have that?"

He sighs. "Gives me a place to be every morning. Provides structure to my day."

A cup of coffee is the highlight of his day? Now I feel bad that I haven't made more of an effort to get to know him through the years. I should have invited him over for dinner from time to time. I will, from now on. I hope he likes Rice Krispies.

On the counter next to his coffeemaker, there's an old black transistor radio complete with the dial for tuning and the strap for carrying. He turns it on.

"We have a few open lines, so give us a call," Smyth says before the station breaks for a commercial.

Mr. O'Brien searches his bulletin board for the phone number.

Nervous about talking on air, I sway in my seat at his table. "Can you offer any advice about keeping my cool on the radio?" I ask.

"How would I know? I've never called in to the show."

I laugh because as he says it, he hands me a scrap piece of paper with the ten-digit number scribbled across it. "You just happen to have this handy and have no idea who uses the alias Frank from South Boston?"

He clears his throat. "Pretend you're talking to a friend."

"Why don't you ever give your real name?"

He smiles. "Carol didn't like me calling in. Said I got too worked up."

"She didn't recognize your voice?"

"Oh, she did, but she pretended not to. She'd bring up something Frank said on air and ask me what I thought about it. It was our little game." He smiles at the memory. It reminds me of something Ben and I would do. "Go ahead. Make your call."

I punch the numbers into my phone. I get a busy signal, which I haven't heard in years.

"Keep trying," Mr. O'Brien says. "It takes a while."

On the sixth attempt I make it through to a call screener. I give him my name and tell him I want to talk to Branigan on air. "He's been waiting for my call," I explain.

He puts me on hold. Mr. O'Brien carries the radio to the table and sits across from me.

Branigan's voice comes out of the speakers and fills the kitchen. "Well, you'll never believe this," he says. "On line two, we have a special guest. Jillian, Nico's ex, err, current girlfriend, is finally calling us. Welcome to the show, Jill."

He sounds so friendly that you'd never guess he spent the last few months ripping me apart. My hand shakes so much I can barely hold on to the phone. I can feel my cheeks burning up. I can't go through with this. I need to hang up. Right now!

"We've been trying to get you to call in for weeks," Branigan says. "What made you do it today?"

I glance at Mr. O'Brien. He nods. I can do this. I take a deep breath. "Because I want to—" There's a horrible echo.

"Jillian, hold on a minute," Branigan says. "You need to turn your radio down. Do that for me right now."

Mr. O'Brien carries his portable radio into the living room.

"So we're glad you've decided to give Nico another chance. I guess it's only fair, seeing how I got another shot at the mixed doubles title, and look how that turned out. I am the club's mixed doubles champion for the tenth consecutive year."

I should have known he'd get that in. "I wanted to set the record straight," I say.

"About the incorrect call you made in the first tournament?"

"No! About me and Nico. We're not trying again. I don't want the ring back, ever."

"That's not what Nico just told us."

"I know. That's why I'm calling."

Branigan pauses. "Nico's lying? Is that what you're telling us?"

"He's not being truthful," I say.

"Nico, what do you have to say about this?" Branigan asks.

Dead silence.

"You have to say something," Branigan persists. "She's calling you a liar."

"It will take some time, but eventually Jillian will take me back," Nico says. "I'm going to work hard until she does."

"Jill?" Branigan says.

"It's never going to happen. I want him and you to leave me alone."

Mr. O'Brien peeks into the kitchen and nods.

"You're not enjoying your five minutes of fame?"

"It's been five months," I exaggerate. "You've been trying to ruin my life all because of a stupid tennis tournament."

"It's not stupid to me," Branigan says. "Did you purposely make an incorrect call?"

"It's possible."

"Possible?"

"Yes, I was angry with you so I called the ball out. It was on the line. I'm sorry."

Someone at the radio station turns on victory music, Branigan talks over it. "Jillian, our little game has officially ended," he says. "Since you're not with Nico, how about we host a contest to give our listeners a chance to win a date with you?"

Mr. O'Brien shakes his head. I don't need his encouragement for this decision though. "Thanks, but no."

After I hang up, Mr. O'Brien offers to make me a cup of coffee in his pod maker. I can tell he has never used the machine before, so I show him how it works. The radio is still on. Listeners are calling to talk about Nico and how delusional he is if he thinks I would forgive him after what his show put me through the past few months.

The last caller to comment on the situation is Ben from the car. "If Jill changes her mind about the win-a-date contest, I want to be the first person to enter," he says.

"I like Ben in the black Dodge Charger," Mr. O'Brien says.

"Me too."

When I leave my landlord's, I text Ben before driving off to work. *If we went on a date, would you disappear in the morning again?*

He immediately calls. First, he tells me the reason for his curt text earlier was because he thought I had reconciled with Nico. He then explains why he left on Saturday. "I got up to make breakfast, but you had no food so I ran out to the grocery store. When I got back, your parents were at your door. I thought if I showed up so early in the morning looking disheveled, with breakfast, they'd figure out I spent the night. I didn't think it would be a good first impression."

A chill runs down my spine as I imagine the icy glare my parents would have given Ben. Just as quickly though, a warmth spreads across my chest: Ben was concerned about making a good first impression on my parents! If our sleeping together was a one-night stand, he wouldn't care what they think. He plans on sticking around! Ben and I are going to be a couple! "So maybe you can meet them another time?"

"I'm hoping to," he says. "But in the meantime, when can I see you again? I still owe you dinner."

"How about tonight?"

Chapter 39

On this beautiful fall day, Mr. O'Brien has his living room windows wide open. His television is loud enough for me to hear the football game that he's watching. The Patriots are humiliating the Bills. A U-Haul box truck bumps up the road, with Ben's car trailing behind it. I rise from the step I'm sitting on as Ben, Lucas, and another friend step out of the vehicles onto the driveway. Ben heads toward the walkway to greet me while his friends circle around to the back of the truck.

Mr. O'Brien steps out onto the porch as Ben pulls me into an embrace. "Need a hand?" the old man asks as the truck's back gate rumbles open.

"The guys and I have it covered, but thank you." Ben walks across the porch to shake my landlord's hand. Lucas carries a large box up the stairs. He bobs his blue cap in Mr. O'Brien's direction.

After six months of dating, Ben is moving in today. Other than the apartment being more crowded with his belongings, it won't be much of a change for us, because he's pretty much been living here since the day he called into the radio show. Before we made it official though, Ben insisted on getting Mr. O'Brien's permission.

We had the old man over for dinner and Ben asked him if he minded if there was another tenant living in his duplex. I expected Mr. O'Brien to lecture Ben about how back in his day a man didn't live with a woman unless he was married to her. Instead Mr. O'Brien pointed out the window at Ben's Charger. "That thing doesn't leak oil, does it?" he asked with a laugh. He slapped Ben on the back. "You better do right by her."

"Count on it," Ben answered.

Ben's other friend struggles to lift a chair out of the truck. Mr. O'Brien and Ben go down to help him. With the five of us unloading, the truck is empty in no time at all. Ben's friends drive off, Mr. O'Brien returns to his apartment to watch the game, and Ben and I unpack his boxes in the living room. The television is tuned to the football game, but neither one of us is really paying attention to it.

"I'll be right back," Ben says. "There's still one more box in my car."

I glance at the television while he's gone. The Patriots' receiver catches a ball near the forty yard line and runs all the way down the field, extending his arms toward the goal line as he gets tackled. "Is he down on the one yard line or did he make it to the end zone?" the announcer asks. "They're reviewing the play now."

Ben returns with a small box. He kneels on the floor in front of me, opens it, and pulls out the most beautiful diamond ring I have ever seen.

Next door, Mr. O'Brien yells, "Touchdown!"

Preview *Waiting for Ethan*

Chapter 1
2012

"Neesha Patel's grandmother ruined your life." That's what my mother says when I point out the obituary. She mutters to herself in Italian, glances at the picture in the newspaper, and then goes right back to making the list of things she wants me to check on when she and my father make their annual exodus to Florida later that day. I slide closer to her on the couch and begin reading the article out loud:

> *Satya E. Patel (known as Ajee), 92, of San Antonio, TX, formerly of Westham, MA, died Wednesday. She is survived by her son, Dr. Kumar Patel of San Antonio, TX, her grandson, Dr. Sanjit Patel of San Antonio, TX, her granddaughter, Neesha Davidian of Canyon Lake, TX, and five great-grandchildren...*

At the mention of the great-grandchildren, my mother looks up from her notepad and frowns. Finally, I think, she's going to show some sympathy for the Patels. I even think I see tears in her eyes. "It sounds like both Sanjit and Neesha have children." I nod, trying to picture my old friend with kids, but all I can see is a lanky fourteen-year-old girl with a long dark ponytail and a mouthful of wires. "Their grandmother is the reason I'll never have grandchildren of my own." Although her words sting, they don't shock me. I am thirty-six and single. My mother long ago abandoned all hope of me ever getting married and having a family, and for this she blames the deceased, a woman I haven't seen since I was fourteen.

"What's going on in here? You're supposed to be packing." My father appears at the bottom of the stairs, dressed in a golf shirt and holding the driver I gave him for Christmas two weeks before. He can't get to Florida fast enough to start playing again.

"Neesha Patel's grandmother died."

My father raises his eyebrows. "Recently?"

"Last week."

"She must have been well over a hundred. She was ancient when she lived here."

"The paper says she was ninety-two."

My father rubs his chin. "That means she was only sixty-nine or seventy when they moved to Texas?"

"Right, Dad. Your age. Ancient."

"I'm only sixty-seven, Gina, and I feel like I'm twenty." He steps away from the stairs and takes a halfhearted swing with his golf club. "It's being active that keeps me so young." He winks. "May I?" He points at the paper, so I hand it to him.

My mother sighs. "Why did they even bother to publish her obituary in the Westham paper? They haven't lived here for almost twenty-five years. People don't remember her."

I glare at my mother. "Mom, everyone remembers Ajee. She was a hero in this town."

My mother rolls her eyes. "She was a nosy old woman, Gina. That's all."

I stand and walk to the living room window. The Patels' old house is directly across the street. The Murphys live there now, but someday Neesha will be back. Her grandmother said so. She said it the same day she told me I would marry a man named Ethan.

⚜ ⚜ ⚜

As we load the last of the suitcases into my parents' car, Mr. and Mrs. Murphy make their way across the street. My father mutters something incomprehensible under his breath. Mr. Murphy makes a beeline up the driveway and heads straight to me. "Gina." He hugs me tightly as if he hasn't seen me in ages. "Are you still on the market?" I nod. "What's wrong with young men today? If I were just a few years younger... But don't you worry. Every pot has a lid." He passes on similar pearls of wisdom every time I see him, which is about once a week when I visit my parents.

Mrs. Murphy follows about four steps behind her husband and zeroes in on my mother. She waves a picture in the air above her head. "I just have to show you my grandson before you leave, Angela." She reaches the passenger door where my mother is standing and hands her a snapshot of a newborn baby. "Born yesterday. Isn't he beautiful?"

My mother looks at me pointedly, and I feel my stomach begin a gymnastic act. How is it possible that Kelli Murphy, the seven-year-old sniveler I babysat for, is a wife and parent, while I'm not only single but haven't had a meaningful date in the last three years?

My mother turns her attention to the photo and then smiles at Mrs. Murphy. My father looks at his watch. He wants to be in Virginia in bed by 10 p.m. because he has a 7:30 tee time tomorrow morning.

"He's a big boy," Mrs. Murphy says. "Nine pounds, six ounces."

"He's beautiful," my mother says.

"He looks like me," Mr. Murphy adds. "Spitting image."

My mother laughs. My father opens the driver's side door.

"They named him Ethan." By the look on my mother's face, you would think Mr. Murphy just said his grandson was named after Bin Laden.

"That's a great name," I say. My mother won't make eye contact with me.

"It's an old name that's come back around," Mrs. Murphy says.

My father leans into the car, puts the keys into the ignition, and starts the engine.

"We have to get going," my mother says. "Congratulations on your grandson."

The Murphys wobble back down the driveway, and my dad jumps into the driver's seat. My mother hugs me. "Strange we should hear that name on the same day we learn of Ajee's death," she says. But I don't think it's strange at all. It's a sign from Ajee. *Don't worry*, she's saying. *Your Ethan will be here soon.*

As the car starts to pull out of the driveway, my mother opens her window. "Gina, if some nice man asks you out this winter, promise me you'll say yes, no matter what his name is."

Acknowledgments

Steve, my rock and beshert. I never would get any writing done without you. You cook our meals, keep the house stocked with chocolate and wine (very important!), keep me calm when things get bumpy, and never complain about the events I skip out on so I can write. You are my unsung hero. I love you, always.

Molly, Lynda, and Ann, our writing retreat in Chicago got this story going. Your encouragement, and the support from the rest of our group, Vicki, Celia, Barb and Carol, have been a gift I treasure.

Susan Timmerman, my work sister, your feedback early in the process helped me develop the story. Thank you for always being there to listen. Our friendship is so special to me.

My writing group at the Hudson library, Tiana, Martha, Jeanette, Neville, and Steve, is an invaluable resource who not only critique my chapters but also coach me on my public speaking skills.

Julie Peterson, You are always a wise sounding board for all things publishing. Thanks for letting me bounce ideas off you, reading my manuscripts and most important, reminding me that the middle is always hard, but somehow I get it done. You have been such a great friend for decades. And to think where it all started.

Thank you to Susan Devane, who read a few drafts and offered enthusiasm and encouragement that fueled me through the writing process. I'm so lucky to have you as my sister and friend. Maria and Michael, I feel the same way about you too. Mom and Dad, thanks for being my biggest cheerleaders and my best marketing team, telling everyone you talk to about my books and insisting they read them.

Liza Fleissig, I wish I could think of a stronger word than thank you to let you know how grateful I am to you. I can't so I will just say thank you for believing in my writing and in me and for standing by me. Your brilliance and dedication never cease to amaze me. Thank you, too, to everyone who works with you at Liza Royce Agency (LRA) and makes it such a special agency.

Most important, I want to thank you, the reader, for choosing my novel. Your reviews and support mean the world to me. A special shoutout to all the book bloggers who have helped promote my novels. I appreciate all you do.

About the Author

Diane Barnes is the author of All We Could Still Have, Waiting for Ethan, Mixed Signals, and More Than. She is also a marketing and corporate communication writer in the health care industry. When she's not writing, she's at the gym, running, or playing tennis, trying to burn off the ridiculous amounts of chocolate and ice cream she eats. She and her husband, Steven, live in New England with Oakley, their handsome Golden Retriever. She hopes you enjoy reading her books as much as she enjoyed writing them.

She can be found at www.dianembarnes.com and on Twitter and Instagram @DianeBarnes777

JOIN THE FUN!

In December, one lucky reader will be selected to have the option of having their name included in an upcoming book. Sign up for my newsletter at **www.dianembarnes.com** for your chance to win!